The BAD MOTHER'S CHRISTMAS

SUZY K QUINN

www.lightning-books.com

British Library Cataloguing in Publication Data
A catalogue record for this book is available from the British Library

Printed by CPI Group (UK) Ltd, Croydon CR0 4YY

ISBN 9781785631603

Author's note

I still cant believe so many people read my books.
Each and every day, I am grateful for you, dear reader.
Thank you so much.
If you want to ask me any questions about the books
or chat about anything at all, get in touch:

Happy reading,
Suzy xxx

Email: suzykquinn@devoted-ebooks.com
Facebook.com/suzykquinn
(You can friend request me. I like friends.)
Twitter: @suzykquinn
Website: suzykquinn.com

Saturday 30th June

Late evening

So I'm engaged to be married.

Again.

I wonder how many marriage proposals happen on family campsites with coin-operated showers?

Am guessing very few.

Feel weirdly nervous, which I'm sure isn't the usual reaction of a blushing bride. I want to marry Alex, but, but...

Rather ominously, Alex and I are sleeping apart on our first night as an engaged couple because my 'two-man' tent doesn't fit two people.

I'm sleeping with Daisy, who is flailing around in her dinosaur sleeping bag like an interpretive dancer.

Alex is lying on cold, grey boarding-school blankets in the back of his Land Rover a few metres away.

Does he know I'm freaking out?

I sort of broached my feelings over the campfire.

'Let's hope we can build a happy family together,' I said. 'Despite our differences.'

Alex said 'hope' was a pointless word. 'We won't hope,' he said. 'We will succeed because we make every effort to do so.'

That freaked me out even more.

It's not marrying Alex that's the problem. It's the 'building a happy family' part.

How can we do that when Alex's mother and I don't get along?

Sunday 1st July
Morning

Woke up at 5 am to find Mum and Dad arguing in hushed voices over a whistling kettle.

Their sticky-up morning hair made them look like angry punk rock stars – Dad the white-haired scarecrow guitarist and Mum the pink-haired lead singer.

'It's consumerism gone mad, Shirley,' Dad whispered. 'Camping is about downsizing. Appreciating nature. The simple things.' He jabbed a knobbly, sunburnt finger at a nearby luxury motor home. 'A big van like that is just an utter waste. Who needs a dishwasher on a campsite? And an electric orange juicer is just ridiculous.'

'You're being very selfish Bob,' said Mum, hands on hefty hips. 'Not everyone enjoys nature. All I'm asking for is somewhere to watch Netflix when it rains.'

As Mum and Dad argued in hissy voices, the motor home's hydraulic door whooshed open and a deeply tanned, white-haired lady popped her head out.

'Would anyone like some homemade hollandaise sauce?' she asked. 'We can't store it – Paul went a bit mad at the farmer's market and filled the fridge with oysters, crab and English sparkling wine.'

Behind her, an elderly man delicately snipped parsley over buttered kippers.

'A spot of hollandaise sounds wonderful,' said Mum. 'It'll go a treat on our bacon sandwiches.'

Within five minutes, Mum had befriended the white-haired

lady and invited herself on a grand-tour of the luxury motor home.

Mum clumped back down gleaming metal steps with the couple's life story.

'Rita and Paul bought that van with Paul's redundancy money,' she told us. They're touring the UK right now, but they'll be off to Holland soon. Their daughter just won a football scholarship in the US so they've got an empty nest. Rita has a grown-up son from a previous marriage; he left the army to move in with an older woman – she has two kids from a previous marriage and a drinking problem. They live in a bungalow with bad damp and last year they had mice.'

Mum went on to describe the motorhome in detail: its shower room, fridge-freezer, two king-sized double beds, fully-stocked kitchen etc.

'Rita's offered to make you a celebration cake for your engagement, Juliette,' said Mum. 'She's got a little baking pantry on board with four sizes of tin. Do you want a three-layer cream Black Forest gateau with kirsch cherries?'

'Who on earth needs a cake to celebrate getting engaged?' Dad demanded. 'Isn't love enough?'

None of us said anything, but we were all thinking the same thing.

A three-layer cream Black Forest gateau sounded *very* nice.

Mid-morning
Just finished breakfast. Alex has gone for a run in his black-ninja jogging gear.

Still freaking out about being engaged.

I thought a good night's sleep might sort me out, but I didn't have a good night's sleep because Daisy cartwheeled in her sleeping bag all night.

Was too unsettled to finish my egg and bacon sandwich this

morning, and also turned down Mum's 'brunch' offer of tea and biscuits.

Mum gets worried when people don't eat and kept shoving her hand on my forehead, asking if I had a temperature.

'Your curls have gone all flat,' she said, tugging at my limp blonde-brown strands. 'That's a sure sign of illness in your case. Unless you've over-bleached it again. You didn't let Brandi do your highlights did you?'

Assured her that I wouldn't be that stupid. At least, not again.

My platinum blonde, hair-extended little sister aspires to turn everyone into a men's magazine pin-up. Turn me into slutty Barbie once, shame on you. Do it twice, shame on me.

'My hair is flat because I couldn't rinse it properly,' I said. 'I ran out of 50 pences in the shower. I'm fine Mum. Honest.'

But I wasn't honest because I'm not fine.

Feel *really* nervous.

Late morning

A minor argument over lunch.

Althea is my best friend and a welcome camping companion, but no one likes aggressive veganism. Softly, softly is a better approach.

True – Mum *has* bought obscene quantities of meat. A whole pig, plus five polystyrene rafts of beef-burgers is ridiculous for one long weekend, even for a big family. And it was silly of Mum to argue that red meat is a health food.

When Mum brought out three buckets of sausages, Althea went into a full activist rant.

'Who needs seventy sausages for one long weekend?' Althea demanded, black hair tumbling over her Che Guevara t-shirt. 'Have you ever seen a commercial pig farm? It's piggy Auschwitz for innocent animals.'

Mum looked every bit the guilty meat-eater, in a red chef's

apron, giant BBQ fork held aloft.

'There are a lot of us here, love,' Mum protested. 'I only brought ten sausages per head. Anyway, all this meat is free-range. The pigs had a good life before their intestines were pulled out and stuffed with their own flesh. I bought them from a farmer friend, Porky George. He's a lovely fellow; very kind to his livestock.'

'No meat farmer is truly kind,' said Althea. 'Do you know how he slaughters his pigs?'

Mum said the pigs were read bedtime stories, then cuddled to death.

Afternoon

It started thundering and raining after lunch, so we're all holed up in our tents or caravans, sleeping or reading until the storm passes.

Dad is in his element, wearing all his hiker waterproof gear and talking about survival skills and the great outdoors.

The rest of us are wishing we were Rita and Bob, snug in a motorhome, drinking tea from real china mugs and watching MasterChef.

8 pm

We're supposed to be barbecuing sausages for our evening meal, but Dad still hasn't managed to start the BBQ because the coals are damp.

Rita and Paul were kind, offering to share their red wine from real glasses, Quattro Formaggi pizza, garlic bread and green salad.

Sadly, Dad declined for all of us, saying we'd rather do *real* camping thank you very much.

We're all still furious with him.

Evening

Separate beds again for Alex and me. Am still freaking out.

I want to marry Alex, but I'm also scared.

When Nick and I broke up, I thought my world had ended. But I stayed strong for my little girl and, through grit and determination, bought a house with two flushing toilets and a fridge full of cash-and-carry cheesecake.

Life isn't perfect, but it's stable. Stable isn't bad, given the last few years I've had. Nick and his mother will be in my life forever, but they're at arm's length – which is bearable.

If I marry Alex, *his* mother will move from arm's length right into my personal space. This could be *un*bearable if we're not getting along.

There's a lot to get my head around. And a stomach full of sausages to digest.

Monday 2nd July

At last!

A good night's sleep.

I moved Daisy to Mum and Dad's caravan last night due to excessive windmilling. It was for Daisy's benefit too: if I got accidentally slapped in the face again, I would have lost my temper.

Alex crept into my tent in the early hours of the morning, saying he wanted to watch my face as the sun came up.

'Do you remember when we were growing up?' he said. 'And you overheard me in the woods singing "The Sun Has Got His Hat On"?'

'Yes,' I said. 'You were a charming falsetto.'

'Bloody embarrassing,' said Alex. 'I thought no one was listening.'

'I already knew tough Alex Dalton had a sensitive side.'

'Yes, you always knew,' he smiled. 'Then and now.' He looked very handsome in the dawn light, with his glinting brown eyes and tousled black hair. However, due to my tiny tent, his elbows and knees were in uncomfortable places. When he finally left, it was a huge relief. His elbow had been on my boob the whole time.

After breakfast (coffee and more sausages), Alex was a gentleman and helped everyone pack up. He and cousin John Boy made a good team, tossing tents and sleeping rolls into the back of vehicles. But then John Boy's leg stump swelled up, and we had to force him to sit on Mum's deluxe padded camping chair.

John Boy didn't want to rest – he usually carries on with physical activity until he's in agony, then unstraps his prosthetic leg and anaesthetises himself with vodka. But with the sun out, he was happy to take off his shirt and tan his tattoos, while Callum and Daisy decorated his metal leg with Disney stickers.

My tent was easy to take down but getting it back into the bag was trickier. Alex spent a red-faced half-hour trying to wrestle armloads of slippery dinosaur fabric into an umbrella-sized bag.

Callum and Daisy got a chant going.

'Rex, Rex, Rex!'

It was quite cute seeing the two cousins getting along because they've been fighting a lot on this trip.

Callum is getting the blame, which is unfair. My seven-year-old nephew may look like a ne'er-do-well in his skull t-shirt, black jeans and bright-orange trainers, but he's very gentle with Daisy, and she did *ask* him to squirt the water gun.

Daisy plays the sweet and innocent two-year-old card with her adorable blonde-brown curls and big, blue eyes, but she is a silent assassin, scratching, biting and stamping Callum whenever adults aren't looking.

As Callum rightly puts it, it's age and gender prejudice – something he'll use his public profile to tackle when he's a premier league football player.

Eventually, Alex used his 'Landie' to drive over the crumpled tent fabric, squashing the puffy nylon into neat, flat folds. He looked heroic in the Land Rover, with muscular arms spinning the wheel back and forth.

Callum was very impressed by 'Rex and his Monster machine'. He enjoys adults who scare him and started following Alex around calling him 'mate' and 'lord'.

Alex offered to come back to the cottage and help me unpack, but I said no – I wanted to spend a bit of time alone to process this huge life change. Although, I didn't say 'process'. I said 'celebrate'.

'I'd rather hoped we'd celebrate together,' said Alex.

'Just give me time,' I told him. 'It's a lot to think about.'

I'm freaking out, freaking out!

Tuesday 3rd July

Back at the cottage. Should unpack the camping stuff but too tired right now. Daisy is napping, and cousin John Boy is in his bedroom also, changing his bedsheets and scrubbing the wooden floor with a wire brush and soap.

John Boy offered to change my bedsheets and scrub my floor too, but I said no. He pays me rent, so shouldn't have to do my domestic chores. Anyway, a wire brush would ruin my carpet.

Too tired to cook tonight, so phoned Mum and suggested a family Chinese.

'I'm not walking up to your house,' said Mum. 'I've been camping all weekend.'

'It's only five minutes away,' I said.

'But it's uphill,' said Mum. 'You should come to us.'

The country track between the cottage and Mum and Dad's pub isn't really uphill. It's just a slight gradient. But I didn't bother arguing because I'm happy to do a takeaway at the pub. It means I can have a pint of Guinness with my egg-fried rice and cashew chicken.

John Boy is coming for the takeaway too. This is good because he'll carry Daisy on his shoulders there and back.

I know it's only a five-minute walk, but it is a *little* bit uphill on the way home.

10 pm
Back at the cottage after the Chinese takeaway.

I toyed with asking Alex over but decided against it. I do need thinking space. Also, takeaway Chinese isn't his thing. He regularly flies to Shanghai, Beijing and Hong Kong, and gets annoyed at English attempts to 'ruin' tasty cuisine.

I was in a world of my own as Mum unloaded the silver-foil takeaway cartons and endured a telling off for not selecting egg or special fried rice.

'*Juliette* Duffy,' Mum snapped. 'Would you pay attention before these spring rolls get cold?'

Embarrassingly, I started crying. This was unexpected for everyone – me included.

Mum felt bad then and emptied all the spring rolls on my plate. Everyone hugged me and asked what was wrong.

'I don't know,' I said. 'I have no idea why I'm crying.'

'It's a big decision, isn't it love?' said Dad. 'You and Alex. Lots of changes. Where you live, who pays for what and a new family for Daisy. Those Daltons have their problems, don't they? It's a great big leap of faith. Who knows how it will turn out?'

I cried even more then.

'It'll be fine love,' said Mum, ruffling my hair, so curls fell all over my face. 'If Catrina Dalton gives you any trouble, she'll have me to answer to.'

Which is pretty much what I'm afraid of.

Wednesday 4th July

Texted Alex to apologise for being 'a bit off' since the camping trip.

He texted back to say he didn't have a clue what I meant.

The good thing about Alex's dysfunctional upbringing? His assessment of 'weird and distant' is decidedly different from mine. A few days apart is normal to him.

'Weird and distant' isn't ideal. But when you get past the weirdness and distance, Alex is a beautiful person. More impressive than anyone I've ever met – except for Daisy, of course.

Alex is going to 'swing by' later to talk wedding plans, so I'd better tidy the house, take out the recycling mountain etc.

Cousin John Boy is a neat and tidy housemate, crushing all his Stella Artois cans and neatly folding his KFC bags in the recycling containers, but my wine and Guinness bottles are more conspicuous.

Where will Alex and I live when we get married?

I can't picture Alex living here.

And I can't imagine living at the Dalton Estate, with its housekeeper, acres of grounds, swimming pool, horses and regular visits from Catrina Dalton.

Better go.

Daisy and I are catching the train to London.

Althea is holding a 4th of July family love-in this afternoon to celebrate America's freedom from British imperialistic tyranny.

The party will be huge, but luckily so is Althea's three-storey Bethnal Green home and rambling 'pot-luck' garden.

Technically, guests should be family only, but Althea has a big heart and many extended family members, including at least 50 randoms she's met at music festivals.

Evening

Just got back from Althea's 4th of July family love-in.

I've never seen so many tissue-paper hearts over one back garden. They were a swaying, swishing pink sky of joy.

Althea looked beautiful in her red sari, with rainbow glitter in her lengthy, black curls and a heart bindi on her forehead. And little Wolfgang was handsome as a moustached, axe-wielding Jack of Hearts.

It was heart-warming to see Althea and her many ex-boyfriends, Wolfgang's dad, Wolfgang's maternal and paternal grandparents, plus a load of festival randoms all sharing the love in a non-sexual way.

Mid-afternoon, Althea made us all join in a big 'love circle' while Wolfgang's dad played 'It's So Easy to Fall in Love' on a sitar.

Althea put her arms around me and Tara, Wolfgang's paternal grandmother, and we all swayed and sang to celebrate love and peace. It was a moment of divine connection – although, I must admit, marred slightly by Wolfgang pickaxing a heart piñata to death in the middle of the love circle.

'This is what I want,' I told Althea. 'Blended family bliss. Me, Nick, Alex and Alex's mother all getting along.'

'So bring the love,' said Althea. 'And the elderflower vodka.'

'I don't see it happening,' I said. 'And my life is messy enough already. I can't bring Daisy into another dysfunctional mother-in-law situation. Two messes do not make a tidy.'

'Then tidy the mess.'

'Do you think that's possible?' I asked.

'Whether you think you can, or think you can't, either way you're right,' said Althea. 'But don't tell anyone I said that.'

'Why not?' I asked.

'It's a quote from Henry Ford,' said Althea. 'The man who ruined the planet with modern motorcars.'

Assured Althea I'd keep quiet.

'Look, families always have issues,' said Althea. 'As long as you've got love, you can do anything. Wolfgang's dad is an idiot. No offence to Tara here. But idiots need love too. So it works. Think positive. Say it to yourself all the time: one big happy blended family.'

'How can I get along with Alex's mother?' I asked.

'You've got to visualise success,' said Althea. 'Imagine you and Catrina Dalton bonding and having a lovely time. You can do anything with visualisation. An example – I visualised Wolfgang playing peacefully with other children at this party. The universe delivered. He shared his flapjack with a soul cousin.'

Further probing revealed that Wolfgang had rammed an unappealing beetroot and carrot flapjack into another child's face. But I suppose it's one up from stealing kids' food.

Maybe Catrina and I *can* get along. It's possible.

But possible isn't the same as probable.

Late evening
Alex just dropped by for a glass of wine, but he's gone now. He has a meeting in Edinburgh tomorrow and is catching the overnight train.

'Say the word, and I'll cancel,' said Alex. 'I promised I'd be around for you more and I mean it. We're newly engaged. The company can survive without me for one meeting.'

I did not say the word.

I still need thinking space and don't mind Alex being away.

However, I did suggest doing a celebratory meal next week.

'Excellent,' said Alex. 'I'll bring Champagne.'

Champagne feels very official.

Almost too official.

Still – have been cheered by Althea's positivity. Anything IS possible. Catrina and I can be friends. I just need to work out how to make it happen.

Thursday 5th July

Morning

Alex just phoned from Edinburgh.

'I miss you terribly,' he said. 'And it's not even lunchtime. I should never have agreed to this work trip. But I have an idea – are you and Daisy free this weekend for strawberry picking? Seasonal *and* child-friendly.'

'It's Nick's weekend with Daisy,' I said. 'I can't commit to anything.'

'Well, perhaps you and I can visit the Tate Modern instead,' said Alex. 'A friend of mine is exhibiting. We can round off the day with dinner at the Oxo Tower. A friend of mine owns the place.'

'No,' I explained. 'I mean *I* can't commit to anything either.'

'Why not?' Alex asked.

'If Sadie is at Nick's house, I'll have to supervise the visit.'

'You won't let Daisy visit her father's house unsupervised if his girlfriend is there?' said Alex.

'Exactly,' I said.

'Isn't Sadie in Dubai?' Alex asked.

'Yes,' I said. 'But Nick and Sadie are always on again, off again. Dubai isn't that far.'

'Do you think you're being reasonable here?'

'Maybe not reasonable,' I said. 'But necessary.'

'This is a slippery slope Juliette,' said Alex. 'If you start dictating to Nick he may very well start dictating back. There's no law against having a mad girlfriend.'

Accused Alex of not being sympathetic.

'I'm trying to be fair,' said Alex. 'You have no legal right to supervise Nick's visits with his daughter.'

'Nick and Sadie are always screaming at each other. It's a toxic atmosphere for Daisy.'

'Nick won fortnightly weekend visitation,' said Alex. 'If you don't like his girlfriend, that's just bad luck isn't it? Something you have to get used to?'

Ugh. I know Alex is right. Decency and fairness are the qualities I love best about him.

I wouldn't swap Daisy for anything, but god – I wish I could change her father.

Friday 6th July

Decided to do a mega-house clean today.

It was on cousin John Boy's prompting – he said if we didn't deep clean the cottage soon, we'd get vermin and dysentery.

'Kitchen worktops should sparkle,' said John Boy. 'Dull equals disease.'

John Boy is fantastic on the domestic front, having been conditioned by the army and a germ-phobic mother to keep things spic-and-span. He always cleans up after himself, arranges his brightly coloured Nike trainers in neat rows and uses a set-square to make his bed every morning.

It's Daisy and I who are the domestic let-downs.

I honestly try to do the washing up straight away, but Daisy causes problems. She has a toolbox of tricks to distract me from domestic duties, including blood-curdling screams and flushing essential things down the toilet.

And of course, Daisy herself is a messy vandal – pulling books from shelves, scribbling on walls and leaving trails of Duplo bricks wherever she goes.

In the process of tidying, John Boy and I discovered that Daisy had chewed a hole in the sofa. I think this means her molars are coming. Either that, or she's picked up bad habits from Wolfgang.

Am still worried about Daisy's misshapen teeth. From her point of view, she has a neat little space that fits her thumb perfectly, but if she carries on thumb-sucking she could have teeth problems when she's older.

Must remember to show her the Tim Burton version of *Charlie and the Chocolate Factory* and point out Willy Wonka's scary round-the-head braces.

Mid-morning

Making good headway with the cleaning and tidying, but am in a quandary re Daisy's favourite soft toy, Curry the Rabbit.

Curry is now a stinky pile of shredded fur and the enemy of a clean, pleasant-smelling house. Even John Boy wrinkles his nose if 'Curry the Babbit' is in the lounge and asks if I've 'guffed or something'.

Daisy refuses to let me wash her stinky rabbit toy – which is probably the right instinct. I'm not sure Curry would survive a wash.

Have decided to hide Curry and hope Daisy forgets about him. It seems the coward's way out, but like Mum says, sometimes motherhood is about survival.

Afternoon

Daisy just had a mega head-banging meltdown because she can't find Curry. Worse – I can't find Curry either. I hid him somewhere clever, but where?

You'd have thought Curry would be locatable by smell, so I must have stashed him in an un-smellable location.

The loft perhaps?

Late afternoon

Alex just called. He asked if I minded him staying in Scotland until next week.

'Work just got hectic,' he said. 'Three senior managers have been poached by rival companies. It's the law of the jungle out there, and there's a tiger on the loose.'

Thought that was a little bit dramatic, but Alex was adamant things could get 'life-threatening'.

Told Alex to take his time dealing with the tiger. I have my own animal dramas, namely a rabbit to hunt down. Also, Mum phoned earlier, begging for help in the pub tomorrow. Something to do with cider and the summer rush. Daisy will be with Nick, so I'll take the opportunity to be a helpful daughter.

Goodness knows, Mum and Dad do enough for me.

Saturday 7th July

00.30 am

Nick just rang, and now I can't get back to sleep.

Shouted at Nick for ringing at an ungodly hour and demanded to know if he was drunk. He claimed he wasn't, but baby Horatio had only just fallen asleep and he hadn't realised how late it was.

'What do you want?' I demanded. 'It had better be important.'

Nick gave me a long speech about Sadie leaving him for the bright lights of Dubai, his psychological issues with parenthood, baby Horatio's dairy allergy and 'emotional and physical fatigue'.

'Are you surprised Sadie left you?' I said. 'Two selfish adults and a baby do not happiness make.'

'Why can't we just get back together, Jules?' said Nick. 'I know I messed up. Sadie was always just a sex thing. I should never have had a baby with her. No offence to Horatio but he's ruined my life.'

'You ruined your own life, Nick,' I said. 'Your best chance at a relationship now is getting back with Sadie, the mother of your *other* child.'

'No way,' said Nick. 'That ship has sailed. It's serious this time.

We've both changed our Facebook statuses *and* profile pictures.'

I knew this already since I Facebook spy on Nick and Sadie regularly.

Sadie's profile image is currently a 'come hither' picture of her big, beautiful, moon face peeking out from under a red fez.

Nick has a wholesome picture of himself, brown hair windswept, blue eyes welling with sadness as he pushes Horatio down a woodland trail.

'Have you called about anything important, Nick?' I asked. 'Or just to complain about your self-made mess of a life?'

'I phoned to ask for help,' said Nick. 'Mum is being unreasonable. She won't take Horry because she's doing a paper-porcelain course in Suffolk. I can't cope with two kids at once Jules; it'll break me. I'm exhausted.'

'I promised Mum I'd help out at the pub tomorrow,' I said. 'I can't let her down. And by the way, my new *fiancé* won't be happy about you ringing me in the middle of the night.'

'You're engaged?' said Nick. 'To the posh twat?'

'I'm getting on with my life, Nick,' I said. 'Just like you did.'

'But why now, Jules? Talk about kicking me while I'm down.'

'You've been down ever since you had Horatio,' I said. 'How is today any different?'

'I had bad news earlier,' said Nick. 'Sadie has a new boyfriend. It looks like she won't be back any time soon.'

'Look, you'll have to get used to having Daisy and Horatio together at some point,' I said. 'I can't help you out every visit. I have Daisy full-time, twelve days out of fourteen. The weekends are when I work and get things done. Why don't you take the kids to Tiny Tumbles? They can run around while you have a sit with a big cup of coffee and stare into space.'

'Yeah, that sounds like a plan,' said Nick, in a tired voice. 'What time do they open? Will they take the kids from 8 am?'

21

'They open at 11 am on Saturdays,' I said.

Nick started to cry.

In the end, I agreed that Nick could pick Daisy up at 10.30 am.

'But you'd better not be late,' I added. 'Or something bad will happen to your testicles.'

10.30 am

Nick just phoned to say he's running late. Leaving the house with a baby is difficult, so I'm giving him leeway. But he'd better hurry up. I wasn't joking about his testicles.

It's been a busy morning already because Brandi and Callum have come and gone.

My little sister and nephew knocked at the door just after breakfast.

Brandi was grey-faced and complaining about Callum's hyperactivity.

'I thought a change of scene might do him good,' she said, finger-combing her platinum-blonde hair. 'He just won't sit still today, no matter what I put on the telly.'

My little nephew proved her point by thump, thump, thumping on the open front door and shouting: 'Open up in the name of the law! We have a warrant!' Then he came spinning into the house with a toy gun to his chest shouting, 'Nobody move. It's a raid!'

John-Boy understood the game straightaway and played the evil drug dealer, appointing Daisy as his side-kick, dastardly Daiz. The three of them were soon wrestling on the kitchen floor, so Brandi and I left them to it.

'The summer holidays are next week,' said Brandi. 'How am I going to cope? It's not even nine o'clock, and I want to throttle him.'

Asked Brandi if she'd stayed up late last night, and she admitted she'd hit a few clubs and slammed three tequilas.

I know Brandi had Callum young, but she does need to be more responsible, move out of my parents' house, finish her beautician training etc.

She's a mother now. She has to understand – her life is over.

'Callum's louder than usual,' Brandi insisted. 'And Mum and Dad have been no help. Neither of them would take him to the park.'

'Why not?' I asked.

'I've burned my bridges with Dad,' Brandi admitted. 'I've asked him for hungover childcare too many times. He told me I had to learn res-pon-sib-il-ity.

'Why wouldn't Mum take Callum?' I asked. 'She's always babying you.'

'Mum was hungover too,' said Brandi. 'She was the one who bought the tequila slammers.'

Brandi shouldn't go out drinking every Friday, but I forgive her because having a baby at the age of sixteen is horrendous. Especially when that baby turns into a highly energetic boy like Callum.

While I was dosing Brandi up on Coca Cola, cheese Doritos, ibuprofen and paracetamol, we realised the house had gone quiet.

Ominous silences are ominous for a reason.

We headed upstairs to find Callum and Daisy chucking handfuls of Rice Krispies around my bedroom.

'We made Rice Krispie land!' they laughed.

It's quite astonishing just how many Rice Krispies come out of one box. Callum and Daisy were so pleased with themselves that it seemed cruel to tell them off. But we had a good go, all the same.

I made Callum and Daisy hoover the bedroom, landing and stairs, but I'm still finding Rice Krispies, even now. And I sense I'm in for a crispy, crunchy sleep tonight, my dreams haunted by the leering faces of Snap, Crackle and Pop.

11 am

Nick just picked Daisy up.

He was twenty minutes late, but I didn't tell him off because he looked awful. Aside from his usual 'Dad not coping and covered in white stains' look, there were weeping, bleeding patches all over his scalp.

'What's wrong with your head?' I asked.

'It's psoriasis,' said Nick. 'Because of all the stress. Don't you start.'

'Start what?' I asked.

'Names have been called. Nick Rotten Bonce and worse.'

'You should see a doctor, Nick,' I said. 'You look terrible.'

'I have,' said Nick. 'Three of them. Mum even got me in with a private specialist. They all said the same thing. The scabby scalp will go away when I manage my stress better. But how can I do that when I'm a single dad, working full-time?'

Admitted I couldn't see a solution short-term. Or indeed, long-term.

Nick left then, waving a sad goodbye as he strapped the kids into his sensible, new Volvo. I think Horatio might have been sick because I saw Nick struggling with a packet of wet wipes.

When Nick and I got together, pre-Daisy, he was a handsome actor with brooding blue eyes, dark eyebrows and tastefully dishevelled brown hair.

Now he is a tired, old dad with white stains all over his tired, old t-shirt.

Karma really is a bitch.

2.30 pm

Mum let me finish my pub shift early, so have decided to relax with my diary before tackling the housework. There is one positive about being a single mother – sometimes you get whole days off when your ex-partner takes the kids.

Of course, there are a million things to do, but I still have the luxury of an uninterrupted cup of tea.

Lovely.

3 pm
Sigh.

Nick just called. He is 'stressed and disorientated' and needs help with the children. He even offered to pay me, which is a new one. Sensed he must be pretty desperate and didn't want to leave Daisy with a nervous-breakdown candidate, so have agreed to meet him.

Evening
Long day.

Met Nick at Tiny Tumbles play area – aka over-heated hell for tired parents.

Tiny Tumbles is the kind of place parents go when they desperately want a break, so it's amazing Nick doesn't have a loyalty card. He'd get 10% off his coffee and a free selfie with the Tiny Tumbles clown.

Daisy was delighted to see me. Nick looked tired and relieved; he needed to change Horatio the moment I arrived, so I chased Daisy around the soft play while he disappeared into the gents.

There were a handful of other parents inside the colourful, padded child cage – mainly dads who looked physically active. They all said the same thing: 'I don't know who's having more fun – me or them!'

I said I was dehydrated and frightened, but they just laughed. Then Daisy went down the mega-scary death slide and goaded me into following her.

'Mummy! Be BRAVE Mummy!'

A queue of kids built up behind me, so I had to go for it –

flinging myself down the vertical slide, eyes closed, heart pounding.

I reached the bottom screaming hysterically, leggings lodged right in my bum crack. It was humiliating, especially when a teenager in a Tiny Tumbles t-shirt helped me to my table.

Daisy was happy in the ball pool after that, discovering inappropriate objects like a germy-looking rubber glove and a packet of nicotine chewing gum.

Eventually, Nick reappeared from the toilets looking stressed. He was half-walking, half-dragging a stumbling Horatio – aka the smartest one-year-old in town. Horatio was a lord among commoners, dressed in navy boating shorts and short-sleeved checked shirt, with a salmon pink jumper tied smartly around his shoulders.

'Horry just won't stay in the stroller any more,' Nick complained. 'He has to walk everywhere. It takes ages. Is it me or is it hot in here?'

'No wonder you're hot,' I told Nick, eyeing his skin-tight black jeans. 'You haven't dressed right for soft play. You need to stop prioritising fashion for comfort. You have kids now.'

Daisy waved at Horatio from the ball pool. 'Bugger, bugger! My baby bugger!'

Nick rubbed his worry-lined forehead, slumped into a plastic seat and said: 'God, I need a break.'

Unfortunately, Horatio had high-tailed it to the café area and was grabbing at chocolate bars and muffins with happy, chubby fingers.

'Shit.' Nick leapt to his feet and sprinted after him. 'Horry. Dude, no. You can't have that. You've just had a chocolate muffin.'

Horry began to wail. It was a heartfelt, emotional cry, as though a dear friend – perhaps someone he rowed with at Cambridge – had passed away.

Nick's face crumpled. 'Dude! Horry! It's OK, mate. It's OK.

Daddy's here. Have the choccy then, don't get upset.'

Horry's tantrum earned him a Toffee Crisp, a Mars Bar and a bag of crispy M&Ms.

When Horatio finally settled in the little kids' car town with sturdy padded sides, Nick sat and stared into space.

I recognised the look. It was the same one I had when Daisy started running around – exhaustion to the point of lobotomy.

Eventually, Nick said: 'So you and fancy pants Dalton got engaged, did you? It won't last. You two are like Sadie and me. On again, off again.'

'We're nothing like you and Sadie,' I said. 'Alex is sane and reliable and responsible.'

'Come on Julesy, you're too different to make it work.'

I didn't reply. The truth is, deep down, I feel like Nick could be right.

Sunday 8th July

Still haven't unpacked the camping equipment. My little red Fiat is full of airbeds, duvets and god knows what else. By the smell of things, there's a half-eaten sausage in there too and possibly some barbecued bacon.

My car now struggles uphill, which can't be very fuel-efficient.

REALLY need to unpack, but when?

Afternoon

Alex just phoned. He had a wedding date in mind: my birthday.

'In three months?' I squeaked.

'What date do *you* have in mind?' Alex asked.

'I don't have a date in mind,' I said.

'Well, what about the venue?' said Alex. 'Do you have a favourite Dalton hotel?'

'I hadn't thought about that either,' I said.

'I thought ladies obsessed over weddings,' said Alex. 'The date, the dress, the venue, the colour scheme.'

Said I wasn't a lady and didn't know anything about colour schemes. Certainly, my wedding to Nick wasn't colour-coordinated. Unless pain, anguish and betrayal have colours.

'Where did you get the idea of colour schemes from?' I asked.

'I've been watching *Don't Tell the Bride*,' said Alex. 'In the spirit of a good SWOT analysis. It helped me understand where other men get it wrong.'

'And where do other men get it wrong?' I asked.

'They go on *Don't Tell the Bride*,' said Alex. 'Juliette, why can't you commit to a date or venue? It feels like you're putting the brakes on.'

'Your mother and I aren't getting along,' I admitted. 'It feels like a red flag.'

'My mother can be difficult,' said Alex. 'And you're opinionated. Those two things aren't a good match. You might have to make your peace with that.'

'Althea says love solves everything,' I insisted. 'If your mother and I spend time together, I'm sure we can bond. Once she apologises for missing Laura and Zach's wedding, of course.'

'I'd let that one go if you want to be friends,' said Alex. 'My mother is far too self-centred to accept criticism. In her mind, she's done nothing wrong.'

'We're both adults,' I said. 'I'm sure we can have a reasonable discussion about my sister Laura's hurt feelings.'

'I thought we were planning a wedding,' said Alex. 'Not a funeral.'

Afternoon
Phoned Catrina. She didn't answer, so I left a message asking her to call back.

I have images of Alex's mother, cocktail in hand, silver-blonde hair swept into an elegant chignon, wrinkling her La Toya nose in distaste upon seeing my number.

I'll keep trying.

Monday 9th July

Laura phoned to congratulate me on my engagement. She'd heard the news from Zach, who learned it from Alex's PA. Which I'm guessing means Catrina must know too.

Once my big sister confirmed I was genuinely engaged, she asked what the clanking sound was.

'I'm doing the recycling,' I said. 'I'm always doing something when people call these days, whether it be housework, chasing a two-year-old or using the toilet.'

'You answer your phone on the toilet?' Laura asked.

'Only when good friends and family call,' I said. 'You should be honoured.'

'Well, congratulations on your engagement,' said Laura. 'I must admit, I was a teeny bit upset to hear it third-hand.'

'It doesn't feel real enough to tell people yet,' I said. 'We haven't set a date. And I won't until Catrina and I get along better.'

'Catrina's tricky,' Laura admitted. 'But it's like anything – you get used to her in time.'

'I don't want to get used to her,' I said. 'I already have one bad mother-in-law relationship. I need to bond with Catrina before the wedding. Fix everything and make it all shiny and perfect.'

'Perhaps you should focus on the things you have control over,' said Laura. 'Like where you're having the wedding.'

'COULD EVERYONE STOP PRESSURING ME ABOUT WEDDING DATES!'

'I asked where, not *when*,' said Laura, in her lovely gentle voice. 'Goodness, you sound ever so anxious.'

'Did you feel nervous when you got engaged?' I asked.

'On the contrary,' said Laura. 'It was the happiest day of my life.'

'You didn't feel worried at all?' I asked. 'Not about anything? What about marrying into the mighty Dalton family?'

'I *did* feel nervous when I first met Catrina,' Laura admitted. 'I'd learned basic Hungarian of course, but it's a tricky language – there are 35 different cases. Imagine what an ignoramus I felt, using the accusative case when I met to be inquisitive.'

'Has Catrina apologised yet for missing her son's wedding?' I asked. 'And making you, his blushing bride, cry in the toilets?'

'Oh, that was such a long time ago,' said Laura. 'Let bygones be bygones.'

'I can't do that Laura,' I said. 'You're my sister. What would you do if someone made me cry on my wedding day?'

'I'd hunt them down and beat them to a bloody pulp,' said Laura, in an uncharacteristically hard voice.

I was a little taken aback.

'All I want is an apology,' I said.

'I wouldn't bother,' said Laura. 'Catrina Dalton is…challenging. Just let her do her thing, and you do yours.'

'But I don't want that,' I said. 'I want a proper healthy mother-in-law and daughter-in-law relationship. Is that too much to ask?'

'With Catrina? Yes. Listen, shall I take you wedding dress shopping? There are some great boutiques in London.'

Had something like a panic attack then, pulled John Boy's KFC bag from the paper recycling and hyperventilated into it.

'You should take up meditation,' said Laura, hearing the brown bag inflate and deflate. 'Or yoga. To handle your nerves.'

'Single mothers don't have time for meditation or yoga,' I said. 'My stress solution is sugar and alcohol.'

'Why don't you have a party to celebrate your engagement?' Laura suggested. 'It might help you get used to the idea. Make it feel more real.'

'I'm doing a meal for Alex tomorrow,' I said, folding the KFC bag for later use. 'At the cottage. Mum and Dad are coming.'

'You're cooking?' said Laura. 'At the cottage? You're cooking for *everyone*?'

Said yes, and there was no need to say it in that tone of voice because I'm perfectly able to put a few pizzas in the oven.

'You're doing frozen pizza?' Laura asked.

'And garlic bread,' I said.

'Home-made or those frozen baguettes?'

'Frozen baguettes.'

There was a long silence, then Laura said, 'Will you at least do a side salad?'

'Of course I'll do a side salad,' I snapped. '*And* there'll be wine.'

'If you're celebrating a new life with Alex, maybe frozen pizza isn't the place to start.'

Afternoon

Have unpacked the larger camping items from the car, which will aid fuel efficiency.

Couldn't find any old sausages or bacon, but the rotten smell lingered even with the more significant items unpacked.

Then I had a light-bulb moment.

Curry the rabbit!

I'd hidden him in the glove box.

Gave Curry back to a delighted Daisy, who called me the 'best Mummy ever'.

Perhaps I should have thrown Curry away. It would have been a kindness, like the time we found a myxomatosis-ridden rabbit in the pub garden. The poor thing couldn't see and was clearly in pain, but the RSPCA wouldn't come out. Mum had to snap its neck to save a long, drawn-out death.

The next time *Watership Down* came on TV, Mum had to leave the room. We heard her sobbing in the bathroom, and she came back red-eyed and complaining of 'hay fever'.

Mum is like all tough people – soft as anything deep down.

Tuesday 10th July

Morning

Cooking the 'celebration meal' this evening but having a last-minute panic. The Co-op has sold out of pepperoni and margarita pizzas, leaving only novelty BBQ cheeseburger flavour.

Also, there are no clean plates or baking trays at the cottage. This is my fault – John Boy mainly eats Pot Noodles, Pop-Tarts and Ginster's pastries, so rarely requires crockery.

Sluts and drunks do indeed leave washing-up until morning. As an unmarried mother who drinks too much and often leaves washing-up overnight, I'm both these things.

Mid-morning

Just phoned Mum, panicking about the meal tonight.

Mum was very soothing until I told her about the Co-op running out of frozen pizza.

'Hang on a minute,' she bellowed. 'You were going to do pizza for this big 'I'm getting engaged' meal? What kind of celebration is that? Why don't you tell your future husband you don't give a shit about him?'

'I don't have time to do a five-course gourmet meal,' I shouted back. 'I am a single mother with a full-time job and camping equipment to unload.'

'When I was your age, I had three kids and a pub to run,' Mum argued. 'And I could still put a decent meal together. Cook Alex something special, for heaven's sakes. Poacher Tony is doing the rounds. He can get you a brace of pheasant for twenty quid. Or duck, if you're after a bigger bird. I suspect Tony gets his ducks from the boating lake in the park, so they're totally free-range.'

The thought of washing-up all the pots and pans, THEN cooking a stolen mallard for eight people made me burst into tears.

Mum relented then, calling me a 'soft sod' and offering to do a meal at the pub.

Accepted immediately and thanked her profusely.

'Oh, it's fine,' said Mum. 'You'd be doing me a favour. Your dad keeps saying I'll never use this new wood-burning pizza oven, so I need to prove him wrong. This will be just the ticket.'

'You just said pizza wasn't fit for a celebration meal,' I said.

'Ah, but this is special pizza,' said Mum.

'How is it special?' I demanded.

Mum said the pizza would have free-range duck on top.

Late afternoon

I'm at the pub, trying to get Daisy to sleep in her travel cot.

Mum, Nana Joan, Callum and Dad are all in the garden, throwing pellets into Mum's new wood-burning pizza oven.

I can hear Callum from here, singing: 'Burn mother flipper, burn.'

Mum has some weird ideas about Alex's 'upper-class' standards and has bought three jars of caviar to go on the pizzas. She's also rolled all the bathroom towels into swan shapes.

Seems ridiculous to talk about 'upper-class' standards when Callum keeps running around with his trousers down singing his bum, bum, b-b-b bum song.

Daisy has been quiet for at least ten minutes, which is a good sign. I'm writing this outside my old bedroom, body tensed as I pray Daisy nods off to sleep behind the door.

There's no noise right now, but I daren't go in and check. When Daisy does drop off, I can go downstairs and pour myself a glass of wine. But it's like baking bread in the oven – check too soon, and you could ruin the whole thing.

7 pm
Quite hungry.

Alex still hasn't arrived.

Mum has already put the food out, having over-catered as usual.

It's a mixed spread, including pizzas topped with king prawn, caviar and smoked salmon, a couple of roast pheasants, a dessert trolley and a 'small' cheeseboard. Which is huge.

7.30 pm
Just realised I didn't give Alex a specific time for dinner. This is bad, as Alex usually has dinner at 9 pm.

Have phoned Alex, but calls are going through to voicemail.

Mum was very distressed to hear Alex might not be here until nine.

'Nine!' she shrieked. 'I can't wait until then. I shall be ill.'

'Why don't we start on these pizzas then?' suggested Nana Joan. 'I'm sure your fiancé won't mind, Juliette.'

We agreed to try one pizza – the caviar one, which smelt disgusting.

Midnight
At the cottage with Alex sleeping beside me.

It's been a long evening.

Alex arrived at the pub around 8.30 pm, while I was upstairs rocking and shushing Daisy and occasionally shouting: GO TO SLEEP!

We'd eaten most of the pizzas by then and carved the pheasants, but – out of respect for Alex – had left the cheeseboard untouched (except for a small triangle of brie Mum ate accidentally).

Alex looked very handsome in the bedroom doorway, wearing his smart suit and holding two bottles of Champagne.

'Juliette,' he said. 'It seems I've missed the meal.'

'You need to go, you need to go!' I shouted, pushing Alex out of the room with urgency. 'Daisy will fight sleep even more if we start talking.'

Of course, Daisy began to scream the minute I closed the bedroom door.

'Mumeeee! MuMEEEE! REX?'

I experienced the usual conflict of emotions. Guilt about leaving my little girl *alone* in a dark room with towels masking-taped to the window. And fury that she wasn't lying down and going to sleep.

'We've just got to make a run for it,' I told Alex, in a faux-bright voice. 'She'll go to sleep. Eventually.'

'CURREEE,' screamed Daisy. 'Want curry!'

'Has she eaten?' Alex asked.

'Curry is her toy rabbit,' I explained.

'Are you sure she's OK in there?' asked Alex. 'She sounds desperate. Can't we bring her this Curry the rabbit thing, or whatever it is? Surely then she'll calm down?'

'She already has Curry the rabbit,' I said. 'Didn't you notice the smell?'

'Well, can't we tell her the rabbit is in her cot?'

'It doesn't work like that,' I explained. 'Daisy will just ask for something else.'

Daisy's wails drifted over the pub garden.

'CURRY! WANT BABBIT! WANT CURRY BABBIT!'

'How can you stand this crying?' Alex demanded. 'Juliette, let me go to her. Maybe her rabbit has fallen out of the cot.'

'I feel sorry for the poor bugger that ambulance is coming for,' said Nana Joan, cocking her head. 'It sounds in a hurry. I hope they pull through.' Then, noticing Alex, she said, 'Hello love. Well, you're a nice filled-out chap, aren't you? Not like that Nick. One punch and down he went.'

'Juliette, I really feel I should see to Daisy,' said Alex. 'If she's crying so loudly, something serious is wrong.'

'Don't pander to the crying,' said Mum. 'Close the door and walk away. Kids need to be ignored every so often. It's good for them. Otherwise, she'll have you running up and downstairs all night long.'

'Isn't that part of being a parent?' Alex challenged. 'Look. Just let me see if I can calm Daisy down.'

He went cantering upstairs, and Daisy's screams were momentarily relieved.

'There,' said Alex, when he came back downstairs. 'That's better. She only wanted to know where her rabbit was, Juliette. Now she'll go to sleep.'

Mum and I exchanged glances.

We didn't have to wait long.

A second later, Daisy screamed: 'SCUSE ME! SCUSE ME REX! WANT WATER. THIRSTY. WANT WATER REX!'

'Well, if she just needs a glass of water…' said Alex.

We let him take Daisy a glass of water. Then a toy she'd left in the garden. Then she wanted a story and milk in a Tommee Tippee and 'just one last cuddle' over and over again.

By ten o'clock, Alex had the sad, tired eyes of a new parent who'd been thoroughly broken in.

'She says she won't sleep unless she can have pizza,' he said.

'How does she know we're having pizza?' I accused. 'I told her we were having courgette and tuna fish, mixed with egg-yolk and broccoli.'

'She's been watching from the window,' said Alex. 'I took down the towels. She asked me to.'

I felt sorry for Alex, but I was angry too.

'You realise I'll be the one picking up the pieces tomorrow?' I said. 'Why couldn't you have listened to me?'

'I have to learn these things for myself, Juliette,' said Alex. 'I haven't had the luxury of being with Daisy since birth. But surely she will sleep better tonight. Now she's been up so late.'

The whole table sucked in their breath as I ranted about the effects of over-tiredness.

'She'll be waking all night,' I said. 'You've knocked her out of her sleep cycle. Over-tired kids DO NOT SLEEP WELL.'

Alex demanded I show him medical studies to prove this.

'The studies are real life mums on Mumsnet,' I said. 'The ones in the trenches.'

Alex raised an eyebrow. 'The trenches. Quite the metaphor.'

'You've been here two hours, and your eyelid is already twitching,' I said. 'You try doing it all day every day and tell me what it feels like.'

Alex told me to calm down.

I screamed that I would not calm down.

There was an awkward silence. Then Alex said, 'I'm told married life has its challenges. Is this the first of them, do you think?'

'Marriage is like Tupperware,' said Dad. 'Half the pots don't have lids, but you wouldn't be without it.'

'What are you talking about Bob?' said Mum. 'Ignore him Alex, and his metaphorical nonsense. My advice for a good marriage? Always say your piece. And if that means keeping your partner awake until 3 am while you shout at them, so be it.'

Dad nodded sagely. 'You have to let them get it out, Alex. Or you'll only suffer later.'

Wednesday 11th July

Alex told me this morning that he 'enjoyed' the family meal.

'But you spent the whole time running back and forth to Daisy,' I said. 'And then I shouted at you. And then Mum gave you pizza with duck and orange sauce on top.'

'Yes, I didn't much care for the duck and orange pizza,' said Alex. 'But the pheasant, king prawn and parmesan was an unexpected triumph. And now it's my turn to throw a celebration meal. You wanted to bond with my mother. So I've booked us all in for a Sunday lunch at the Mayfair Dalton.'

'This Sunday?' I asked.

'No, the end of the month,' said Alex. 'My mother can never be mobilised that quickly. The Mayfair Dalton is serving roast pheasant, believe it or not.'

'You're not fed-up with pheasant then?' I asked.

'A man who is tired of pheasant is tired of life,' said Alex.

'I think your mother and I should clear the air before we meet up for lunch,' I said. 'I've tried calling her.'

'And how has that worked out?'

'Not well. She doesn't answer or return my calls.'

'My mother is notoriously hard to get hold of,' said Alex. 'Don't take it personally. Just meet for lunch and do your bonding there.'

'I feel we should talk privately first,' I said. 'About her missing Laura and your brother's wedding.'

There was a long silence, then Alex said: 'So what are you saying? Are you going to phone my mother and criticise her for failing to attend Zach and Laura's wedding? And you think that will clear the air? I seriously wouldn't recommend that. Anya handles criticism badly. You'll make an enemy of her for life.'

It always confuses me when Alex calls his mother Anya. Why can't the Hungarians use an M word for mother like the rest of Europe?

'So what else am I supposed to do?' I said. 'Not mention Laura's wedding at all? Just squash my angry feelings into an angry ball and glare at your mother over the lunch table?'

'Yes,' said Alex. 'That's how we do things in our family.'

Thursday 12th July

Just tried Catrina's mobile again. She didn't answer but Monique, her assistant, did.

'Ms Dalton is in bed recovering from lunch,' said Monique. 'I'll tell her you called.'

Precisely what Catrina needed to recover from was unclear. But I'm guessing cocktails.

Friday 13th July

Morning

Catrina just phoned.

Returning the call was an error on her part – she thought I was Juliette Lewis, the actress.

It was a little humiliating explaining that I was a different Juliette, the one engaged to her son, Alex.

'On, Juli-*anne*,' said Catrina, in her strong Hungarian accent. 'Yes, I did hear about the engagement. Vell, darling. Engagement doesn't always end in marriage. I should know. I should *know*.' Then she started to sob. 'Carlos made so many promises. But now he is off with that young girl, photographed in all the papers. So humiliating for me. He thinks of nobody but himself.'

'Look, I may as well get this out of the way,' I said. 'Now Alex and I are engaged, you and I have some things to clear up. I want to talk to you about my sister's wedding.'

'Who is your sister?' Catrina demanded.

'Laura,' I said. 'She married your other son. Zach. But you didn't attend their wedding.'

'Zachary is married already?' said Catrina.

'Yes,' I said. 'Earlier this year.'

'Monique probably forgot to tell me,' said Catrina. 'I have a full diary and some health problems.'

'Laura gave you the invitation in person,' I said. 'She told me.'

'Wedding invitations can be hard to recognise, these simple things with string and recycled paper. Everyone trying to pretend they don't have money. When I married Harold, wedding invitations were gold and silver. So glamorous. So beautiful.'

'You must have known about the wedding,' I insisted. 'You sent a wedding gift.'

'Monique probably sent Champagne,' said Catrina. 'She always sends Champagne. Or perfume. Very French.'

'The wedding gift was the sort of present you would send,' I said. 'It was a solid silver goulash kettle from Budapest.'

'Oh yes!' said Catrina. 'The goulash kettle. So elegant. I nearly kept it for myself. But I have so many. I'm afraid I have to go now. I get tired in the afternoons.'

'It's only 11 am,' I said.

'Oh yes, vell,' she said. 'Morning. Afternoon. It's all the same.'

Then she hung up.

Saturday 14th July

Shift at the pub tonight.

Alex asked if he could see me, but told him I was working. It's true – I am working. But I'm also in need of more thinking space after the phone call with Catrina.

I already have a bad mother-in-law, aka Nick's mother, Helen. Do I really want another one?

Fun shift at the pub trying all the new summer ciders. Mum bought ten cases of mixed fruit flavours from the brewery this week in a misguided effort to be healthier.

'Doctor Slaughter has been on at me again about my weight,' said Mum. 'So I'm having these ciders instead of beer. They count towards one of my five a day.'

'It would be better if you stopped drinking altogether,' I said.

'Rubbish,' said Mum. 'People who drink alcohol live longer. It's a medical fact.'

'I think they're talking about moderate drinkers,' I said. 'Not people who drink all their weekly recommended units in one night.'

'Don't get on at me, Juliette,' said Mum. 'I take my health seriously. Look, I've bought a Fitbit.' She waved her large wrist at me, showing a gleaming, top-of-the-range, touch-screen Fitbit with built-in heart monitor. It would have been a useful purchase if Mum hadn't turned off its health features.

'I couldn't be doing with vibrations every hour, telling me to move,' Mum explained. 'And the heart monitor was just depressing. Who wants to know they have below-average cardio health? I don't like being bullied into walking either, so I turned off the pedometer thingy. If I've sat on my arse all day, that's my business.'

Sunday 15th July

Morning

Have phoned Catrina again and left a message re meeting in person to talk. Clearly, a phone call won't work because Catrina can hang up whenever things get complicated.

I've left five messages now, and it's getting a bit humiliating. I could wait until Catrina, Alex and I meet for lunch in a few weeks, but it seems inappropriate to have a delicate conversation over a fancy meal, especially pheasant.

Phoned Alex to complain, and he sympathised.

'Anya can be hard to get hold of,' he said. 'She has a full diary and even fuller cocktail cabinet. A difficult combination.'

'But she has an assistant,' I said. 'Surely calling someone back isn't such a big deal. Especially in the age of mobile phones.'

Alex said he'd see what he could do.

Afternoon

Alex has called his mother. He got through on the first attempt, which makes me both suspicious and annoyed.

'Anya has agreed to meet us for lunch in the village tomorrow,' said Alex.

'Us?' I queried. 'We already have an 'us' lunch at the end of the month. I want to talk, just Catrina and I.'

'Accept the offer, Juliette,' said Alex. 'You wouldn't go into a boxing match without a referee.'

'I wouldn't go into a boxing match full stop,' I said. 'I'm too pretty to be punched.'

'So why are you?' Alex asked.

'I don't want to fight with your mother,' I said. 'I want to bond with her. But to do that, we need an honest, open conversation about the past so we can move forward.'

'To my mother, that's a fight,' said Alex. 'I hope you have a good pair of boxing gloves.'

I don't, but I'm sure I can borrow some. Mum and John Boy have five pairs of boxing gloves between them.

Monday 16th July

Lunch with Catrina and Alex didn't happen.

Alex phoned mid-morning to say his mother had gone AWOL.

'Monique tells me Anya went to London,' said Alex. 'I imagine she's making a mockery of her recovery.'

'What recovery?' I asked.

'She stayed at the Priory recently,' Alex explained. 'After Carlos left, my mother spiralled into bad cocktail habits.'

Thought this was an odd comment, since Catrina already had bad cocktail habits. She drinks every bit as much as Yorkie, who is a medically diagnosed alcoholic. The only difference is she uses fancier glassware.

'Maybe it's for the best that Anya has done a bunk,' said Alex. 'It sounds like you were spoiling for a fight.'

'No I WASN'T,' I said. 'Just a discussion.'

'Which would turn into a fight,' said Alex. 'Reasonableness is not part of my mother's makeup. Look Juliette, she isn't going to change. No matter what you say to her. She's not going to recognise any wrongdoing. That would be death. Anyway, she's emotionally fragile right now. Not up to a confrontation.'

'Why does it have to be a confrontation?' I asked. 'Why can't your mother just apologise for upsetting my sister and we all move forward?'

'Can't you just tolerate my mother, as your sister does?' said Alex. 'And focus on the positives of joining the Dalton family?'

'Like?'

'Like staying for free in many excellent hotels.'

In the end, Alex and I had lunch – just the two of us.

We ate at the village deli, while Dad took Daisy to the park for a picnic. Daisy's molars are still coming through, so I didn't want her eating the tablecloth or the salt and pepper shakers.

43

Alex was disappointed not to see Daisy – which was quite sweet. He kept asking how her words were getting along. Could she pronounce 'parmesan' yet, after his hours of tuition?

Told him she was getting there.

Tuesday 17th July

Althea visited today, bringing obscene quantities of tofu.

'This will cure all your hormone problems,' she said. 'It's a vegan miracle.'

'I don't have hormone problems,' I said.

'Yes you do,' said Althea. 'All women do. We've messed up our divine design with chemical hair dye and white bread.'

I have to admit, Althea is looking well on her tofu-heavy diet. Her thick, black curls were shiny and luxuriant under a pink cowboy hat, and her curvy figure rocked a tight-fitting European Union t-shirt.

Told Althea I'm getting cold feet about the wedding.

'Well you do have shit to sort out,' Althea conceded. 'You and Alex are from different worlds. How are you going to handle finances once you're married? Are you going to keep working at the pub, or will Alex pay your way like some archaic statement of patriarchal ownership?'

'I don't know,' I said. 'It feels like a weird idea, someone paying my bills.'

Nick never supported me in any meaningful way, although admittedly he did buy Tesco Express Prosecco if he won a leading role.

'It's not the money side of things,' I said. 'It's my relationship with Alex's mother.'

'You're over-thinking that,' said Althea. 'I already told you. Bring the love and you'll be fine.'

'I can't love Catrina until she apologises to Laura,' I said.

'Then you won't be fine,' said Althea. 'Find the love first, not second. Negative emotions carry cancer.'

'I'm not just going to sweep her bad behaviour under the carpet,' I said. 'A discussion needs to be had.'

'Choose love, Juliette,' said Althea. 'And let it go. Let it go.'

Then she started singing, *Let It Go*.

Wolfgang joined in with his growly voice, and Daisy demanded I sing too. Felt forced into singing my agreement, but deep down I haven't let it go.

Words must be spoken before bonding can take place.

Althea left promising she'd visit soon with wedding-dress fabric samples. Felt doubly worried – first about wedding planning and second about the type of fabric Althea will bring. Pink, neon taffeta does not an elegant bride make.

Wednesday 18th July

Alex just phoned from work to pressure me into a wedding date.

'We really should get something in the diary,' he said. 'The decent venues get booked up months or years in advance.'

'You're a leisure-brand magnate,' I said. 'Surely you can get last-minute bookings at Dalton hotels.'

'Certainly not,' said Alex. 'I can't cancel other people's bookings. Admittedly, I've ring-fenced a few weekends just in case, but it's already getting awkward. We've had to turn down Princess Eugene, and she's well-known for holding a grudge.'

'Why do we have to move at one-hundred miles an hour?' I asked, grabbing John Boy's KFC bag for more hyperventilating.

'What are you talking about, Juliette?' said Alex. 'We haven't even set a date. We're not moving forward at all.'

'How can we?' I said, between inhales and exhales. 'Things need to be smoothed over with your mother. She wouldn't even turn up to a lunch date.'

'You're marrying me, not my mother,' said Alex.

'But your mother stays at the Dalton Estate.'

'Yes, she comes and goes. She's always welcome.'

'I'm not doing another mother-in-law from hell popping-in situation,' I said. 'Your mother and I need to have an adult discussion, smooth things over and get along.'

'So what do you propose?'

'I've tried calling your mother,' I said. 'She just hung up. So I'm going to visit her in person.'

Alex sighed. 'One of my favourite things about you Juliette is that you know your own mind. I'm not going to stop you. But don't say I didn't warn you.'

Thursday 19th July

Callum has been given twenty school tadpoles to take home for the school holidays.

They're 'late bloomers' which, according to Dad, means they'll die soon.

Luckily, Callum doesn't know what 'mortality' or 'failure to thrive' means and took Dad's comments in a positive way. He's sure all his 'boys' will turn into big, strong frogs.

Callum has named all the tadpoles (Destroyer, Judge Dredd, The General etc.) and can identify them by appearance and personality.

The tadpoles are currently on the bar in the pub, being made a fuss of by Mum, Dad, John Boy and the regulars.

John Boy has become especially fond of the tadpoles and chatted to them throughout our afternoon shift.

'Look at old Destroyer,' said John Boy. 'Pushing everyone around. He's the real boss of the tank. But little Judge Dredd there is my favourite. He's a wily one, he is. A real survivor.'

John Boy is taking Callum to Aquatic Land tomorrow to browse fish-tank furniture. Callum has his heart set on a glittery porcelain castle and some pink-plastic seaweed.

Friday 20th July

Nick just called, on the pretence of organising visitation tomorrow, but really he wanted to complain about Sadie.

'She's moved in with some old, overweight billionaire in Jumeirah Beach,' he complained. 'It's all over Facebook.'

It sounds like Sadie is living the shallow high life she's always craved, driving a leased white Mercedes and living in a gleaming glass apartment in one of the world's tallest buildings.

'Is her new boyfriend aware she has a baby son?' I asked.

'Who knows?' said Nick. 'Sadie hasn't done FaceTime with Horatio in weeks. She just texts pictures of herself and her new fat boyfriend.'

Couldn't resist looking on Sadie's Facebook profile to see how old and fat her new boyfriend is. The answer is: very on both counts.

There are various shots of Sadie, draped over her tubby designer-suit man in expensive-looking restaurants and hotel bars. She looks tanned and toned, but her smile is strained.

How could she abandon her son like this?

Hope Sadie stays in Dubai for a long time. Horatio is better off without her.

Saturday 21st July

Nick picked Daisy up first thing, so I had a day to myself. Should have spent it tidying the house, but Alex swept me off my feet and took me on a Thames riverboat cruise.

We had a delicious seafood lunch and took in the sights, with Alex pointing out plots of land he's bought and sold over the years.

It's funny. On paper, Alex and I don't work. But the children in us have always been best friends. He sees the real me, and I the real him.

When the boat docked at Blackfriars, Alex told me anecdotally that his father was in hospital nearby at London Bridge.

'Your father's in hospital?' I asked.

'Yes,' said Alex. 'But it's nothing to worry about – he's been in and out of hospital all year. His new girlfriend calls an ambulance at the drop of a hat.'

'Do you want to visit him?' I asked. 'Bring flowers or something?'

'No,' said Alex. 'The last thing my father wants is his son seeing him in his pyjamas. I had thought about building a few bridges this year, though. His new girlfriend seems to have softened him a little.'

'So why not drop by the hospital?'

'That's a step too far.'

'Why is he in hospital anyway?' I asked. 'What's wrong with him?'

'Suspected heart attack.'

'Oh, my goodness!' I said. 'Aren't you worried?'

'*Suspected* heart attack, Juliette,' said Alex. 'Before you fly off the handle, you might want to ask what the doctors diagnosed.'

'Which is?'

'Severe indigestion.'

Sunday 22nd July

Alex stayed over last night, which was sexually awesome – BUT there was a downside.

He wakes at 6 am, just like Daisy.

Had hoped for a lie-in on my parenting day off, but no such

luck. The shower woke me at six, and then Alex suggested we go for a ten-mile run to blow off the cobwebs.

As I was pulling the duvet over my head, Alex's phone bleeped loudly and he announced he'd received a bizarre email. He turned it into a *Breaking Bad* cliff-hanger, saying over and over again: 'This is very strange, *very* strange …'

'What's strange?' I asked, pulling back the duvet.

'This email from my father,' said Alex. 'He's out of hospital. Reading between the lines, they sent him on his way with a box of Gaviscon and a warning to stop wasting their time. Anyway, he's invited us to his house in Guernsey for Christmas.'

'Us?' I said.

'Yes,' said Alex. 'Alex plus fiancée…' He paused. 'The invitation said Juli*anne*. So I'm guessing my mother has told him about you.'

'Do you want to go to your father's house for Christmas?' I asked.

'Of course not,' said Alex.

'Yesterday, you were talking about building bridges,' I said.

'Not that many bridges.'

Monday 23rd July

Start of the school summer holidays today.

Had an irate phone call from Brandi first thing, begging me to come and help with Callum.

'It's only 9 am and I've already lost all my patience,' she screamed. 'If someone doesn't help me, I'm going to kill him.'

Told Brandi I'd be over in five minutes.

At the pub, Callum was running around like Dennis the Menace on fast-forward. I had to pull him down from the ceiling, literally: he'd squashed himself between that and the top bookshelf.

'What on earth did you give him for breakfast?' I asked Brandi.

'He made his own breakfast,' said Brandi. 'Sugar sandwiches

with golden syrup, chocolate sauce and condensed milk. And don't look at me like that. It's Nana's fault. She texted him the recipe.'

'Why did you let Nana text him recipes?' I demanded. 'Her diet is 80% Murray mints, 20% bananas. Plus a pinch of sugar from the sugar bowl whenever she passes the kettle.'

'She's healthier than Mum,' Brandi insisted. 'At least she has the bananas.'

Tuesday 24th July

Hottest day of the year so far, and the weather says it's going to get hotter.

Alex surprised me by popping over for lunch. He brought Cobb salad, crusty French bread and some wedding 'save-the-date' cards designed by his marketing agency.

The visit wasn't an especially welcome surprise because I was walking around bra-less in a Spice Girls t-shirt, fanning myself with one of Daisy's colouring books when Alex arrived.

'Bad time?' he observed.

'Yes,' I said. 'But it's good for you to see me in my natural state. It'll help prepare you for married life.'

Alex told me I looked beautiful in my natural state, then spread out five different 'save the date' designs on the breakfast bar and asked which I liked best.

Grabbed John Boy's trusty KFC bag for a quick inhale and exhale.

Alex hugged me and asked if there was anything I wanted to talk through.

Said yes – I'd hoped his mother would have returned my calls by now, but she hasn't. And I'm dreading doing an unannounced visit.

Alex quietly unpacked lunch, then said, ' Is this *really* just about my mother? Or is it marriage full stop?'

'Maybe it's about acceptance,' I said. 'If your mother accepts me, it's like your whole family does.'

'You don't have to see my mother,' said Alex. 'It's a big house. When she stays, you can keep your distance. And I can visit my mother alone in London –'

'I don't want that,' I said. 'Divided birthdays and Christmases. I want everyone to get along. Blending. Really blending.'

Alex put comforting arms around me and gave Daisy some French bread to pick at.

'What do you think, Daisy?' Alex asked her. 'Do you think Mummy's being silly?'

Daisy said, 'Yes Rex. Mummy silly.'

Which I thought was very unsupportive.

'Relationships will always have problems, Juliette,' said Alex. 'If you want to wait until everything is perfect, you might be waiting a long time. Better commit to working through problems when they arise.'

It sounded reasonable, and quite healthy for Alex.

'I've had enough uncertainty,' I said. 'I want a nice mother-in-law-daughter-in-law relationship for a change. Is that asking too much?'

'Life is uncertain, Juliette,' said Alex. 'One never knows what's around the next corner. Sometimes you have to jump in. Risk-aware, not risk-averse.'

'This is a marriage we're talking about, not a business acquisition,' I said.

'The principles are similar,' said Alex. 'It's all about calculated risks and long-term return. I took a huge financial risk buying out the Dalton Group. But it *was* calculated. I was aware of the worst-case scenario.'

'Which was?' I asked.

'Complete financial ruin.'

'I don't want to be ruined,' I said, reaching for the KFC bag again.

'My father had a saying, growing up,' said Alex.

'Was it: *Glare at the staff and they bring your coffee quicker?*' I asked.

'No,' said Alex. 'He said, safe is risky and risky is safe.'

'And what does that mean?'

'It means playing it safe is the biggest risk of all. Life knocks everyone down. If you play it safe, you're not ready for the knocks. But take the risks and you'll be in the driving seat.'

It was a stirring speech, diminished only slightly by the Rice Krispy on Alex's shoulder.

'Of course, my father probably regretted that advice,' Alex mused. 'Because I took a big risk and bought his company from under him. But back to marriage. Personally, I think I'm a solid investment. Proven growth and high dividends.'

'I think you're medium risk because of your mother,' I said. 'And before I commit to investing in you, we need to work on being one big, happy, blended family.'

'Noted,' said Alex.

'So I need to visit your mother.'

'Christ,' said Alex. 'Are you going to go through with that? I've already told you it's a terrible idea.'

'I think a reasonable conversation –'

'This is where you're going wrong,' said Alex. 'My mother is never reasonable. I wouldn't waste your time.'

'I have to try,' I said. 'She's not answering my calls. Knocking on her door is the only way forward.'

'Just make sure you wear plenty of padding.'

Wednesday 25th July

Stopped by the Dalton Estate to see Catrina in an effort to make our relationship better.

I've definitely made things worse.

On the positive side, I had the foresight to drop Daisy with Dad first. So I spared my two-year-old daughter the sight of grown women flinging drinks at each other.

Ugh.

Alex did warn me.

Afternoon

Daisy is sleeping. Time to write about my horrendous meeting with Catrina.

The negative signs were there from the start because Catrina was shouting into her phone when I arrived at the Dalton Estate.

Note to self. If someone is screeching 'For god zakes, what kind of imbecile enjoys French people?' hold off the problematic conversation for another time.

Ditto – if someone is drinking cocktails at 11 am.

Catrina was lounging on the lawn in her bikini and gulping a Martini as I crunched down the gravel path towards the main house.

Offered a tentative: 'Hello?' and Catrina gave an exaggerated startle, then flung her mobile phone to her prosthetically enhanced chest.

'What are you doing here?' she demanded.

'I hoped we could talk,' I said. 'Your son and I are getting married, and –'

'Which one are you?' asked Catrina, squinting into the sun. 'The one with Zach or the other one?'

'I'm Juliette. The one with Alex.'

'Oh yes. I remember now. Julianne. From the cruise.'

'Jul*iette*,' I said. 'My name is Juliette. Not Julianne.'

Catrina didn't invite me to sit down, so I perched on a nearby rattan sun lounger and began my prepared speech.

'Alex and I are engaged,' I began.

'Yes,' said Catrina, lifting her floppy sunhat. 'I know. So what? Do you know how many engagements I have had in my life? Do I come to people's homes and tell them all about it? What is the use of this? Don't you know Harold is in *hospital*?'

'Actually, he's out of hospital now,' I said. 'Alex told me.'

'Why has no one told *me* this?' Catrina demanded. 'That new *American* girlfriend, shutting me out. Such a silly woman with her bright clothes and dyed hair. To dress that way at her age – so ridiculous. We have a saying about women like that in Hungary, but it is too good for her. So I will use the English. *Filthy* American gold digger.'

'Why don't you call Harold?' I asked. 'See how he's doing? He only had indigestion.'

'Don't be ridiculous,' said Catrina. 'I can't call him. I'm his ex-wife.' She blinked then and said: 'Why are you here again?'

'I thought we should do some bonding,' I said. 'We'll be family soon –'

'I already have a family darling,' said Catrina. 'At my age, you don't have room for more.'

'Legally you'll have to make room,' I said. 'When Alex and I marry, I'll be your daughter-in-law. And on the subject of daughter-in-laws, I'm hoping you might apologise to my sister for not attending her wedding.'

'Who?'

'My sister. Laura. She married your son Zach.'

'Oh, *Zach's* new wife,' said Catrina. 'Why would I apologise? I gave her names of good Catholic churches for the wedding, but she didn't listen. How could I attend a *civil* ceremony in a *hotel?* Harold felt the same way.'

'At least Harold came to the reception,' I said.

'Vell, it's too late for me to do that now,' said Catrina. 'Water under the bridge. Nobody cares about something that happened so long ago. Unless they are very petty.'

'Laura is kind and forgiving,' I said. 'But that doesn't mean you don't owe her an apology.'

'She won't be getting one from me,' said Catrina. 'And I don't like being spoken to in such a way. I tell you, Alex will be hearing of this. You don't want to make an enemy of me. You will live to regret it.'

'You don't want to make an enemy of me either,' I said. Not sure what I meant by that, but it was the best I could think of under the circumstances.

Catrina sat bolt upright with her Martini then, like a cat arching its back.

Working in a pub, I have an instinct for when people are about to throw drinks and Catrina had that look.

I grabbed Catrina's glass, but we ended up tussling, and the Martini spilt all over Catrina, the olive and lemon peel resting on her tanned cleavage.

Thought it best to leave then.

Couldn't think of much to say on my way out, so opted for, 'You should probably wash that bikini – strong alcohol isn't good for printed fabrics.'

I didn't wait for a thank you.

Evening
Phoned Alex to tell him what happened, but Catrina had got to him first.

'My mother tells me you threw a drink in her face,' he said. 'And called her an ignorant Hungarian slut.'

'No. I didn't.'

'Maybe she's thinking of an argument with someone else,' Alex reasoned. 'She does have a fair few of them. Well. I did warn you.'

'I didn't mean for it to be an argument,' I said. 'But I had to be honest. Your mother does owe Laura an apology.'

'You'll learn,' said Alex. 'My mother is unreasonable. You can't reason with unreasonable. Don't waste your time.'

'But I want us to get along in time for the wedding,' I said.

'Well, you've made a great start, Juliette. Ten out of ten. So has this incident with my mother made you any more certain of the wedding date? Or have things gone the other way now?'

'It's not a business meeting Alex, it's a wedding,' I said. 'There are emotions involved.'

'Exactly,' said Alex. 'Much more difficult to schedule.'

Thursday 26th July

Althea called round today with a bunch of fabric samples for my wedding dress.

Seeing the samples sent me into a panic, and I ended up wailing and pacing back and forth like a caged animal. John Boy's KFC bag had been recycled, so I was all at sea.

Althea made camomile tea to calm me down, then berated me until I breathed normally.

'What's going on Julesy?' Althea demanded. 'Is Alex being a distant, moody arsehole again?'

Said no. Alex has phoned every day, talking about weddings and suggesting dates.

'Things were already bad with his mother,' I said. 'But now I've made them much worse. Reassure me. Tell me it's fixable.'

'It'll be fine, Julesy,' said Althea. 'I see a lot of light pink sparkly waves around you. Remember – you and his mother are one. You have to let go of the separateness illusion.'

Am clinging to Althea's positivity by my fingernails.

There *has* to be a way to repair the damage.

Once I'd finished my camomile tea, Althea and I assessed fabric samples again.

'Why don't you have any white fabric?' I asked.

'Don't you know what white symbolises?' said Althea. 'Virginity. How sexist and archaic is that? Why not make a statement with harlot red? Tell the world you won't be judged for sexual promiscuity.'

'I like the colour white,' I said. 'It's princessy.'

'Well, to tell you the truth, Wolfgang used all my white taffeta for his Wizard of Oz costume,' said Althea. 'He's playing Dorothy. I never thought he'd use the whole lot, but he wanted such a big tutu in the end. You know how he is – he likes to make an entrance.'

Have a vision of Wolfgang wearing a skirt the size of a table and knocking other kids off the stage. And almost certainly, that vision is accurate.

Friday 27th July

Alex phoned. He's going to come over after work with a bottle of wine and 'supper'.

Could do with two bottles of wine but didn't want to ruin Alex's civilised dinner arrangements with my low-brow drinking habits.

'Are we still having Sunday lunch with your mother this weekend?' I asked.

'I thought, given recent cocktail throwing events, best not,' said Alex.

'I didn't throw a cocktail,' I insisted. 'I just misjudged things a little.'

'I've been thinking,' said Alex. 'Would you like to be introduced to my father while my mother cools down?'

'I've met your father before,' I said. 'He was awful.'

'Mr Dalton senior is a little less vicious than usual these days,' said Alex. 'You wanted happy families, Juliette. Why not start at the top?'

'Your father is someone I'm happy to ignore,' I said. 'He used to hit you with a cricket bat.'

'It wasn't just a cricket bat,' said Alex. 'There were coal tongs, a riding crop...a ladle on one occasion. But my father is from a different generation. Everyone was more brutal in his day. He thought he was doing it for our own good. I don't dislike him because he beat us as children.'

'So why do you dislike him?'

'Business-related and family reasons. Power games. The way he throws his weight around. But he's getting better since the new girlfriend came on the scene. More human. And the cricket bat was a long time ago.'

Told Alex I'd rather try and get along with his mother first. One maniac at a time.

I've called and called Catrina since the Dalton Estate drink-throwing incident, but once again she's not answering.

Will keep trying.

Saturday 28th July

Just put Daisy to bed, having talked to her about weddings, marriage, life changes, etc.

Daisy was fascinated by the idea of moving into 'Alex's castle' and asked if we would become princesses.

'Not princesses,' I said. 'But I imagine we'll have fun if we move in with Alex.'

'Why?' Daisy asked.

'Because he has a swimming pool, stables, a gym room and many, many bedrooms. And there'll be a housekeeper to look after everything.'

'What's a housekeeper?' Daisy asked.

'Someone who does all the jobs you don't want to do, then turns invisible,' I said. 'Alex's housekeeper is called Mrs Hawks. I've never met her, so she must be very good at her job.'

'Castles cold Mummy,' said Daisy. 'They peas in the bed. We get bruises. Ouch!'

Assured Daisy that Alex's house was well-insulated with 100% pea-free beds.

'Will On Boy live in Rex's castle too?' Daisy asked.

'No,' I said. 'He'll stay here and get a friend to move in.'

Daisy asked lots more questions about the wedding then, some trickier than others. Disney has badly mis-sold weddings to children, in my opinion. Had to explain there would be no talking animals, mermaids, etc.

'The wedding is just a big party with flowers and cake and all our friends,' I told Daisy.

'Can I invite friends, Mummy?' Daisy asked.

'Yes,' I said. 'Of course you can. Who would you like to invite?'

'Daddy,' said Daisy.

Rapidly back-pedalled.

'I'm not sure Daddy would like that, Daisy,' I said. 'Maybe he can come to your birthday party instead. What about inviting Wolfgang to the wedding? He's your friend.'

'Don't be silly Mummy,' said Daisy. 'He eat the flowers. And the nighty man.'

Assuming, by 'nighty man', she meant the vicar.

Sunday 29th July

7 pm

A family emergency.

Callum is in accident and emergency with a head injury. He got into a fight with three big boys who pushed him down the playground slide.

Callum kept the injury secret at first, attempting to fix it himself with a tube of Loctite superglue.

I've agreed to be on stand-by, because Brandi and Callum have already been at A&E for three hours and there don't seem to be any doctors around.

'If we're not seen by midnight, would you do the graveyard shift?' Brandi asked. 'I can hardly keep my eyes open.'

'Surely you'll be seen by midnight?' I asked.

'I don't know,' said Brandi. 'They're talking about a ten-hour wait. How many hours are there between eight and midnight?'

I love my little nephew but hope my late-night services won't be called upon. Daisy will be OK at home with John Boy, but the thought of spending the early hours of the morning with a stir-crazy Callum in A&E is unappealing.

He's bad enough on a twenty-minute bus journey.

Monday 30th July

Midnight

Am writing this in A&E, having been called in to wait with Callum.

There's a mixed crowd in the A&E waiting room. Most are over-anxious parents with perfectly healthy children. Some are parents with sick kids and good reasons to be anxious. The rest are trampoline injuries.

Callum has already made a friend: a girl called Angel Rain who looks like Moana.

Angel Rain had breathing difficulties earlier, so her parents have brought her in to be on the safe side. She's had problems with her heart and lungs since birth.

Have said Angel Rain can go ahead of us because her need is greater.

This confused Callum a great deal.

'Do the good kids get seen first here then?' he asked. 'And the naughty ones last? Like at school?'

Explained that Angel Rain was sicker than Callum, so needed more urgent attention.

'And you're not *that* naughty, Callum,' I added. 'Just high-spirited and full of Coco Pops in the morning.'

'I am naughty,' said Callum. 'Miss Bullard is always sending me out of class.'

'Why?' I asked.

Callum detailed his many classroom misdemeanours, including shouting 'Bullard!' when the teacher's back was turned, drawing blue felt-tip all over his stomach and running around the classroom going 'WAAAAAAHHH!' with his shirt pulled up.

'Why do you do stuff like that?' I asked.

'I'm just bored,' said Callum. 'School isn't my thing. I'm no good at reading and writing, Aunty Julesy. And it's no fun being the thick kid. There should be a different kind of school for kids who can't sit still. Because we are special in our own way.'

Sometimes Callum is wise beyond his years. Other times, like yesterday afternoon in the park, he can be incredibly stupid.

2 am

Awful thing just happened.

Angel Rain turned blue and started gasping for breath.

Her poor parents – I felt so sorry for them. They were beside themselves.

Callum and I hammered on the security door that separated the riff-raff from the medical staff, but the doctors and nurses had obviously trained themselves to ignore banging because no one came.

Luckily, one of the nurses happened to be coming out for a break, bag of chocolate Maltesers in hand, so we forced her back inside to get a doctor.

Angel Rain is being seen now, thank goodness. She and her parents have disappeared through what Callum calls 'the sliding door of doom'.

They haven't returned, so I hope she's OK. Seeing a child dangerously ill puts things in perspective. In the scheme of things, Callum is blessed. Even if he does have a head full of superglue.

4 am

Still haven't been seen.

Phoned Mum to request a change-over so I can go home and sleep.

'There's only one doctor on duty,' I told her. 'It's taking forever.'

'You're lucky there's even one at this time of night,' said Mum. 'Doctors in NHS hospitals are rare as hen's teeth these days. It's a national disgrace. We should all pay more taxes and get it sorted. Let me put my bra on. I'll be right down.'

6 am

Home now but sleep is alluding me.

Callum was finally seen at 4.30 am – just after I phoned Mum.

An upbeat man called Dr Chang looked Callum over, cheerily adding more glue to his wound.

'You did the right thing with the superglue, Callum,' said Dr Chang. 'We use something very similar here. Maybe you'll be a doctor when you're older.'

Callum said he was too thick to be a doctor and hated school.

'I didn't like school either,' said Dr Chang. 'I used to study at home. Four hours every night. There's a lot of time in the day if you look for it.'

Callum said he liked watching TV in his spare time.

I told Dr Chang that he seemed remarkably perky for a man who'd been working sixteen-hours straight and thanked him profusely for the overtime.

'There was no choice.' Dr Chang laughed maniacally. 'If I didn't do overtime, there would be no one on duty.'

Mum arrived halfway through Dr Chang's examination, having somehow barged her way through the watertight security door. She located us by swishing curtains aside and calling out, 'Julesy! Callum!'

When Mum found us, she shook hands with Dr Chang, sat heavily on a spare wheelchair and opened up a bulging picnic bag.

Dr Chang accepted a sausage roll, a bag of salt and vinegar Hula Hoops and a foil carton of Capri Sun. Then he asked Callum how the injury happened.

Callum tilted his head reflectively and said, 'I was talking when I should have been listening.'

'Callum started a fight with three big boys,' I explained.

'Teenagers,' Callum added proudly. Then he started saying things that defied physical possibility.

'They pushed me down the slide, and I shot into the air, flew all the way to the roundabout and that's where I hit my head.'

Callum is just like Mum. Why tell the truth when fiction is so much better?

A positive end to the early, early morning – Dr Chang told us that Angel Rain is fine. He wasn't supposed to talk about other patients, so used sign language. We surmised that Angel Rain used some kind of large asthma inhaler for her chest and is now sleeping. Which is great news.

Afternoon
Aww.

Woke to find seven missed calls from Alex.

Explained about the Callum A&E visit and that John Boy has been looking after Daisy while I caught up on sleep.

'I was worried,' said Alex. 'If you hadn't picked up this time around, I would have come to Oakley and hunted you down.'

I appreciated the stalker sentiment and told Alex I missed him.

'But there's no point coming to see me today,' I said. 'I'll be unconscious. I'm going to check on Callum later, then have a very, very early night.'

If I didn't have a daughter, I'd have forgone a lot of sleep to stare into Alex's beautiful brown eyes. But as a mother, your priorities change.

Sleep first. Romance second. Sex last.

Evening
Callum is doing fine – his head injury is healing well. It turns out the superglue he used really did the job. The doctor hardly added any of his own.

Callum now wants to volunteer at the hospital to help children like Angel Rain.

'They're short-staffed, aren't they?' he said. 'They could use someone around who knows how to use superglue.'

Talked to Callum about the big boys in the play park, and his story changed yet again. This time, he claimed to have jumped down the slide to run away from the boys, then 'brained' himself somersaulting over the fence.

Mum asked Callum if there was something he wasn't telling us.

Callum looked scared, then said all in a rush: 'One of the big kids hit me with a baseball bat, but you can't tell anyone because Chris Whippy said he'd come after my family if I grassed him up.'

Mum has gone to the park right now, looking for Chris Whippy. I pray for his sake she doesn't find him.

8 pm
Home now.

It didn't take long for Mum to sort out the boy who hurt Callum. She came back from the park after twenty minutes, swinging Chris Whippy's baseball bat.

'Those boys won't be messing with you again,' said Mum, ruffling Callum's curly, black hair, then tucking the baseball bat under the bar with the last-orders weapons. 'I've told them to find a new patch.'

'Weren't you worried about those boys being tooled up?' Brandi asked. 'I nearly took my earrings out and went over to look for you.'

Mum laughed. 'It was only teenagers with a baseball bat, love. You wouldn't believe the weapons I've confiscated over the years. Yorkie routinely carries a double-edged hunting knife. And Mad Dave's crossbow is out in the garden shed with all the camping equipment.'

Tuesday 31st July

Chris Whippy's parents turned up at the pub last night looking for the woman who stole their son's baseball bat.

The dad, a tired, shaven-headed man in a Chelsea football shirt, clearly wanted to leave well alone, but the mum was on the warpath.

'Tell that woman to give my son his baseball bat back,' she demanded. 'Or I'll give her a good kicking.'

Had to laugh. I mean, honestly. Fancy coming to our pub and

threatening violence. Brandi lives for the days she can pull out her hoop earrings and throw herself into a scuffle. And Mum is both fat enough to do damage and extremely handy with a beer-tap wrench.

Told Chris Whippy's mum her son wouldn't be getting the baseball bat back because he had put my seven-year-old nephew in A&E.

Chris Whippy's mum wasn't sure what to do then. You could see the cogs turning – albeit slowly. She'd come into the pub an avenging angel but was now the mother of a nasty piece of work.

'Shall we move on?' I suggested.

'All right,' said Chris Whippy's mum. 'Sorry he hit your nephew. I can't control him these days. I do everything for that boy, but I get no thanks. He'll learn soon, just like I did. School days are the best days of your life.'

Felt sorry for her then, because anyone who misses school must be really miserable.

Wednesday 1st August

Nick seems to be getting it together re being a fully functioning adult and parent. He just phoned to say he'd pick Daisy up at 8 am this Saturday morning.

'Has your mum agreed to take Horatio then?' I asked.

'No, she's not babysitting right now,' said Nick. 'She's got some personal stuff going on.'

'What personal stuff?'

'Private family stuff,' said Nick. 'I can't talk about it. She's not ill, but she needs looking after.'

Weird to think of Helen needing looking after. It brings to mind a fanged spider wrapped in a fluffy heart blanket. Maybe she's lost an important client. Or her expensive home has been painted the wrong shade of Farrow and Ball.

Impressively, Nick has made solid plans for Daisy and Horatio this weekend. He's bought a paddling pool, a load of plastic toys and some strong 'Bullet' coffee from Tesco.

Evening
Laura just phoned. Zach is visiting his father in hospital, so she's feeling lonely.

'I don't mean to sound selfish,' said Laura, 'but Zach works all day. And now I've lost an evening with him too.'

'Harold Dalton is in hospital again?' I asked. 'What's he in for this time?'

'Oh, there's nothing wrong with him,' said Laura. 'His new girlfriend is being overly anxious again. It's nice she cares, but I wish she cared about my family time too. The doctors say Harold has more indigestion. Either that or constipation. Nancy is demanding they run test after test, but it's all in her mind. Sorry. I know that sounds callous.'

Sounds like Harold Dalton's new girlfriend is as insane as Catrina. He certainly knows how to pick them.

Thursday 2nd August

Alex just phoned. He's invited me to a wine tasting at the end of the month.

Accepted the invitation, then asked about his father.

'Laura told me he's back in hospital,' I said.

'I didn't know that,' said Alex. 'He must have run out of Gaviscon.'

'You didn't know?' I asked.

'No,' said Alex. 'Does that make me a monster?'

'Of course not,' I said. 'You're one of the least monstrous people I've ever met.'

'The shareholders might disagree with you,' said Alex.

'Well they'd be wrong,' I said. 'You're incredibly kind. But you hide it behind a stern exterior. Of course, if your father is seriously ill, then you are a monster.'

'He isn't,' said Alex. 'If he were, the legal team would have been in touch.'

The wine tasting will be at the Bond Street Dalton. It's a free event for Alex and his team. Every summer, international wine merchants gather at a Dalton hotel to tempt the Dalton Group with their wares.

Will have to talk to Laura about how to elegantly spit out wine. There has to be a technique that doesn't make me look like John Boy at a football match.

Hope Alex doesn't expect me to know about wine. Aside from the colour difference, I haven't got a clue. Although I know more than Brandi, who thinks rosé is red and white wine mixed together.

Alex said a limo driver would take me home after the event, so I needn't worry about public transport late at night.

'We won't be spending the night together?' I asked.

'I'm flying to Stockholm the next morning,' said Alex. 'Another work thing. But I can cancel the trip if you want me to. Again, just say the word.'

Once again, I didn't say the word. I still have a lot of thinking to do.

Evening
Just watched *Legally Blonde* with John Boy. I enjoyed it for the frothy girly fun, and he enjoyed it because he fancies Reese Witherspoon.

Realised that lovely Reese got remarried and became a blended family. And she always looks happy. If she can do it, surely Alex and I can.

Friday 3rd August

Three of Callum's tadpoles have died – Prince Nassim and the two 'brothers' Darth and Vader.

Callum took it very hard when he saw the lifeless bodies. He dug a little grave for them in the garden and has given the other tadpoles extra food because he thinks they could be traumatised.

Forget what a sensitive little soul Callum can be sometimes. He hides it well, with swearwords and violence, but he's like Mum and John Boy – a real softy deep down.

Daisy wasn't upset about the dead tadpoles, laughing heartlessly as John Boy struggled to fish out the bodies with a sieve.

They do say two-year-olds are selfish, but I hope she isn't a psychopath. From what I've Googled, it can be genetic, and Nick isn't a good provider of robust mental-health genes.

Dad has come up with a solution for Callum's grief – a free summer holiday club called Artz Kidz at the local gallery.

'Little Callum can express his feelings through creativity,' Dad enthused. 'And communicate his pain and loss in more productive ways than thumping and kicking the sofa.'

Brandi is totally on board because Artz Kidz offers free childcare three days a week. For her, creativity is just a side benefit.

Evening

Alex is off to New York tonight. He didn't ask me to 'say the word' this time because the trip is urgent.

'How is your dad doing?' I asked. 'Is there any news?'

'Yes,' said Alex. 'The diagnosis is official: another case of indigestion. The only thing my father is suffering now is acute embarrassment. If he's not careful, his next diagnosis will be boy who cried wolf.'

Saturday 4th August

So hot today.

Alex phoned from New York and confirmed it was 'hot as hell' in the Big Apple too.

Thank goodness I live in the countryside with something like a breeze, but it's still boiling.

Before Nick picked her up, Daisy spent the first part of the morning completely naked, singing 'Feeling hot, hot, hot' with sweaty blonde-brown hair stuck to her head.

John Boy is walking around with no shirt on, but that's not unusual. What's strange is Mum, who usually loves the heat, complaining and Googling air-conditioning units.

'This hot sun is fading my hair like nobody's business,' she said. 'I've had to ditch the pink and go bottle-blonde again. It's just too much maintenance.'

If Mum thinks she maintained her pink hair, she's kidding herself. It always looked washed-out. No doubt, she imagined herself a vibrant-pink pop princess like Katy Perry, but the reality was the shade white t-shirts go when washed with pink underwear.

Evening

John Boy and I just watched the Brady Bunch movie. Another happy blended family – but no mention of extended family members.

Maybe Mr and Mrs Brady have difficult in-laws hidden away in the background.

Sunday 5th August

Surprise party for Dad in the pub this afternoon.

Laura came with baby Bear, and Nana Joan drove to the pub on her new electric scooter.

She looked very cool astride her black-leather-upholstered Easy Rider with flame motif and monster-machine tyres. She's had a new platinum-blonde bobbed hairdo and completed the biker-chick look with a synthetic-leather pink jacket.

Alex offered to do a FaceTime appearance from New York, but I told him not to bother. We'd never hear him over the live folk band.

Helped Mum secretly decorate the pub, while Laura, baby Bear and Daisy distracted Dad upstairs.

Along with promotional Carlsberg and Pimm's bunting, Mum hung a giant picture of Dad behind the bar. In the life-size photo, Dad is on his bicycle wearing a neon-yellow cycle helmet, hi-vis jacket, hi-vis sash, hi-vis bicycle clips, hi-vis trousers and trainers with reflective stripes. He looks like a novelty 'Terry the Traffic Cop' garden gnome.

'Just wait until you see what I've bought your dad for his birthday,' said Mum, as we hung the picture. 'A brand new, light-weight aluminium bike with disc brakes. It's called 'Road Slayer' and cost over £1,000. He's going to love it.'

It's sad that after decades of marriage, Mum doesn't understand Dad at all. Dad loves maintaining his old pushbike, which he's had since he was eighteen. Most replacement parts don't exist any more, so Dad has fashioned brake pads from blackboard wipers and made good use of duct tape and coat hangers.

Predictably, when Mum presented Dad with the gleaming, new Road Slayer bike, Dad was dismissive.

'I've already got a bicycle, Shirley,' he said. 'What do I need another one for?'

Mum went off in a strop temporarily but rallied when Brandi brought out the birthday cake, which was Mohito-flavoured and filled with real booze.

'What's wrong with a good old-fashioned jam sponge with a

sprinkle of sugar on top?' said Dad.

'Oh shut up, Bob,' said Mum. 'A birthday isn't all about you. The rest of us want to enjoy ourselves too.'

Monday 6th August
Morning

Alex is back from New York and phoned me from Heathrow Airport.

'I'm coming to see you tonight after work,' he said.

'Aren't you jet-lagged?' I asked.

'If I'm honest, yes,' said Alex. 'But I love you and want to show commitment to our future marriage.'

Can't wait to see him. And if he falls asleep early, there's a benefit: I can watch *Love Island*.

Evening

Alex is here but jet-lagged and asleep on the sofa. I've put a blanket over him and left him to it, but am hoping he'll wake in the night and join me upstairs for hot reunion sex.

Then again, I'm pretty tired myself. A full-eight hours sleep is also an exciting option.

Tuesday 7th August
Morning

Very surreal morning.

Had a call from Harold Dalton's assistant, Miss Ling. She phoned just after Alex left for work and invited me to Harold Dalton's Guernsey home for Christmas.

Asked Miss Ling how she got my phone number. She laughed and said, 'We have our ways.'

Which sounded a little sinister.

However, Miss Ling assured me that the Dalton Group haven't spied or phone-tapped since the mid-1970s.

'Mr Dalton – that is *Harold* Dalton – wanted to make doubly sure you and Alex received his Christmas invitation,' said Miss Ling. 'Harold wants to bring the whole family together this year.'

'I'm not family,' I said. 'At least, not yet.'

'Mr Dalton wants to *welcome* you to the family,' said Miss Ling.

'Why?' I asked.

'You're engaged to his son.'

'He didn't welcome my sister,' I said. 'She was engaged to his son too, and she has much neater hair than me.'

Miss Ling gave an indulgent chuckle and said: 'Mr Dalton's recent hospital stays have changed his outlook. He knows he's not going to live forever. We understand you have a young daughter. She'll be most welcome. Harold enjoys children at Christmastime.'

'What about the rest of the year?' I asked.

'As long as they have clean hands and keep their voices down,' said Miss Ling.

This is a very odd development.

Very odd, indeed.

Evening

Finally got through to Alex, after calling and calling all afternoon.

Alex was very apologetic when he finally picked up. However, I've done him a massive favour by alerting him to a phone-reception black spot in the Chelsea Dalton conference room.

'Your dad's assistant called,' I said. 'She invited me to Harold's house on Christmas Day. It's a bit weird, don't you think? What's going on?'

Alex went silent for a moment. Then he said: 'My father is getting on in years. Maybe he's feeling the cold hand of death on his collar. Miss Ling called me this morning too. I did wonder why.'

'You didn't speak to her?'

'No. I never take calls from my father or his staff members. It's better that way – fewer arguments. I'll give my mother a call and find out what's going on. She is intimately connected with the inside workings of the Dalton family. She'll know what this is all about.'

'Your mother?' I said. 'She and your father divorced years ago. What's she going to know?'

'Oh she'll know,' said Alex. 'She keeps a firm finger on the family pulse. My father's will changes regularly. She needs to keep abreast of things.'

'You mother is in your father's will?' I asked.

'Of course,' said Alex. 'They were married. And speaking of marriage, have you decided on a date yet?'

Gave a strange laugh.

After a long silence, Alex said: 'Look, Juliette, if you've changed your mind, just tell me.'

'I haven't changed my mind,' I said. 'But your mother and I still need to make amends.'

'Why are you fixating on that?' Alex asked. 'Life isn't perfect, Juliette. And families are the least perfect thing of all. Just bite the bullet and pick a date.'

It was a silly way to phrase things. Who likes biting bullets?

Wednesday 8th August

Told Mum and Dad about Harold Dalton's Christmas Day invitation.

'His assistant phoned me personally,' I said. 'Harold wants to welcome me to the family.'

'You'd have thought the old bugger would phone you himself,' said Mum, 'if he wanted to welcome you to the family. So are you going there for Christmas then?'

'No way,' I said. 'That would be horrendous.'

'Oh, it might not be so bad,' said Mum. 'You wouldn't be short of grub, that's for sure. But then again, you're trying to get along with Alex's mum, aren't you? Maybe you should spend Christmas with her instead.'

'The getting along part is not going well,' I said. 'Last time I saw Catrina, she tried to throw a drink over me.'

'What kind of drink?' Mum asked.

'A Martini,' I said.

'At least it wasn't anything sticky,' said Mum. 'Poor old bird. She has a few screws loose. Don't take it personally. Some of my favourite customers have chucked drinks at me. If I took it to heart and barred all of them, I'd be out of business.'

Thursday 9th August

Lovely day with Alex. We took Daisy to the zoo.

While Daisy was preoccupied with the foul-smelling chipmunk enclosure, I asked Alex if he'd spoken to his mother about Miss Ling's phone call.

'She didn't know anything,' said Alex. 'I have no idea why my father wants to bring us all together.'

'What's your mother doing on Christmas Day?' I asked.

'Anya usually goes to my father's house with the rest of the Dalton clan,' said Alex.

I was shocked by this. 'Your mother goes to her ex-husband's house on Christmas Day?'

'Yes,' said Alex. 'I think it's a case of keeping your enemies close.'

'What about your little sister?' I asked. 'Will Jemima go to your father's house too?'

'Jemima will be in France over Christmas,' said Alex. 'She's staying with her father in Paris right now and they're getting on like a house on fire. She's starting school there next term and moving in with her father permanently.'

'What does your mother think about that?' I asked.

'She sees the merit of Jemima being in Paris,' said Alex.

'I couldn't imagine Daisy living away from me,' I said. 'It would feel all wrong.'

'My mother's skills don't lie in childcare,' said Alex. 'We're big on delegation in my family. Why not hire professionals to do the job?'

'I'm not any good at childcare either,' I said. 'But I still want to be with Daisy.'

'You and my mother are very different,' said Alex. 'Actually, that's one of the things I love most about you.'

'Do you want to spend Christmas with my family at the pub?' I asked.

'I'd be delighted to,' said Alex. 'As long as there's nothing breaded on the menu.'

Honestly!

Talk about snobby. Just because Mum and Dad run a pub, doesn't mean we only eat chips and scampi. Mum, in particular, has very high-brow tastes and regularly shops in Waitrose.

Having said that, I'd better talk to Mum about Christmas Day food *just* in case. Mum probably won't cook an oven-ready Christmas dinner, but a good Cash and Carry offer could sway her.

Should also talk to Mum, re the novelty wooden penis on the Christmas tree. It's off-putting, especially if we have turkey.

Afternoon
Popped into the pub to ask (instruct) Mum and Dad on the Christmas dinner this year.

Mum said she'd already ordered the meat for Christmas Day.

76

'I'm doing a twelve-bird roast,' she said. 'Something for everyone.'

'What's a twelve-bird roast?' I asked.

'Turkey stuffed with a goose, chicken, pheasant, partridge, pigeon squab, Aylesbury duck, Barbary duck, poussin, guinea fowl, mallard and quail,' Mum explained. 'With layers of sausage meat in between.'

'That's a shocking amount of food,' I said. 'It works out more than one roast bird per person.'

'Don't be silly love,' said Mum. 'A quail is ever so small. Barely even a starter. Which reminds me – starters. What do you fancy? Lobster?'

I suppose at least lobster and twelve roasted birds aren't breaded.

Friday 10th August

Lunch shift at the pub today.

Mum put her giant club sandwiches on the menu with two kinds of bacon, so we were hectic all afternoon.

Callum sloped in from Artz Kidz holiday club just after three, helped himself to a J20 and bag of crisps from behind the bar, then sat on a stool and wrote poetry. After twenty minutes of a furrowed brow, he asked me some interesting philosophical questions to help stimulate his creative brain.

They were:

+ When are we all going to die?
+ Did my bruise go down the plughole?
+ Is the world bigger than the sky?
+ Why can't I marry my teaching assistant?
+ Are God and Santa Claus the same person?
+ Do tadpoles go to heaven, even if they push other tadpoles around?

I think Callum is in an existential frame of mind because three more of his tadpoles have died. His sadness has led him to question the meaning of life and death.

Wish I had more answers for him.

Saturday 11th August

Alex landed, having been in Berlin yesterday on a 'short hop' meeting.

He called from the airport to complain that we haven't seen enough of each other.

'But you're travelling,' I said.

'Yes, but you didn't tell me not to,' said Alex. 'You didn't say the word.'

'I don't mind you travelling right now,' I said. 'I'm happy to have a bit of space. Can you please ask your mother again about taking my calls?'

'I can ask again,' said Alex. 'I doubt she'll listen.'

'Isn't there anything you can do?' I asked. 'It's all a bit humiliating, fifty calls in.'

'Try for a hundred,' said Alex. 'That's my mother's usual caving-in point. Listen – I'm going to come and see you tonight. Are you at the cottage?'

Told him yes, but that he should stay in London.

'You'll tire yourself out, coming straight here after an international meeting.'

'Nonsense Juliette,' said Alex. 'It was only Berlin. Practically on the doorstep.'

He's going to drop by for a quick hello, then head back to London for a dinner meeting with colleagues.

It will be nice to see him.

Afternoon

Called Catrina again.

Her assistant, Monique, said Catrina was in Spain, buying art with her ex-boyfriend Carlos.

'And she left her mobile phone with you in the UK?' I asked.

Monique said no, she was in Spain with Catrina.

'Well, can I speak to Catrina then?' I asked.

Monique said that was impossible. Catrina wasn't available for transatlantic calls.

I said that Spain, being in Europe, wasn't transatlantic to the UK. And also, if Monique could talk on Catrina's mobile, surely it wasn't a huge step to put Catrina herself on the phone?

Monique hung up then.

Will keep trying.

Sunday 12th August

A low day for Alex and me.

If things had gone to plan, we'd be holding a new-born baby right now. Feeling very raw and emotional. Miscarriages are awful. Just awful.

Of course, babies hardly ever come on their due date, but that's not the point. I keep thinking about what our baby would have looked like. Would he or she have had Alex's brown eyes? My light, curly hair? Mum's hefty hands?

Alex came over first thing to make breakfast and look deeply into my eyes.

I don't know if he's feeling as sad as I am. Maybe this sort of thing affects men differently.

Phoned Mum to have a cry and she told me life always works out for the best in the end.

'It was a terrible thing to happen, love,' she said. 'But try and focus on the positive. Count your blessings that you don't have a crying, shitting baby screaming the place down and you can sleep all night long. You're getting married. Focus on that.'

It was good advice.

Alex, Daisy and I have our whole future ahead of us. No sense thinking what might have been.

Monday 13th August

Alex left for Paris today. He talks about international travel like he's catching a bus into town.

'Paris is just down the road,' he said. 'Only a train ride away. But you say the word Juliette and I'll cancel the trip.'

Once again, I didn't say the word.

And once again, Alex didn't look happy.

Pub shift tonight.

The bar is pretty empty, so I've had a lovely time reading Brandi's *Heat* magazine from cover to cover while sipping Guinness.

Heat magazine revealed that Will Smith and Jada Pinkett Smith are a blended family. Will Smith has a son from a previous marriage, but now he's married to Jada and they're all living happily ever after. Happy blending is possible. It's possible.

Tuesday 14th August

Aww.

Alex came home early from Paris, especially to see me. He phoned from my front doorstep and said: 'Guess where I am right now, Juliette?'

Guessed the obvious: plane, airport, Champagne bar, marble-floored lobby etc.

'None of the above,' he said. 'I'm outside my favourite house in the world.'

I still couldn't guess where Alex was, so he knocked on the front door.

'Hang on a minute,' I told him. 'I might have to call you back. There's someone at the door.'

Was a bit embarrassing, finding Alex on the doorstep. He looked exhausted but happy, and we embraced like black-and-white movie stars. Then Daisy came rushing up shouting, 'Rex! Rex!' and he swept her up into his arms too and spun us both around.

When Alex released us, he told Daisy he had some toys for her.

'Mrs Hawks had a clear-out,' he said. 'They're things I used to play with as a boy. I thought you could make good use of them.'

Alex went to his car, then returned to our messy house with a box of musty-smelling mint-condition antique toys.

'These have been in my family for two generations,' he told Daisy. 'You can play with them and carry on the Dalton tradition.'

Daisy ooed and aahed over collectable Dinky cars (including a 'much sought-after' Bedford-end tipper) a Bayko building set and an evil-looking clockwork Mickey Mouse from the 1940s – all in their original boxes.

'Why the toys grey?' Daisy asked.

Alex explained the toys were from his father's time when colour was a luxury.

'How did you keep these old toys in such good condition?' I asked Alex. 'They're pristine.'

'The threat of a severe beating helped.'

'Daisy will ruin these,' I said. 'She'll destroy the boxes first, then move on to the mechanical parts.'

Alex said it didn't matter. 'They're hers to do whatever she wants with.'

'But they're family heirlooms,' I said.

'Daisy is family,' said Alex. Which I thought was very lovely.

Alex is on his way to New York now.

It was literally a 'flying' visit, ha!

Wednesday 15th August

Met Althea for lunch today in Bethnal Green.

I wanted to talk about Alex's mother, my insecurities, failures and feelings of guilt, but Althea shouted at me.

'Stop with the guilt and self-flagellation,' she said. 'Live in the moment. Don't let yesterday trouble today. I drank a whole bottle of homemade sloe gin last night. Do you think I feel guilty? No way.'

Asked Althea why she'd drunk so much gin in one sitting.

'I'm creating award-winning vegan booze for the Bethnal Green Fair next week,' she said. 'You get points for consistency. I had to make sure the gin at the bottom tasted the same as the stuff at the top.'

Maybe women judge each other for good reason, i.e. to stop mothers drinking whole bottles of gin.

Althea has decided not to enter her sloe gin in the vegan booze competition though, because it's too boring.

'I've invented something much better,' she said. 'Tofu rum. It's delicious.'

'What's does it taste like?' I asked.

'Like Bailey's Irish cream,' she said. 'Only lumpier.'

Thursday 16th August

Shopping in London today for Mum and Callum's birthday presents.

Mum is hard to buy for because she gets everything she wants the moment she wants it. Callum is much easier. He loves any toy that is noisy/messy/irritating.

In the end, I bought Mum a large box of diabetic chocolates. Will hide the word 'diabetic' with Daisy's sparkly glitter pen because Mum refuses all diabetic, decaffeinated, zero-sugar, diet, alcohol-free products, claiming she takes her drugs straight.

Have bought Callum the 'Pie Face' game, which slaps people with whipped cream. Am predicting a 'favourite aunty' prize on Sunday.

Dropped in on Laura for lunch. She didn't seem herself during our visit, and admitted she was feeling sad.

'What are you feeling sad about?' I asked.

Laura said she didn't know. Everything was perfect. Except that Zach was away a lot on business, she didn't have any local friends and was cripplingly lonely.

'But I'm just making a fuss,' she said, dabbing her eyes with an Orla Kelly handkerchief and cuddling baby Bear. 'How can I be lonely when I have this little guy?'

Baby Bear is huge now, with a giant blond head and rosy red cheeks. He looks sturdy and handsome, the picture of health.

'A baby isn't company,' I said. 'I mean, they don't say a lot, do they?'

Laura said Bear babbled away like a beautiful brook. But I think she was missing the point.

'Can't Zach be at home more?' I suggested.

Laura said no, Zach's job was 'fairly intense'.

'Anyway, this is our agreement,' she said. 'I do the childcare while Zach builds the empire.'

Told Laura she should talk to Zach, but she insisted it was the wrong time.

'He's far too busy with the wind-turbine stuff,' she said. 'I need to support him, not give him problems.'

Laura is a lot nicer than I am, but it's not always for the best.

Even I know that you should ask for what you want in life, and I've made a real mess of mine.

'I'll call and visit more,' I told Laura. 'And you should talk to Zach.'

Seeing Laura proved what I've always known. A fancy life in a fancy house does not happiness make. It's people who make you happy.

Or unhappy.

Evening
Alex just phoned.

He's back from New York tomorrow night and wants to see me. Advised him to stay in London; I'm working in the pub anyway, so it's not as though we'll have much time together. However, he insisted on coming straight from the airport to the cottage.

Aww.

Friday 17th August
Bloody Nick.

He's messing me around re having Daisy tomorrow because there's a bar opening on the South Bank tonight and he has a VIP invite.

'How does that stop you seeing Daisy?' I demanded. 'Tonight and Saturday morning are completely different times.'

'I think I'm coming down with something,' said Nick. 'The South Bank event might wipe me out.'

'So basically, you're predicting a hangover tomorrow,' I said.

Nick didn't reply, which meant yes.

'What's all this about, Nick?' I said. 'You've been doing so well at being a sensible parent. Don't fall down now. You're nearly there.'

'It's all this stuff happening with Mum, Jules,' said Nick. 'It's bad.

Really bad. I need to let loose for a night.'

'What stuff?' I asked.

'I can't say,' said Nick. 'It'll probably come out soon. You know how Great Oakley is. Secrets don't stay secret for long.'

'Why don't you just go out tonight and not drink?' I asked.

'Don't be stupid Julesy,' said Nick. 'There'll be complimentary cocktails. You know how I am around free drink. I have to get my fifty quid's worth.'

'Then don't go,' I challenged.

'I need a night out,' said Nick, sounding close to tears. 'It's relentless, this parenting stuff. I've forgotten the person I used to be. I'm just this sad, grey, old man getting through the day. One endless cycle of cooking, cleaning, buying new baby clothes because the old ones are covered in sick, trying to get Horry to sit still for FaceTime with Sadie while she lives it up in Dubai. It never ends. And I'm doing this *alone*. I JUST WANT SOME TIME FOR MYSELF!'

I was unsympathetic. 'That's parenthood,' I said. 'You wouldn't be doing it alone if you hadn't run off with my bridesmaid.'

'Look – tonight is important for my career,' said Nick.

'What career?' I said. 'You're working in Henry's plastics factory. Your acting days are over.'

There was another long pause, then Nick said, 'That's part of the stuff with Mum. I can't count on working at the factory forever. I have to think bigger. Look, all the top names in London theatre will be there tonight. I need to make some connections again – I've been out of the game for way too long. It's sink or swim.'

'Don't theatre directors have better things to do than visit bar openings on a Friday night?' I asked.

'A bar with free cocktails?' Nick snorted. 'Get real. Come on Julesy, I'll make it up to you.'

'It's Daisy you have to make it up to,' I said. 'When she's sixteen and seeing irresponsible men, you can explain *you* were her irresponsible male role model.'

'I'm a great dad,' Nick insisted. 'How many kids can say they have an actor for a parent? Not many.'

'You're not an actor any more –' I started to say. But I was cut off by the wail of baby Horatio in the background.

'OK buddy,' said Nick. 'Just dip your dummy in the syrup and put it back in again.'

I wonder what 'stuff' Nick is talking about re Helen. Maybe he and his stepfather had an argument. Or perhaps he's just full of shit and wants a night out.

Probably the latter.

Evening
Alex dropped by the pub during my shift.

He came straight from the airport in his business suit and looked a little out of place, perching at the bar with the regulars. Like seeing caviar in Asda.

You could tell Yorkie, with the few rotten teeth he has left, felt intimidated by Alex's flashy pearly whites, and Mick the Hat complained that the pub was 'going too upmarket' and headed home to drink Special Brew.

Alex ordered a double whiskey to sip rather than gulp and asked me how I'd been.

I went into a big long rant about Nick and his South Bank event and how he's sidestepping childcare tomorrow.

In some ways, I suppose it's a step forward, i.e. Nick planning for a hangover. But it's still infuriating.

'How about I have Daisy tomorrow?' Alex suggested.

'You've been travelling back and forth all week,' I said. 'Don't you want to rest?'

'I'll be fine after a good night's sleep,' said Alex. 'A solid five hours and I'll be right as rain.'

'But can you handle a two-year-old for a whole day?'

'Of course,' said Alex. 'I run hotels all over the world.'

I told him he'd just set up a perfect sit-com scenario with that bold statement and should expect chaos.

'I looked after Jemima growing up,' said Alex. 'She could be very demanding, but a good carrot-and-stick program worked wonders. I'm sure Daisy will be the same. Listen – if we're going to be sharing a life together, I'll be Daisy's stepfather. I want to spend time with her.'

Invited Alex to stay overnight at the cottage, but he'd promised to see his mother in London for a 'late supper'.

'Give her my regards,' I said coolly. 'And ask her to return my calls once in a while. Once would do, actually.'

'You two still aren't friends yet?' said Alex, raising an eyebrow. 'You surprise me.'

'Should you be heading back into London?' I asked. 'You've already travelled from the airport to here. You'll wear yourself out.'

'I made my mother a promise,' said Alex. 'And she's feeling lonely right now.'

'Poor thing,' I said. 'All alone with nobody to throw drinks over.'

'Listen, I know you want to get along with Anya,' said Alex. 'I'll talk to her. Let me see what I can do.'

Alex is a good man. Pretty much the opposite of Nick, who, despite his temporary scrubbing up, seems to be sliding back into his old ways.

I just hope Daisy behaves herself tomorrow and doesn't cover Alex in toilet paper.

Saturday 18th August

Alex arrived at 7 am while I was still in bed pretending to be asleep.

Daisy and I were playing a game. It was called 'Mummy hopes Daisy stops pulling her eyelids open, believes Mummy is asleep and goes back to bed.'

So Alex's curt 7 am knock on my door was unwelcome.

Stumbled downstairs and found my handsome fiancé on the doorstep in his running gear. He'd been for a seven-mile run around the fields, having been too jet-lagged to make his usual ten.

'Did I wake you?' he asked.

'Technically, no,' I said. 'But I was enjoying being in bed.'

Daisy toddled to the stair-gate then, shouting, 'Rex! Rex!'

'Daisy, I'm here to look after you today,' Alex announced. 'Let's start by making you a wonderful, healthy breakfast.'

Alex made poached eggs with a homemade hollandaise sauce, which we all enjoyed. Daisy even ate the 'bunny oak' (runny yolk) because Alex said it would make her strong as an ox.

After breakfast, Alex announced he was taking Daisy to the park, the library and then back to the park for a picnic lunch.

'Two-year-olds are a lot to manage,' I said. 'Call me if you need help.'

'It'll be fine,' said Alex, giving my arm a reassuring squeeze. 'You wait and see.'

Afternoon

Alex just called from A&E. He's taken Daisy there because she hurt her arm in the playground and was 'screaming in agony'.

I wasn't worried because I could hear Daisy's cries in the background and knew they were fake. When she's in real pain, she doesn't sing 'tra la la' at the end.

'She sounds fine,' I told Alex.

Alex barked, 'For God's sake, Juliette. Something could be broken. I don't know why these doctors are taking so long.'

Asked Alex to put Daisy on the line.

'I'll try,' he said. 'But she's very distressed, poor little thing.'

Daisy came onto the phone. 'Hurt arm Mummy,' she said. 'Need bandage.'

'Daisy, does it really hurt?' I asked. 'Or do you just want a bandage?'

'Wheelchair,' she said. 'Want wheelchair. Like On Boy.'

Am going up to A&E now to reassure Alex and persuade him to bring Daisy home.

Alex is annoyed with me for not being worried, and I'm annoyed with him for not seeing through a two-year-old who wants to play hospitals.

Afternoon

Poor Alex. He's embarrassed, but I did warn him.

Arrived at A&E to find Daisy in no pain whatsoever, holding a book in one hand and a bag of dry-roasted peanuts in the other.

I asked her to lift both hands above her head, which she did with ease, asking if we were playing Simon Says.

'See?' I told Alex. 'She's fine.'

'Human beings release natural painkillers during bone trauma,' Alex barked. 'Let's hope you haven't made her worse.'

'She doesn't have a broken arm,' I said. 'She's just pretending. Did you see her fall?'

'No,' said Alex. 'But I certainly heard it.'

'Daisy,' I asked. 'What did you fall off?'

'The slide,' she said, adding, 'No! The roundabout.'

'And did you hurt yourself?'

'Yes,' said Daisy, nodding sagely, curls bouncing up and down.

'Does it still hurt now?' I asked.

'No,' said Daisy, shaking her head, eyes big and earnest.

'She just wants her arm in a plaster cast,' I told Alex. 'Or to have her own crutches or wheelchair. She's not really injured. Look at her. If she'd broken something, she'd be pale and she wouldn't be moving that arm. She certainly wouldn't be using it to lift peanuts to her mouth. Let's get her home.'

While we were talking, Dr Chang appeared at the sliding doors and called Daisy's name.

'Hello again,' he chirped. 'If you've brought another picnic, I wouldn't say no to a KitKat. It's been eight hours since my last break.'

'You've had time off since we were last here, haven't you?' I asked.

'The odd hour here and there,' said Dr Chang, giving a stressed laugh. 'You learn to sleep standing up on this job.'

Dr Chang confirmed that Daisy was faking her injury and totally fine.

'She was so believable,' said Alex, shaking his head with bewilderment. 'Anybody would have been fooled.'

Reassured Alex that he is a good man trying to do the right thing.

Which he is.

Sunday 19th August

Mum and Callum's birthday.

Nick should have had Daisy today, but he's still hungover after Friday night.

'I'm getting old, Julesy,' he said. 'Hangovers last two days now. Have pity.'

Told Nick off for being irresponsible, but actually I was happy to take Daisy to Mum and Callum's joint birthday party.

Daisy wanted to dress herself this morning, which I foolishly encouraged. From the neck down she looked adorable in a velvet party dress, but from the neck up she'd added a swimming cap, Where's Wally glasses and glitter makeup.

It was kiddie chaos at the pub, because Callum had invited his whole class.

'Kids parties are proper events now,' Brandi explained. 'They cost a bomb. You need a proper entertainer, a colour scheme, place settings, a shop-bought piñata, jigsaw sandwiches and pricey presents in the party bags like little mini Lego sets.'

'Says who?' asked Dad.

'Everyone,' said Brandi. 'You get mum-shamed if you don't toe the line.'

'What rubbish,' said Dad. 'Show a bit of backbone, Brandi. This is all one big capitalist con to make weak-minded people buy things they don't need. What's wrong with a slice of cake and a balloon at the end of a party? Some nice wholesome games and a little sing-song?'

'It's different when you're a single mum,' Brandi insisted. 'You don't want people thinking you can't afford things. It's embarrassing.'

'But you *can't* afford things,' said Dad. 'You put everything on credit cards.'

The entertainer, Mr Bubble-tastic, called in sick just before the party – which caused a bit of panic. Mr Bubble-tastic had a migraine, which I imagine is a common ailment among children's entertainers.

Dad sort of saved the day by stepping in to do the entertainment. He kicked off with a 'Speed Bonny Boat' singalong, then made the kids do 200 star jumps before playing 'Dorothy, where's my button?'

Callum wasn't impressed. He kept saying, 'This is lame, Granddad. Why can't we play with Nana's laser guns?'

'We don't need that plastic rubbish,' Dad replied cheerfully. 'Ring-a-ring-a-roses is as fun today as it's ever been.'

Fortunately, the party food cheered everyone up. This was Mum's domain, and she'd gone over the top as per usual, buying a huge chocolate-fudge gateau, an additional tiered birthday cake, buckets of sweets, over 300 biscuits (10 per child) and an arm-length gala pie.

The kids were pretty hyper by the end of the party. I felt sorry for the parents picking them up but also glad they were leaving.

When the kids left, the adults immediately broke out the alcohol, like drug addicts getting their fix.

I had to be moderate because of Daisy, so only had one Prosecco and a small shot of Jägermeister. However, Laura, who had left baby Bear with the Spanish nanny, took part in Mum's 'all the colours of the rainbow' shot challenge and got totally hammered.

I've never seen my big sis so drunk before and was a bit worried. Laura was, of course, polite and lovely as always, but slurred her polite, lovely words and cried when it was time to go home.

'I'm so lonely,' she sobbed. 'I don't want to go back to London. I want to stay here with all of you.'

'We'll work something out to cheer you up, love,' said Mum. 'But I can't think of anything at the moment. I'm too drunk.'

Poor Laura.

Home now.

Daisy sleeping.

Pretty sure Mum's party will still be going, but I'm happy to be in bed. Motherhood makes you appreciate bed a lot more than a party.

Monday 20th August

Nick just phoned.

He was wild with jealousy, asking why I'd let 'fancy pants Dalton' look after 'our precious child' over the weekend.

'What's wrong with Alex looking after Daisy?' I asked.

'Oh come on Julesy,' said Nick. 'What does he know about kids? He'll have given her Eggs Benedict for breakfast, then bored her to death about hostile hotel takeovers.'

I kept quiet about the Eggs Benedict.

'If you can put a veto on Sadie, I get the same right of veto,' Nick insisted.

'I thought Sadie was still in Dubai,' I said.

'She is,' said Nick. 'But she has to come back eventually.'

If Nick thinks Sadie is returning any time soon, he doesn't know her at all. Now she's got herself a boyfriend meal ticket, she'll be riding the expat gravy train into the sunset.

'It's ridiculous to compare Alex and Sadie,' I said. 'Sadie is totally nuts. She can't even care for her child. Alex is a decent guy.'

'Not the point,' said Nick. 'If you get a veto, so do I.'

So Alex's doom-filled prophecy has come true.

Told Nick that I would happily allow Sadie to be around Daisy from now on.

Felt entirely comfortable saying this, because I'm confident Sadie will stay in Dubai a long time.

Tuesday 21st August

Phoned Althea to talk (laugh) about Alex's day with Daisy.

We had a good chuckle about Alex's A&E visit paranoia. Then Althea relayed her own story about Wolfgang's father taking him to the emergency room.

'He'd only swallowed a Sharpie lid,' she laughed. 'Talk about paranoid!'

I stopped laughing then, picturing a bullet-shaped Sharpie pen lid.

'A Sharpie lid is pretty big,' I said. 'I would have taken Daisy into

A&E if she'd swallowed something that large.'

'Oh, Wolfgang's always swallowing stuff,' said Althea, dismissively. 'It all comes out the other end. A pen lid is small-fry compared to some of the other stuff he's got down him. Sixteen-stud Lego bricks. A doll's leg. He's swallowed half a pack of dominoes before. I only worked it out when I noticed the double six was missing.'

I do admire Althea's laid-back attitude to parenting, but Wolfgang is clearly built to last. You only have to look at his flowing, black Fabio locks, huge front tooth and large, athletic thighs to know he's a hardy sort. A real tank of a child. I imagine his intestines making short work of those dominoes, crushing them to fine powder.

Wolfgang will probably grow up to be a tough Bear Grylls-style outdoor explorer, enduring rugged terrain and living off insects and cactus juice.

Or he might get into hard-core drugs, resist arrest and end up in prison.

It could go either way.

Wednesday 22nd August

Mum has invited Laura over for tea tonight and asked if Alex, Daisy, John Boy and I would like to come too. She's cooked an enormous meal out of boredom and needs people to eat all the food.

I explained that Alex was abroad, but said the rest of us would love to come.

'Bit of a pain Alex being away so much, isn't it?' Mum mused. 'I thought the plan was for him to settle in the village now you're engaged?'

'I don't mind him working,' I said. 'I need breathing space right now.'

'That's the trouble with businessmen,' said Mum, as though I hadn't spoken. 'Your father is the same – obsessed with the pub.

Try as I might to have a conversation with him, it goes in one ear out the other. I'm starved of attention.'

'Dad pays you lots of attention,' I said. 'Making you cups of tea, running you baths, picking you wildflowers, writing you poems.'

'He loves this pub more than me,' Mum continued. 'Always wittering on about its history and those civil-war bullet holes in the Tudor beams. I don't even believe they're bullet holes. I think they were someone putting in a phone line.'

Found out the other side of the story from Dad.

Apparently, Mum had tried to talk to him while he was doing the stock check. He asked her to wait five minutes, but she got annoyed and went on a day-long rant.

Truthfully, it's Mum who doesn't pay Dad attention, frequently roaring at him to shut up when *The Apprentice* is on and forgetting their wedding anniversary more often than not. But she can't/won't see it.

Still.

Dad loves her all the same.

Late evening

Lovely evening at the pub with the family, and hopefully we cheered Laura up a bit. She did seem happier after being showered with family love.

The meal was a little stilted to begin with because Mum was ignoring Dad after the stock-check argument. But all the food was at Dad's end of the table, so Mum had to ask him to pass the lasagne, wheel-shaped garlic bread, salt, pepper, tortilla chips, grated cheese and extra white sauce.

Dad offered her the salad bowl too, but she stiffly declined.

Despite my protestations, Daisy brought Curry the rabbit to the meal – which was a problem because he's still very smelly. Worse, Daisy kept telling everyone that Curry couldn't eat because Mum's food gave him diarrhoea.

Daisy was quite specific about Curry's bowel trouble, talking about the colour and texture of his 'toilet droppings'. She added that the diarrhoea made him 'fart lots and lots', imitating his farty noises as best she could.

This led Callum to ask an important question: Why can't animals hold their farts in?

Dad talked at length about sphincter muscles, even drawing a little diagram.

It would be nice if our family could get through one meal without talking about toilet habits.

I'm sure the Daltons don't have conversations like this over dinner.

Thursday 23rd August

Lunchtime shift at the pub today.

Daisy and I arrived to find Callum very sad. Almost all his tadpoles have died now, even 'Destroyer', whom Callum was sure had begun to grow legs.

Only Geronimo and Judge Dredd remain, and Judge Dredd is a half-ounce weakling who seems unlikely to flourish.

Dad hasn't helped matters, making insensitive comments about the finite life of August tadpoles and the likelihood the last two will die soon too.

'These are the runts, Callum,' said Dad. 'They'll be dead before the summer's out. Mark my words.'

However, Callum is sure his last tadpoles will survive the winter.

'Nana says love makes things grow,' said Callum. 'And I've given these tadpoles so much love it's unbelievable. They get fed better than I do.'

No one wanted to tell Callum that his feeding choices might be a mortality factor. Fish fingers are enjoyable for seven-year-olds, but crunchy breadcrumb is a poor nutritional choice for a tadpole.

And the fish element borders on cannibalism.

Friday 24th August

Mum wants to do a 'wet the baby's head' party for baby Bear.

'It'll cheer Laura up,' she said. 'She deserves to be made a fuss of. She's ever so low.'

It's almost a year since baby Bear was born, but Mum will grab any opportunity to combine cake and booze.

I agree that Laura needs love and attention, but I'm not sure Prosecco is a good idea, given how drunk Laura got the last time I saw her. Drowning your sorrows works for an hour or so, but your problems feel a lot worse the next morning.

Saturday 25th August

Mum has put Laura's 'wet the baby's head' party on Facebook, which makes it official. She has already set to work on decorations and fetched the promotional Pimm's bunting and Carlsberg World Cup flags from the garden shed.

'You can't use those decorations for a baby celebration,' I said. 'They advertise alcoholic beverages. It's inappropriate. And the colours are all wrong – baby parties should be decorated in pastel pink, blue or yellow.'

'The baby's not going to know, is it?' said Mum. 'It's not as if it can read. And anyway, baby's see in black and white until they're three months old.'

'Baby Bear is nearly a year old,' I said. 'His birthday is on the same day as mine.'

'Is he really that old?' said Mum, visibly taken aback. 'Babies grow quick, don't they?'

It's true – baby years do go fast. But you feel every single minute of them.

Sunday 26th August

Nick had Daisy today to make up for missing last weekend.

Felt a bit put out, because Daisy told me she had 'best day ever ever'.

Nick's mother took Horatio, so Nick indulged his little princess in a classic access-dad weekend. They saw a West End musical, bought Indian sweets on Brick Lane then whizzed around Globe Park on an electric scooter.

It's easy to be fun when you only see your daughter once a fortnight. Try doing it every day, Nick. Then you'll be an angry, miserable, boring parent like I am.

Monday 27th August
Bank Holiday Monday

Summer festival in the pub garden today.

I helped out in the outdoor Pimm's bar, while Daisy and Nana Joan danced to the Queen cover band.

The pub garden looked brilliant with all the bunting and fairy lights, but Mum had bought two new paddling pools, which caused an argument.

'We have hundreds of paddling pools in the shed already, Shirley,' Dad raged. 'This is consumerism gone mad. In my day, you paddled in a washing-up tub full of rainwater.'

'We don't have any paddling pools, Bob,' said Mum. 'You're thinking of the blow-up doughnut.'

Dad marched into the garden shed then and pulled out all the inflatable stuff. It was a fine haul purchased by Mum over the years, and included four ring-shaped paddling pools, a flamingo paddle palace and a one-metre deep 'mega paddler'.

Mum did an about swerve and pretended she was concerned about paddling-pool fashion. 'Inflatable pools change every year,' she claimed. 'What will people think if I put out last year's stuff?'

But Mum has never really cared what people think. If she did, she wouldn't wear skin-tight lycra and no bra in the rain.

It turned out to be a wonderful afternoon, getting paid to run the Pimm's tent while Daisy played under the half-watchful, half-drunk eye of Nana Joan.

And speaking of half-drunk – really should try and phone Catrina again.

SURELY she'll crack eventually.

Tuesday 28th August

Catrina is still not taking my calls.

My last drop-in visit was a total disaster. What's the next step? I have no idea.

Phoned Althea for advice and was greeted by a weird 'slap slap' noise.

Asked with some trepidation what the noise was, because Althea often takes calls in situations where other people would leave their phones well alone.

Althea has answered her phone in the cinema, during medical consultations and a past-life regression session before. Once, she answered the phone with dentist putty in her mouth and asked the dental assistant to translate her sign language. And there's always a 50% chance she'll be on the toilet.

On this occasion, Althea was in a spa being coated with health-giving mineral mud. Wolfgang was there too, having a mani-pedi.

'I think you're insecure about marrying a Dalton,' said Althea. 'Getting along with Catrina represents acceptance. So love and accept yourself on the inside and everything will fall into place. Looking for happiness outside never works.'

'And if I can't find love and acceptance on the inside?' I said.

'Then don't marry Alex,' said Althea. 'And you won't need to worry about his mother.'

'I had that solution last year,' I said. 'But I want a happy marriage and family bliss.'

'Well there's only one solution left,' said Althea. 'Throw Catrina a love bomb and make sure she catches it.'

'She won't speak to me,' I said. 'She's still not taking my calls. I thought she would have cracked by now.'

'Why don't you ambush her at a social event?' said Althea. 'Somewhere she can't leave in a hurry.'

'A public event could be bad,' I said. 'Catrina is very concerned about her reputation.'

'Well there's your trump card,' said Althea. 'Her fear of social embarrassment. Get yourself invited to one of her events and make sure she knows you're coming. Then she'll have to talk to you beforehand so you don't embarrass her in public.'

'Sounds a bit devious,' I said.

'Sometimes, you have to embrace your dark side,' said Althea.

'But how are we going to end up at the same event?' I said. 'We move in totally different social circles.'

'You have to think this through,' said Althea. 'You have Alex in common. There must be something you can wangle an invite to.'

'Yes,' I said. 'Christmas Day with Harold Dalton. Catrina is going, and Alex and I have been invited too.'

'Sounds perfect,' said Althea. 'Give a big thumbs up to the invitation and make sure Catrina finds out. I bet she'll take your calls after that. Now quit talking and start doing. Only don't tell anyone I said that last part.'

'Why not?' I asked. 'Is it another Henry Ford quote?'

'No, Walt Disney,' said Althea. 'A man who enslaved young women with stereotypical princess imagery.'

'Why do you keep quoting people you don't like?' I asked.

'Blame Instagram and Pinterest,' said Althea. 'I go on there for alternative non-pink cupcake designs or canal-boat interiors and get bombarded with great quotes. It's only after I've been inspired that I realise I don't like who said it.'

Althea had to go then because Wolfgang wasn't behaving. He'd just glugged some massage oil and was now quite literally mud-slinging.

Althea wasn't worried about the massage oil because Wolfgang is always downing her essential oils at home. However, she felt the mud-slinging was anti-social.

Evening
OK.

Daisy in bed.

Time to get ready for wine tasting with Alex. Have to make myself look vaguely presentable. Actually, very presentable – we're doing the wine tasting at the Bond Street Dalton.

Need to find the dental floss and dig out a decent bra that doesn't give me quadruple boob.

Wednesday 29th August

Such a sore head this morning.

In the cold, hard light of day, alcohol is alcohol. It doesn't matter how much you posh it up: the hangover is the same.

Wine tasting was an interesting experience. It's funny watching people in smart clothes, pretending not to be drunk.

In my parents' pub, being drunk is socially acceptable. Something to be tolerated with politeness, because there for the grace of God were you last weekend.

At the Bond Street Dalton, everyone was drunk but trying not to show it. It was like watching a bunch of toddlers playing tea parties, while lacking the ability to do basic things like putting a wine glass on a flat surface or text messaging without swaying around.

Sampling the wine was fun though, and I picked up some useful knowledge. Basically, the hotter the country, the nicer the wine.

Alex suggested I spit wine into a giant FA cup-type thing so I wouldn't get too drunk, but I reminded him that my parents run a pub so I can hold my alcohol.

I never should have said that.

Expensive wine is powerful. There wasn't one bottle below 14% proof.

It didn't help that the setting was so formal. A dropped fork rang out in that room. So did a smashed glass.

By the time we reached the New World wines, Alex started pressuring me about wedding dates again. Well, perhaps he wasn't pressuring me, and maybe my response was a little loud. But anyone's voice would have rung out in that banqueting hall.

'Juliette,' said Alex. 'Is there something you want to tell me?'

'I don't want to get married this year,' I said. 'Not while things are still bumpy with your mother.'

'If you're not sure about getting married this year, then you're not sure about getting married,' said Alex.

Was drunk enough to say, 'Yes, that's probably true.'

Alex's lips went all tight then, and he said, 'Is this about me travelling? Because I told you – I can spend more time in Great Oakley. I keep offering.'

'No,' I said. 'It really is just about your mother. And…I suppose feeling, through her, that your family accepts me.'

Alex did some thoughtful sipping and spitting, then said: 'It's going to be a little tricky for you to get along with my mother, don't you think? Since she's not speaking to you.'

'Yes,' I said. 'But I have an idea. A way to bring your mother and me together.'

'Which is?'

'We go to your father's house on Christmas Day.'

'Why on earth would you put us through something like that?' Alex asked.

'Two reasons,' I said. 'First, if your mother knows I'm coming on Christmas Day, she'll have to talk to me beforehand.'

'Why?'

'She's not going to want drink-throwing in front of your family, is she?'

Alex thought for a moment. 'My father has warned her about drink-throwing before. She does listen to him – he dangles the shiny carrot of inheritance over her. And the second reason?'

'Your mother will have both her sons with her on Christmas Day,' I said. 'And I'll have been part of making that happen.'

'I suppose…yes, she would like that. Especially with Jemima being away.'

'We have to try something, Alex,' I said.

'I think you're overly concerned with my mother,' said Alex. 'But I'll do this if it makes you happy. So if you and my mother get along and no one throws cocktails on Christmas Day, will you give me a wedding date?'

'Yes,' I said. 'Absolutely.'

'Then it's a deal,' said Alex, shaking my hand. 'The wedding date can be my Christmas present.'

'Bit of a rubbish Christmas present,' I said.

'No,' said Alex. 'Actually, it's the best present I could wish for.' Then he checked his watch and said: 'It's nearly time for my

Stockholm flight. I'd better call your driver. It's getting late and you're just too beautiful when you're drunk. And even more honest, if that's possible.'

'I'm not drunk,' I insisted. 'And of course I'm honest. Who isn't honest?'

'Lots of people,' said Alex.

When the driver arrived, Alex kissed me and said, 'Listen – are you sure you'll be OK?'

Assured him I'd be fine and wouldn't be sick in the car.

Thursday 30th August

Went to the pub for lunch today and told Mum and Dad about Christmas at Harold Dalton's house.

'Could be a good idea,' said Mum. 'You've been so anxious about the wedding. If you and Catrina buddy up, it could help you turn a corner.'

'I'm not anxious about the wedding!' I screeched.

'Then why haven't you set a date yet?' Mum challenged.

'I will,' I said. 'If Christmas Day goes well, I've promised Alex I'll set a date.'

'Sounds like you're waiting for a happiness guarantee,' said Dad. 'Trust me love, you're not going to get it. They'll always be bumps in the road. It's not about avoiding them. It's about being strong enough to take life and come up fighting.'

Friday 31st August

Busy and hot shift in the pub tonight.

Magner's cider was a big winner, so I had to keep trekking down to the cellar to bring up more bottles. Was very tempted, once down there, to stay and enjoy the cool air but obviously I couldn't leave the bar unattended. Yorkie has been known to stick his mouth under the beer taps if not correctly supervised.

Poor John Boy – the sweat-inducing temperature made his leg stump dressings wet and gave him painful stump rash.

John Boy would have carried on working with a grimace on his face, but I forced him onto a barstool and plied him with heavily iced rum and Coca-Cola.

I could tell John Boy was in a lot of pain because he asked for quadruple measures of rum.

Alex is back from Stockholm and staying with me tonight. He arrived at the cottage this afternoon and is there right now, while I'm here making myself unattractively sweaty.

Could shower and beautify myself here before I go home, but feels weird showering at gone midnight.

Alex will probably be asleep anyway.

Midnight

Alex is totally passed out. Completely. He didn't flinch when I shouted, 'Alex. ALEX! It's me Juliette.' Or wake up when I used Daisy's trick of pulling his eyelids open.

So no sweaty sex for me this evening.

Maybe it's for the best – I'm overly warm already and I'm sitting still. Even sleeping beside another human being belting out body heat feels unappealing, let alone jiggling around. Should have put my pillowcase in the freezer, as per Mum's tip, but too late now.

Saturday 1st September

Uh oh.

Nick's mum and step-dad have split up.

When Nick collected Daisy this morning, he broke down and told me the whole sorry story. 'I can't do it any more,' he wailed, jiggling a startled Horatio in his arms. 'I'm not strong enough, Julesy, I'm not strong enough.'

'Parenthood isn't optional, Nick,' I said. 'You just have to get on with it.'

'It's not parenthood this time,' said Nick. 'It's Mum. I can't be her rock. I've had enough.'

'What on earth are you talking about?' I asked. 'You're no one's rock. You're more like a blood-sucking leach.'

Then it all came out. The 'personal stuff' Nick was banging on about last month.

Henry has left Helen for another woman.

'I've lost my cushy management job at the plastics factory,' said Nick. 'Henry says it's inappropriate because his new girlfriend works there. Mum's been leaning on me for emotional support. It's like blackmail. She'll only take Horatio if I listen to her badmouth Henry for hours on end. I'm emotionally drained, Julesy. But what else can I do? I can't have Horry Horry Vom Voms all day every day. I need a break.'

'Why don't you see this as a challenge?' I suggested. 'A way to help you grow as a person?'

'But what if I don't want to grow?' said Nick, his eyes wild. 'What if I want to stay a child?'

'As long as you're alive, you're growing,' I said. 'You'll get through it. You don't have a choice.'

'Listen, don't go around gossiping about Mum, yeah?' said Nick. 'She doesn't deserve that. She's a good person deep-down.'

Promised. But had my fingers crossed behind my back.

I have to say, I felt sorry for Nick. He looked terrible – really run-down and ill, with dark sunglasses hiding his eyes and an even scabbier scalp than ever.

Before Nick left, he asked if I was still seeing 'Dalton'.

'Yes,' I said. 'He's upstairs sleeping right now, actually.'

'What a lazy bastard,' said Nick.

'He usually gets up at 6 am,' I said. 'But he's been travelling.'

'Probably for the best we haven't bumped into each other,' said Nick. 'You don't want any locked antlers, do you? Two stags fighting.'

It was an interesting analogy. If Alex were a stag, he'd be gleaming chestnut gold, and disembowel Nick instantly with strong, sharp antlers. Nick would be a mangy creature with sad, wet eyes and a scabby coat.

Mid-morning

Phoned Mum and told her about Helen and Henry splitting up. After hooting with laughter, Mum promised she would find out all the gory details via the village grapevine, which she ensures wraps its branches around the pub at all times.

Afternoon

Alex woke just before lunch, showered, dressed, kissed my cheek and left for London, saying he had some loose ends to tie up before a trip to Tokyo later this week.

'It's Saturday,' I said. 'Who works on a Saturday?'

'You do,' said Alex. 'So do your parents. There are no weekends in the hospitality trade. The hotel world doesn't rest. Well, we hope our guests rest very well, but you get my meaning.'

'You should have a break,' I said. 'You've been travelling all week.'

'What would I do with a break?' Alex asked. 'You said you needed space. I'm giving it to you. I may as well use this time to super-charge the business.'

I have to say, Alex seemed refreshed and full of energy, despite all the travelling.

As mentioned earlier, Alex is a vibrant stag with a glossy, chestnut coat. And big, strong antlers.

Afternoon

Dropped by the pub this afternoon.

Mum has found out all the gossip about Helen and Henry and offered to share the news over a box of Celebrations chocolates.

Apparently, Henry has run off with a 26-year old librarian called Elizabeth whom he met via the village amateur-dramatics society. Quite the scandal, her being so much younger. The pair got close while rehearsing *A Midsummer Night's Dream*; Elizabeth played Titania, Henry played Bottom.

Elizabeth has a homely face and figure, but she scrubs up well as Titania, in a vast, flowing red wig. I've seen her on posters around the village, pouting in red lipstick and offering grapes to Henry, who is dressed as a donkey.

It's weird how an old, fat man like Henry can land a girl in her twenties, but I imagine owning a factory helps.

'Helen's distraught,' said Mum, cackling and rubbing her hands together.

Aside from Helen's karmic punishment, this is bad news. It means Nick is an out-of-work actor again, and Helen is being an emotional drain on her son, rather than propping him up financially.

Texted Helen to offer my apologies, but truthfully it was a 'sorry not sorry'.

Helen really did have it coming.

Late afternoon

Just noticed all the *Midsummer Night's Dream* posters have been ripped down from the church and train-station notice boards.

Suspect Helen has been on a rampage.

Evening

Tried calling Catrina. No answer yet but am hopeful. Phoned Alex to make sure he's filtered the Christmas Day news back, and he said yes and that he was on his way to the cottage.

Better tidy the kitchen. And scrub the toilet.

Sunday 2nd September

Morning

Alex just left.

He came over last night with a lovely Italian dinner (seafood linguine with crab claws, tiramisu for dessert), and we talked about Christmas plans in Guernsey.

Am feeling hopeful about Christmas, despite no contact from Catrina. Alex assured me that his mother knows our plans and seemed more receptive to the idea of meeting up with me.

After dinner, Alex and I went to bed and had an amazing, intense sexual experience – until John Boy crashed into the cottage at 12 am and peed loudly with the toilet door open. It's quite incredible how much wee men can hold in. Every time I thought John Boy had finished, he started up again.

Alex and I managed to carry on the sexual experience, but it wasn't quite so amazing or intense after that – especially as I was trying to remember if I'd heard John Boy flush the toilet.

Alex has left for London now, with assurances that he will speak to his mother again and push for a peace-offering lunch.

I'll keep trying to phone her too.

Monday 3rd September

5 pm

Just finished my lunchtime shift at the pub.

Capllum went back to school today, so Brandi was celebrating with rosecco when I arrived.

I have to admit, the pub was much calmer without Callum

tearing around. John Boy was sad though, missing his 'little mate' and their chats about lost love.

Callum still holds a candle for Angel Rain, the Moana lookalike he met in A&E. And John Boy misses Gwen, the university student whose name he has tattooed on his arm.

'I'm surprised you haven't moved on yet,' I told John Boy. 'Gwen was hardly your type, long-term.'

John Boy demanded to know what I meant.

'You usually go for girls who look like they work on cosmetics counters,' I said.

Fortunately, John Boy took this as a compliment.

Tuesday 4th September

Got through to Catrina!

I was so excited when she answered the phone that I nearly dropped my cup of tea.

Catrina told me to stop calling her.

'We need to make peace at some point,' I insisted. 'I'm marrying your son, and this year we'll be spending Christmas together.'

Catrina said something in Hungarian then. I think it was a swear word.

'I want us to get along,' I said. 'Or would you prefer to spend Christmas Day glaring at each other?'

'If you glare at me, I will throw another drink,' said Catrina.

'Why don't we meet for a cup of tea?' I suggested.

'I will throw the tea!' said Catrina.

Then she hung up.

I could look at this as a bad phone call but am choosing to see the bright side. At least Catrina picked up the phone.

Wednesday 5th September

Great news.

Alex has persuaded Catrina to meet me for lunch. Her assistant will phone with details.

'I have some work news too,' said Alex. 'This Tokyo trip – it's turned into a three-week thing. I wondered if you and Daisy would like to join me.'

'I'd love to Alex,' I said. 'But Mum and Dad need me at the pub, and I can't take Daisy away from Nick that long.'

'Well, I'll miss the pair of you,' said Alex. 'Hopefully you and my mother can make peace while I'm away and we'll all spend Christmas together. And live happily ever after.'

Here's hoping.

Evening
No call from Catrina's assistant.

Thursday 6th September

Alex has left for Tokyo.

He'll be there for three weeks, negotiating European distribution for a Japanese grapefruit drink.

The time difference means he will be sleeping when the UK is awake, but he assures me he'll phone whenever he can.

Still no call from Catrina's assistant.

Afternoon
Oh Callum!

My silly little nephew is back in hospital again. He climbed the garden fence this morning with his tank of tadpoles, trying to show them next door's frog pond as an incentive to grow. Then he slipped.

Ironically, the tank landed upright on soft earth and didn't break, but Callum's head hit the fence, and his baseball-bat wound started gushing blood. He also hurt his ankle somewhere in the fall – Mum says it's swelled up like an egg.

Callum has suspected concussion and a complicated break, so he's staying overnight on the children's ward.

Asked Brandi if Callum would be scared, staying overnight on his own, but she just laughed.

It was a bit of a stupid question. Most likely, Callum will be scaring other people.

Evening

Some nice news.

Angel Rain, the girl Callum met in A&E, is staying on the children's ward. She's had an operation since we last saw her and is recovering well. However, she's likely to need more surgeries in future because she has ongoing health issues.

Callum is a fast worker when it comes to girls and has already invited Angel Rain on a movie date. They're watching *Goosebumps* on Callum's iPad tonight, before lights out at 8 pm.

Friday 7th September

Morning

Mum and I just got back from visiting Callum in hospital.

Callum was happy enough, enjoying the Mr Bump-style bandage wrapped around his head and the moon boot on his foot.

Someone – I suspect Brandi – has written 'silly sod' on the bandage.

Once we were settled on wipe-clean blue chairs by Callum's bedside, Mum unloaded a random selection of what she called 'medical essentials'. These included:

- Thick-cut chicken sandwiches lavished with butter
- An orange mousse chocolate bar with a special-offer sticker on it
- Two scotch eggs rolled in black-pudding crumbs
- A can of Kombucha, also with a special-offer sticker on it
- Two bottles of Actimel yogurt drink
- Adult painkillers

'Why on earth have you brought adult painkillers?' I asked. 'You can't give those to Callum.'

'Silly me,' Mum chuckled. 'He can't swallow the tablets at his age, can he? Don't worry – I'll crush them up in some orange juice.'

'Callum is being medicated by trained staff,' I said. 'Giving him adult drugs is dangerous.'

Mum put the painkillers away, muttering about health and safety gone mad. Then she gave Callum a wink and said, 'If you're in pain, let me know. I'll sort you out, all right?'

It was like a mafia boss doing a drug deal.

2 pm

Alex just phoned. It's late evening in Tokyo and he'd been out for a cook-your-own-beef dinner with some business colleagues. Alex was offered raw beef and vegetables, which he cooked himself in a pan of boiling soup.

'I wish you and Daisy were with me,' said Alex. 'The meal was a lot of fun. And Mr Yamakoto and his staff have been very kind – letting me talk incessantly about the pair of you all night.'

I miss Alex, but he was wrong to wish Daisy and I were with him. Daisy can't be trusted around raw meat or boiling water. I can't even relax with a cup of tea in my own home.

Alex asked if I had a lunch meeting with his mother 'in the diary yet'.

'Your mother's assistant still hasn't called me,' I said. 'And she had better call back soon Alex, or I'll have to revisit the Dalton Estate and start throwing my own Martinis.'

'Anya says it was a vodka tonic,' said Alex. 'But I take your point. I'll see if I can get through to her.'

Saturday 8th September

Visited Callum again today. He claims to have double-vision and nausea, so the hospital staff are keeping him in for observation.

Callum looked perfectly well to me and was propped up in bed, sipping a cup of tea and reading the *Mirror* newspaper when Mum, Dad, Daisy and I arrived.

Callum doesn't mind being in hospital, but he is worrying about his tadpoles. He asked if we could bring Geronimo and Judge Dredd onto the children's ward.

'Unfortunately not, Callum,' said Dad. 'Hospitals are sterile environments.'

'But the nurses will understand,' said Callum. 'They've got kids of their own.'

Assured Callum that the tadpoles would be fine with John Boy.

'That's bull-hang,' said Callum. 'They'll think I've abandoned them.'

Mum said she'd tell the tadpoles that Callum would come back soon.

Callum rolled his eyes. 'Don't be silly, Nana. They don't understand English.'

Callum has to stay in hospital one more night, but will probably be home tomorrow if he's well enough.

He has already decided he won't be well enough. He has a lunch date planned with Angel Rain.

Sunday 9th September

Callum should be officially discharged from hospital today, but he has 'blagged' himself another night's stay by claiming more double vision.

When we visited him this morning, he was chivalrously carrying Angel Rain's tray of Rice Krispies and toast to her bed.

Initially, I wanted to tell Callum off for taking up a hospital bed, but the nurse told me bed shortages weren't a problem. It's doctors they're short of.

Have told him not to ask for anything from the overworked nurses, stressing that hospital is not a room-service situation. He can't ring his buzzer every time he fancies another cup of tea.

Met Angel Rain's parents and they assured us that Callum wasn't making too much of a nuisance of himself.

Angel Rain is recovering well, but her heart condition needs lots of monitoring and tests. She's been in and out of hospital since she was born.

'The doctors told us she wouldn't survive her first year,' Angel Rain's mother told us. 'But she proved them all wrong. Now she's a schoolgirl, laughing and playing with the other children. Our little miracle. Maybe she's living on borrowed time, but we thank every day the lord keeps her with us.'

Callum says Angel Rain is 'amazing' and 'so strong'. It's true. She endures her medical condition with patience, courage and dignity.

It puts life in perspective, meeting children like Angel Rain. I moan about all sorts of things. The weather. Running out of phone charge. John Boy's snoring. But when I think of what Angel Rain's parents are going through, I realise how selfish and ungrateful I can be.

3 pm

Another goodnight text from Alex.

He must have been pretty sleepy because he made lots of spelling mistakes – unusual for him.

He wrote: 'I've been very busty'. Which I took to mean he was very busy.

Monday 10th September

Callum is back from hospital.

He's already missing Angel Rain, but was happy to see 'the kids' again, aka Judge Dredd and Geronimo.

Callum has been spoiling his two remaining tadpoles rotten, giving them large pinches of luxury fish food, writing them a poem about the seaside and propping Mum's iPad against the tank so they can watch *The Little Mermaid*.

It seems cruel to tell Callum that his last two tadpoles are likely to die soon. It's already autumn. If they were going to turn into froglets, it would have happened by now.

Dad says there's an outside chance the tadpoles will remain dormant and turn into frogs next year, but he's putting money on them dying before winter.

It might be kinder if he stopped telling Callum this.

Tuesday 11th September

Daisy reached another developmental milestone today.

Taunting.

When she saw Callum hobbling around in his moon boot she said: 'Callum can't walk. Callum like baby. I walk better than Callum.'

I'm hoping her next developmental phase will be empathy. But I'm told that doesn't happen until kids are at least three.

Late morning
Catrina's assistant finally called.

We've booked a lunch this Saturday at the Mayfair Dalton, which is famous for its cocktails. Must remember to wear waterproof makeup.

I'm seeing Althea later, so will ask for advice – re the Catrina lunch. I do want to make friends and move forward, but also need to discuss Laura's wedding. And sort of suspect the two things can't go hand-in-hand.

Althea is an excellent person to talk to about relationships. She has hundreds of friends, because nobody dares fall out with her.

Afternoon
Just got back from Althea's.

Wolfgang was very upset when we arrived because Althea had snapped his recorder over her leg in a fit of rage.

'I don't know what got into me,' said Althea. 'I'm not into censorship. It's not who I am. But that screechy whistling was driving me mad.'

She's made amends to Wolfgang by ordering him a violin, but I fear it will suffer a similar fate.

Talked to Althea about the Catrina lunch, and she suggested I smoke cannabis beforehand to stop me losing my temper.

'It's hard to get angry when you don't know what's going on,' she reasoned.

But I'm scared of cannabis, due to a traumatic teenage experience. The first time I smoked weed was behind the village Co-op with some friends from school. We did laugh a lot, but when I got home, my dad was wearing his old school uniform and burgundy-red cap.

Looking back, it must have been Comic Relief day, but it felt like the world was trying to freak me out on purpose – especially when

Dad made me guess the bird on his school cap.

After a lot of confused stabs in the dark (Flamingo? No…they're pink…) Dad finally told me the answer, giving a disappointed shake of his head.

'It's a curlew Juliette,' he said. 'The noblest of British birds. You can identify them by their long, slender bills and mottled feathers.'

Had to endure a long lecture about recognising curlews before I could escape upstairs to whimper under my duvet.

That experience was a better cautionary tale than any of the anti-drugs lectures we had at school. I never tried cannabis again after that, sticking to legal drugs: a four-pack of Guinness and the occasional bottle of Merrydown cider or strawberry 20/20.

Wednesday 12th September

Brandi has bought an Amazon Echo to cheer Callum up. He's miserable not being able to tear around the place and wreak havoc due to his debilitating moon boot. It goes against all his natural instincts.

The Amazon Echo was supposed to be for wholesome things, like audiobooks, animal quizzes etc. However, Callum has already worked out that Alexa will play fart sounds, and purchased the 'big fart pack add-on'.

Arrived at the pub to find Callum and Mum helpless with laughter, as Alexa said in her pretty robot voice: 'I have another one brewing'.

Scenes like this make me nervous about spending Christmas with the Daltons. Alex and his family are formal people. They know not to swear at the dinner table, and I doubt they find fart noises funny.

Must watch *My Fair Lady* again.

Thursday 13th September

Nana Joan came over today with a kneeling scooter and wheelchair for Callum. Her old people's home gets a bulk-buy discount on mobility goods, so Nana bought the goods at cost price.

Callum doesn't need any mobility aids since he already has crutches but was delighted nonetheless.

'These are the best presents EVER,' he said, as we pushed him around in the wheelchair. 'I feel like a little prince.' Then he progressed to the kneeling scooter, bombing up and down the garden making vroom, vroom noises.

I cautioned Callum about going too fast and risking re-injury, but it was no good. The way he sees it, if he injures himself, he gets to see Angel Rain again.

Friday 14th September

Thought it was about time I had my straggly half-blonde, half-brown hair cut and dyed, since I'm having lunch with Catrina tomorrow. The roots are getting ridiculous – like I'm wearing one of Dad's brown bobble hats.

Unfortunately, making a last-minute hairdresser's appointment is always a big mistake.

Good hairdressers get booked up weeks in advance, so I ended up with a teenage trainee who'd Cruella Deville-dyed her hair half-black, half-blonde.

Maybe I was expecting too much, with my picture of Kate Hudson's smooth beach waves. But I'm not a million miles away from her hair type – give or take a few heaped teaspoons of Frizz Ease.

I knew the haircut was bad when Dad complimented my 'new do'.

'Oh, very sophisticated love,' he said. 'You don't see hair like that much any more, except on older women.'

Mum laughed when she saw me. 'Who did your hair?' she said. 'I'll beat them up for you.'

Brandi delivered a stinging comment too, telling me I looked like a poodle in the rain.

I'd hoped to glam myself up for the Catrina meeting tomorrow, but now if I wear makeup I look like a sexy Shetland sheep.

On the positive side, Catrina probably won't notice. That's the bonus with self-centred people – other people's bad haircuts, labels sticking out, mascara slippages etc. pass them by.

Saturday 15th September

Morning

Nick just picked Daisy up. This gives me most of the morning to prepare myself for lunch with Catrina. Normally, it would be nice to have preening time, but I'd rather not look in mirrors right now.

Mid-morning

Arg!

Alex's mother just cancelled lunch.

We were so close! Sooooo close!

Catrina had, in my opinion, a spurious reason for cancelling. Harold Dalton remarried yesterday, which has thrown Catrina into an 'emotional turmoil'.

'He didn't even tell me,' said Catrina. 'I found out on the radio. Can you imagine?'

Apparently, Harold Dalton married his new fashion-designer girlfriend, Nancy Jane Box, yesterday in Barbados. Nancy Jane Box is now Nancy Jane Box Dalton and will be changing all her branding.

I hope her dresses come with big labels.

'Was Alex invited to the wedding?' I asked.

'Who knows with Harold?' said Catrina. 'Who ever knows? I have such a headache. I have to go and rest. But we'll do lunch soon, darling. How about Friday?'

Said that would be fine.

Am choosing to take a big positive from the fact Catrina:

a) Phoned me personally

b) Called me darling

OK, so she calls everyone darling, but I'm still choosing to see it as a positive.

Mid-morning

Alex just phoned from Tokyo. He knew his father had got married.

'Did he invite you to the wedding?' I asked.

'Yes,' said Alex. 'Surprisingly, he did.'

'But you chose not to attend?'

'I have too much going on to fly out to Barbados on a week's notice. My father understood. He knows about putting business first.'

'He only gave you a week's notice?' I asked.

'It was all he gave anyone,' said Alex. 'The wedding was an overnight decision. A shotgun affair. I do hope Nancy isn't pregnant.'

'Could she be?' I asked.

Alex laughed. 'She's too old to be pregnant. Young for my father, but well past child-bearing age. She's in her forties.'

'Women still have children in their forties,' I said.

'Not women who've overindulged in substances for most of their thirties,' said Alex.

'What about Zach?' I asked. 'Did he go to the wedding?'

'He's not keen on my father's new girlfriend. Well, wife now. So he chose not to put in an appearance. From what I hear, my aunts were there and Ronald, my father's business partner. Other than that, it was a quiet ceremony. Except for the steel-drum band.'

'I suppose your father will see you at Christmas,' I said.

'Yes,' said Alex. 'And you too. How are things going with my mother?'

'She cancelled our lunch date when she found out your father had remarried,' I said.

'Ah ha,' said Alex. 'But you're going to reschedule?'

'That's the plan.'

'Aim for a Japanese restaurant if possible. Anya can't do much damage with chopsticks. Steak restaurants are right out.'

Evening

Nick just called. A TV contact he met in a bar has offered him a 'life-changing' audition on a Manchester soap opera.

Nick wants to head up north tomorrow for the Monday audition.

'So you want me to have Daisy tomorrow?' I asked.

'Would you?' said Nick. 'This is for all of our tomorrows. If I get this part, we'll be on easy street.'

'If you get this part, you'll have to move up north,' I said. 'Far away from your daughter.'

'I'll still get weekends off to visit,' said Nick. 'And they've got a crèche for Horry. He'll have a load of little actor-buddy kids to play with. Look, don't worry, yeah? If I move up north, I'll still do my weekends with Daisy. I love my little girl.'

I'm not worried about Nick moving up north because I know he won't get the part. Soap opera realism is not his skill set. He's an over-actor, better suits TV commercials and theatre.

Sunday 16th September

Took Callum to see Angel Rain today.

Daisy came too. She was very excited to visit a real-life hospital. Two-year-olds think children's wards are fun places filled with wheelie beds, kind nurses in uniform, chocolate vending machines and kiddie magazines. They don't see the grey face of sickness and disease.

Angel Rain was writing a wish list when we arrived, noting down everything she wants to do when she leaves the children's ward. The list included practical choices, like Disney Land, and far-fetched requests like riding a unicorn.

'She's just really thankful for everything,' said Callum. 'Even though her life's pretty shit right now. Most people would be moaning about being ill, but she looks out the window and sees the stars. I love how she sees the world. She never sweats the small stuff.'

Felt a little bit ashamed when Callum said that because I'd just shouted at Daisy for not finishing her over-priced hospital-restaurant lunch.

I felt incensed that Daisy had chosen something I *knew* she wouldn't like (olive pasta) when there were kids' cheeseburgers and chips on offer. And the olive pasta cost £12, whereas all the kids' meals were £6.

But when you meet children like Angel Rain, you know there are more important things to worry about than wasting a plate of pasta.

Anyway, I had a Tupperware tub with me so I can always have the pasta for dinner.

Monday 17th September

Callum is back at school again after his period of convalescence. Brandi has spent the morning catching up on emails from school.

'Education is supposed to be free in this country,' she moaned. 'But it's like Ryan bloody Air with all the add-ons. They're always asking for something. One pound to throw a wet sponge at Callum's teacher, one pound to dress as a superhero, one pound for National Book Day, bake-sale cupcakes from a nut-free kitchen and three clean plastic ice-cream tubs with the labels soaked off for some recycling sculpture. I've got a full-time job. I don't have time for all the admin.'

Told Brandi that if she didn't like it, she should vote for a political party that put more money into the school system, rather than do what she usually does – not vote at all.

'What have pot-a-lic parties got to do with schools?' Brandi asked.

Sometimes I despair of my sister. Maybe it's a good thing she doesn't vote. There probably should be some IQ criteria. Certainly, people should be able to pronounce 'politics' correctly before being allowed in a polling station.

Tuesday 18th September

It's only 8 am, and I've already lost all my patience.

All of it.

Have foolishly decided to potty-train Daisy while Alex is in Tokyo and it's still sunny outside. Mum said this would save on laundry because I can let Daisy run around naked.

Stripped Daisy off first thing this morning and told her to tell me when she needed a wee.

'Need a wee,' said Daisy.

Put her on the potty. She didn't go. This continued for an hour.

The tenth time Daisy told me she needed a wee, I told her she didn't need to go and had turned this 'WHOLE IMPORTANT DEVELOPMENTAL THING INTO A SILLY GAME!'

She cried, then weed on the floor.

Deeply frustrated.

Baby Bear is already partly potty-trained, and he's not even one. Laura does some sign language thing so he raises his hand when he wants to go.

Everyone says Daisy will get potty-training eventually.

But when? Isn't one day of wee all over the floor enough?

Wednesday 19th September

1 pm

Sleepy phone call from Alex. He's been up since 4 am and only just finished his meetings now, at 9 pm.

'The Japanese work extremely hard,' he said. 'Their work ethic is impressive.'

Then he fell asleep mid-phone call.

After shouting, 'ALEX!' a few times, I gave up and let him rest.

Alex won't be back for another week or so, and am really missing him now.

It's true what they say. Absence makes the heart grow fonder. Although there is a lot of wee around the house, so it's OK that Alex is absent at this precise moment.

11.45 pm

Just got back from working at the pub.

Mum was showing off her new sat nav to the regulars when I came on shift.

'It tells you where the speed cameras are,' Mum boasted. 'So I'll save a fortune on speeding tickets.'

Dad objected, both to the 'unnecessary' purchase and the product's morality.

'You shouldn't be speeding in the first place, Shirley. If you're adhering to the legal speed limit, speed cameras should not be an issue.'

He's emailed his MP about the sat nav, which has made Mum furious.

'You're a grass Bob,' she shouted. 'Telling that MP that your wife breaks the law.'

They were still arguing when I left after last orders.

I wonder what the Daltons would make of all the arguing in our family? I imagine they don't fight at all, just stay tight-lipped then subtly adjust their wills to leave out offending parties.

Thursday 20th September

Daisy is so clever.

She's started hurting herself on purpose to get treats.

Offered her hummus and rice cakes for lunch, and she tried to hurl herself from the high chair.

'What are you doing?' I screeched.

'Want On Boy,' she said. 'Want biscuit.'

Didn't know what she was talking about. Then it clicked. Whenever Daisy scrapes a knee or stubs a toe, John Boy gives her a chocolate biscuit to 'calm her down'.

Must talk to John Boy about spoiling Daisy, but I doubt he'll listen. To him, a chocolate biscuit isn't a treat. It's a common foodstuff, like rice or pasta.

John Boy has chocolate biscuits for breakfast if there's no time for his usual: two bowls of Frosties with five heaped teaspoons of sugar on top.

Friday 21st September

Visited Laura in London today.

Althea and Wolfgang were shopping in nearby Soho, so they ended up joining us for lunch.

On reflection, this was a bad idea.

Laura and Althea have such strong views about food and nutrition that they always end up arguing.

Laura champions grass-fed beef, oily fish and bone broths for 'the broadest spectrum of natural nutrition'.

Althea believes that all animal products, no matter how free-range, contain cancer-causing sadness.

It didn't help that Laura was boiling a pot of cow bones on her halogen stove when Althea and Wolfgang arrived.

'Why are you cooking up dead cow?' Althea demanded, sneering at the cast-iron pot of scummy boiling bones.

'I'm making bone broth for Bear,' said Laura. 'It's a wonderful source of natural collagen.'

'Your body makes its own collagen if you eat lentils and leafy greens,' Althea boomed. 'And *those things* don't contain harmful hormones that inflame the body and imbibe the carcinogenic sadness of the slaughtered herd.'

Althea then pulled out her collection of gruesome animal-torture pictures and convinced Laura to sign up for a 30-day vegan challenge.

'Your family deserve a break from sad cow,' Althea declared. 'I stopped eating meat twenty years ago and have never looked back.'

Eventually, after a lot of haranguing, Laura agreed to the challenge and congratulated Althea on two decades of vegetarianism.

'It's impressive,' said Laura. 'Staying well-nourished without animal products in our society is a challenge.'

'No it isn't, Althea insisted. 'People have been circumstantially vegan for centuries. Do you know what millions of peasants lived off in Tudor times? Vegetable soup. These days we have it easy. Linda McCartney sausages be praised!'

I kept quiet.

The truth is, Althea isn't a totally committed vegan OR vegetarian, despite her many militant outbursts. She often forgets her veganism if, for example, she's at a music festival, is feeling hungover and has camped near a bacon sandwich van.

Saturday 22nd September

Daisy has hit the terrible twos, big time.

She wants to do everything herself right now and literally turns red with rage if I say no. It's a big problem because most of the things she wants to do are way beyond her two-year-old ability.

For example, she wanted to pour her cereal milk this morning. Foolishly, I tried the 'laid-back Althea' thing and let her have a go. The result was a two-pint carton of milk emptied all over the breakfast bar.

Daisy has no concept of 'slow' or 'just a little bit' or 'STOP RIGHT NOW. IT'S GOING EVERYWHERE!'

'No Mummy,' Daisy screamed, as I wrestled the milk from her. 'I do it. I DO IT!'

I don't want to crush Daisy's confidence but frankly, aged-two, she does lack ability.

Althea says I should be 'risk-aware, not risk-averse' and allow Daisy more 'challenges', but Daisy doesn't have the co-ordination to slice apples, strike a match or pour boiling water from the kettle.

It's not fair to compare Daisy to Wolfgang, who fries beetroot crisps and cuts down garden weeds with a small machete.

Wolfgang is one of those hardy children who breeze through injuries. He's fallen out of a ten-foot tree and bounced before.

Daisy would have broken something, having already lost a few fingers from the machete.

Mid-morning
Just asked Mum for advice re the terrible twos.

'It's easy disciplining a two-year-old,' Mum declared. 'Just tantrum right back at them.'

But I don't want to do that. I remember Mum's counter tantrums when we were growing up. They were embarrassing, especially when she beat her shoe on the supermarket floor.

Sunday 23rd September

Angel Rain was discharged from hospital today. She's recovering well and may not need surgery again for a while.

Callum is sending her grinning selfies, plus photos of flowers and colourful stones from the pub garden.

All in all, the romance seems to be good for Callum. It's stopped him playing violent computer games and punching sofa cushions. Maybe all he ever needed was a nice girl to look after.

Monday 24th September

Really missing Alex.

We never speak for long on the phone, but by the sounds of things, he is working extremely hard.

Catrina hasn't booked in for another lunch yet. Am pretty sick of chasing her so will wait until Alex returns and take things from there.

Tuesday 25th September

Lunchtime shift in the pub today. It was a welcome distraction from missing Alex and good to have help with Daisy – who is driving me mad with terrible twos tantrums.

This morning she weed in her potty (yay!) then wanted to tip the wee in the toilet herself (boo!). I ended up fighting Daisy for the potty, which, as I kept shouting, was messy and unhygienic.

I've never seen myself as a softly-spoken, gentle, apron-wearing mother, but screaming my head off while covered in wee was a low moment. And now I know why mothers wear aprons.

Bumped into Mum on the way to the pub. She was jumping off the no.67 bus with a pint of milk and share-size bag of limited-edition caramel M&Ms.

'Where have you been?' I asked.

'To the newsagents,' she said.

'That's three-minutes down the road,' I said. 'Why on earth did you take the bus?'

'The government have given me a free bus pass,' said Mum. 'Why not use it?'

'Free bus passes are supposed to help pensioners in poverty,' I said. 'You're taking up space on the bus that could be used by someone with mobility trouble. Not to mention lowering your daily step quota. If you're going to buy a big, share-size bag of chocolate, you should get off your backside and walk for your treat.'

Mum has made a minor effort to be healthier this year (by joining a wine club and buying iceberg lettuce), but she still has type-two diabetes and a lot of bad habits.

Confiscated her M&Ms and told her she couldn't have them back until she'd walked for half an hour. Then I Facebook shamed her by posting a photo of her hopping off the bus, chocolate in hand.

Mum responded with this Facebook comment:

My daughter says I can't have chocolate. Does anyone know a good cocaine dealer?

Wednesday 26th September

Finally!

Catrina has recovered from the 'shock' of Harold remarrying and asked her assistant to rebook lunch.

Monique called this morning and asked if I could make the Bond Street Dalton.

Today.

Explained that I was working but could do Friday.

Monique said: 'Catrina won't be happy about that.'

'Why not?' I asked. 'It's incredibly short notice. And Catrina cancelled herself last time for a very spurious reason.'

'No, Catrina won't be happy about you working,' Monique explained. 'She's very against women working.'

'Why?' I asked.

'Ms Dalton believes a woman who has to work has failed in life.'

'That's an interesting philosophy,' I said. 'I believe a woman who marries for money has failed in life.'

Really need to think before I speak. Especially before lunch with Catrina.

Monique 'liaised' with Catrina's diary, then confirmed Catrina could indeed make Friday.

'Do not cancel again,' Monique warned. 'She will be very upset.'

'I didn't cancel in the first place,' I said. 'I just couldn't do zero notice.'

'That's not how Catrina will see it,' said Monique.

'I'm not going to cancel,' I said. 'I've been waiting long enough for this showdown – I mean, lunch.'

Hopefully the word showdown isn't easily translated into French.

Thursday 27th September

Very tired.

Did a long lunch shift in the pub yesterday, followed by an evening shift until midnight. The pub should have closed at eleven, but Yorkie had been laid off, so was celebrating.

At midnight, Mum had to pull the persuader from behind the bar and tell him to bugger off home on pain of injury.

Between my lunchtime and evening shift, I caught up with little Callum – who's feeling sad.

He'd hoped to take Angel Rain to the school disco next week. However, her last surgery hasn't quite healed as expected, so she needs one more corrective operation.

Callum is especially low because Angel Rain hasn't seen his tadpoles yet, and Dad callously told him they'll *definitely die* now autumn leaves are falling.

Callum is writing Angel Rain a ballad about tadpoles, which he and John Boy will record on MP3 and send to her. Not sure Callum really knows the difference between ballads and rap, but his heart is in the right place.

Friday 28th September

Feeling very ill!

Should have been having lunch with Catrina today, but had to cancel due to unexpected stomach cramps and diarrhoea.

Phoned Monique and could almost hear her head shaking down the phone line.

'She will not be happy,' said Monique. 'Not happy at all.'

'It's in her best interests,' I said. 'If I turn up at a restaurant with my rotten bottom, it will be bad for all concerned.'

Monique took a moment, probably translating from English

to French. Then she said, 'I will try to convey the seriousness to Catrina.' And hung up.

Not sure where the stomach bug came from but think it's probably viral. The last meal I ate was John Boy's 'army spaghetti Bolognese', made from Campbell's meatballs, Supernoodles and Heinz tomato soup. All that stuff has an epic shelf life, so I can't imagine it harbouring germs.

Have been on the toilet all day, with Daisy crashing in making various demands and accusing me of being smelly.

'Mummy, read me a story. Mummy do me princess hair. Mummy, Mummy, *portant* Mummy. Poo Mummy! *Stinky* in here Mummy. Very very stinky. POO Mummy, you *stink*.'

It is both tiring and humiliating.

Mid-morning
Nick just phoned. He is sick too and so is Horatio.

'It's coming out of both ends,' said Nick. 'Mum won't help out while I'm ill – she doesn't want to catch anything. Have pity on me. I can't handle two kids tomorrow.'

'I'm sick too, Nick,' I said. 'I was looking forward to using the toilet in peace.'

'Please Julesy,' Nick begged. 'I'm at breaking point. I've had a year and a half of Horry's vomit to clear up. Now I have my own too. I'll make it up to you.'

Agreed in the end, because Nick sounded so pitiful. Also, John Boy said he'd take Daisy this afternoon, so I can hug the toilet in peace.

He's going to teach her how to do commando rolls, which is excellent. Just the thing to tire her out before bedtime.

Saturday 29th September

Feeling better today. Have managed to keep food down and no more running back and forth to the toilet.

Fancied some fresh air, but didn't dare venture far from the toilet, so ended up doing some gentle gardening with Daisy.

She enjoyed playing with slugs and snails in the garden, and befriended a ladybird named 'Raspberry'.

Sadly, she killed Raspberry by accident.

'Raspberry all flat,' she announced, holding up her little Croc sandal. 'Very flat.'

Poor Raspberry's lifeless body stuck to the bottom of Daisy's shoe.

'Daisy, did you tread on Raspberry?' I asked.

She nodded earnestly. 'Yes. I kill her.'

'Why?' I asked.

'Want to see if her shell hard, Mummy,' said Daisy. 'Like Batman.'

Had to explain that a ladybird's shell isn't made from titanium plating and that a two-year-old's sandal is a death sentence.

'Raspberry has gone to sleep now,' I said in a gentle voice. 'And she won't wake up again. Aunty Althea says she'll become part of the grass, the flowers and the trees.'

Daisy thought for a moment, smiled and said: 'I find new ladybird. With very, very hard shell.'

Psychopath or resourceful?

Hard to say.

Sunday 30th September

Lovely news today.

Angel Rain's corrective surgery was successful and she's recovering well. She's not quite up to visitors yet, but her parents say Callum can see her next week.

Nick is feeling better and has taken Daisy for the day, so I can spend time sterilising the toilets.

Alex back tomorrow.

Can't wait.

Monday 1st October

3 am

Just received a bleepy text from Alex and am now wide-awake, thinking about all the things I need to do tomorrow.

His message said:

Boarding the plane. Home in 13 hours. Do you need catering for Daisy's birthday? If so, I'll call my assistant and arrange. I miss you and love you, your future husband, Alex.

Not sure why he wrote 'your future husband Alex'. It's not as if I'm going to forget who my future husband is. The catering Daisy's birthday offer was thoughtful, but I politely declined.

After experiencing the horror of Callum's mega-party, a simple cake and nice tea at the pub will suffice for Daisy.

I'm going to take the easy route this year and buy her cake (a *My Little Pony* Jam Cream Sponge) and present (*My Little Pony* Mega Collection) from a supermarket and have them delivered.

Dad told me off for not making a homemade cake, but I can't compete with the perfect, shop-bought versions. The chances of me icing a recognisable Fluttershy are zero, so best leave it to the experts – aka, Tesco, Sainsbury's and Asda.

Afternoon

Alex is back from Tokyo.

Just received this text message:

The eagle has landed.

Texted back, asking if the eagle needed to sleep off jet lag, but Alex is coming straight here from the airport again.

Panicked, because I hadn't got any decent food in. Rushed to the Co-op with Daisy in tow and grabbed a Thai curry ready-meal, microwave rice and prawn crackers. I also selected a special-offer white wine (slightly warm) from the ineffective fridge. This selection is well below Alex's usual Michelin restaurant standards, but sadly the Co-op doesn't sell Michelin-star ready meals. Potentially there's a gap in the market there.

Am microwaving Alex's dinner now.

Can't wait to see him.

8 pm

Am worried about Alex.

He seemed disorientated when he arrived at the cottage and kept saying he felt too hot. Being too hot is impossible in my house because I've inherited Dad's meanness with the central heating and always run it a few degrees lower than average.

He was clean and fresh, having used the power shower on his first-class flight, but his eyes looked *very* tired. And while we ate our Thai ready-meal dinner, the cracks began to show.

I expected his fine pallet would detect microwave food immediately, but he declared the food to be 'a triumph'.

'This food?' I asked. 'This ready-meal Thai curry?'

'If it's a ready meal, it's the best I've ever eaten,' he said.

Kept asking him if he was OK and he said yes, but he had a lot to think about re the business.

He actually said that.

'I have a lot to think about re the business.'

After the first glass of wine, he kept accidentally lapsing into Japanese. After the second glass, he rested his hand on his palm and fell asleep at the table, nearly nose-diving into coconut curry sauce.

John Boy checked Alex's vital signs and confirmed he was 'just knackered', then army-lifted him upstairs and into my bed.

He is there now.

Hope he's not coming down with something.

10 pm

Phoned Mum hoping for reassurance about Alex's health and wellbeing, but she made me feel a lot more worried.

'If he's feeling hot, it could be the beginnings of a nervous breakdown,' she said. 'Your Uncle Ralph had one of those during his workaholic years. He was always talking about feeling hot. In fact, he was sweaty for months. Sweaty Ralph we called him. Until we found out about the breakdown, of course.'

Mum said Uncle Ralph had to go to the doctor and take antidepressants.

'Get Alex to the doctor's sharpish,' said Mum. 'He needs looking over by a medical professional.'

'But what if he won't go?' I asked.

'You're his fiancée,' she said. 'Make him go.'

Tuesday 2nd October

Alex has gone to work in London.

He left before I woke up, having scribbled a note in Daisy's fluffy rainbow notepad:

Gone to London. Shares are down. A lot to think about re the business, Alex.

Mid-morning

Have called and called Alex, leaving messages on both his mobile and at all the Dalton Hotels, but no word back.

Laura assures me, via Zach, that he is OK and just 'working

hard'.

'Zach is keeping an eye on him,' said Laura.

'I think he should see a doctor,' I said. 'Can Zach make him see a doctor?'

'Doubtful,' said Laura. 'Zach is the little brother. Older ones never do what younger ones tell them.'

'But you listen to me,' I said. 'You always do what I tell you.'

'You think I listen to you,' said Laura. 'But actually, I'm just being polite. I always do my own thing.'

So after all these years, my big sis has been lying to me. It's quite a blow.

Phoned Mum – once again, hoping she'd make me feel better. Once again, she didn't.

'You and Laura should sort out arguments between yourselves and don't tell tales,' she said. 'You know my motto when it comes to sisters. If it ain't bleedin', don't tattle.'

Afternoon

No word from Alex and he's still not answering his phone.

Just spoke to Laura and demanded she put Zach on the line.

Zach thinks Alex is in meetings because he's not answering his phone. He admitted that Alex seems 'out of sorts' and is keeping an eye on him. Dalton Group share prices have dropped a few points recently, and Alex is taking it badly.

'Share prices are always fluctuating,' said Zach. 'That's the nature of the beast. But our shares always go up over time. Alex knows that. Normally, he's the one rallying the rest of us. I don't know what's got into him. But I'm sure it's just tiredness. Our cousins in Tokyo worked him very hard. I barely heard from him when he was over there.'

I'm sure Zach is right, but I've never seen Alex quite this tired before.

Evening

Alex finally phoned back.

He was slurring his words because he was so exhausted.

'I just have a few things to wap up here,' he said. 'And then I'm coming to Oakley.'

'You should stay in London and rest,' I said. 'The last thing you need is more travel.'

Alex tried to protest, saying he had to be in Great Oakley for Daisy's birthday tomorrow, but I put my foot down.

'You're too tired,' I said. 'And blirthday isn't a real word. Sleep and catch up with us at the end of the week. And Alex – maybe you should see a doctor.'

Alex laughed. 'Juliette, I'm just jet-lagged and tired and working hard. Nothing sweep can't fix.'

Told Alex to rest, and he promised to call 'flirst' thing tomorrow.

Hopefully, after another good night's sleep, he'll be back in the land of the living.

Wednesday 3rd October

Daisy's birthday

Alex hasn't called yet, so assume he's still sleeping and am letting him rest. He certainly needs to.

Dad called at 8 am to sing happy birthday and tell Daisy that kids today are spoilt rotten. He was on the train to London for his annual eye-clinic visit, so the signal kept going in and out.

'No doubt you'll have a big cssssssshhh!…of presents, Daisy,' he said. 'I hope you appreciate cssssshhh!… In my day, an orange cssssssh!… a treat.'

The poor-phone-signal lecture went over Daisy's head because she asked why Dad was talking about 'a peach cake' (appreciate), when she'd asked for a 'hello' one (meaning a yellow sponge).

Mum forgot Daisy's birthday completely and was in a roadside cafe enjoying a bacon bap when I called.

'Why didn't your bloody dad remind me?' she bellowed. 'I'm on my way to a brewery in Norwich. Fancy Bob dropping me in it like this.'

Reminded Mum that Dad had a hospital appointment this morning, so wasn't obliged to be her alarm service.

'He could have at least sent me a text,' said Mum. 'It was very thoughtless. Daisy won't take it badly, will she? She knows I've got a bad memory.'

This is true. Mum has a terrible memory. She forgets my, Laura, Brandi and Dad's birthdays and often her own too. And she can't use online banking, which requires the triple memory whammy of unique ID, password *and* passcode.

6 pm

Alex still hasn't called. He must still be sleeping – he has at least 70 hours to catch up on.

Nice birthday tea for Daisy at the pub. Mum didn't make it back in time, but Nana Joan dropped by on her Easy Rider scooter. We knew when Nana had reached the high street because of all the car horns beeping.

Nick arrived halfway through the birthday tea with Daisy's present: the same *My Little Pony* Mega Collection I bought her. The only difference was, Nick hadn't wrapped it or taken the price sticker off.

He claimed he'd been confused by my text message and thought I'd instructed him to buy the *My Little Pony* Mega Collection, when in fact I texted DO NOT BUY in big shouty capitals. His excuse was being baby-tired – which I suppose I have to allow, considering all the stupid mistakes I made during Daisy's first year. And continue to make, even though she's two.

We're back at the cottage now, and Daisy is still awake, playing with her two *My Little Pony* Mega Collection sets.

Hope Alex calls back soon. Still feeling worried about him.

Late Evening

Mum has just done a birthday drive-by. She came crashing into the cottage with an armload of birthday bits-and-pieces just as I was putting Daisy to bed.

Mum bought Daisy:

+ A 'Now You Are Two' picture book
+ A giant 'Two Today' birthday card
+ A saucer-sized 'Two-Year-Old' badge
+ A sparkly, silver TWO helium balloon.

'Daisy is three today,' I said.

'Blimey,' said Mum, 'That crept up quick. What am I going to do with this cake, then?' She pulled out a number-two shaped cake covered in fondant icing.

Tried to cut the cake to look more like a three but failed – so Mum and I ate a big slice each from the middle to obscure the number entirely. The cake looked like a number eleven after that. However, Daisy can't count past ten so this is probably OK.

Thursday 4th October

7 am

I'm in complete shock.

Harold Dalton passed away last night.

Alex just rang to tell me.

Harold was the sort of man you expected to go on forever, complaining and gritting his teeth in disapproval wherever he went.

Alex is with Zach, Catrina and Harold's new wife right now.

They're at the hospital, putting things in order.

I asked Alex if he needed me with him, but he said no. There are lots of journalists hanging around and security is challenging.

Alex tried to make a joke, saying the nation was desperate to know if Harold Dalton had finally popped his clogs so they can break out the Champagne.

Which is actually quite sad.

Afternoon

Alex called again. His voice sounded strange and flat, and he said he was on his way to the cottage to see Daisy and me.

'How are you feeling?' I asked him.

'I don't know,' he said. 'I honestly have no idea.'

Should do a quick house-tidy before Alex gets here. Create a state of calm in a world that must feel chaotic to him right now.

Will start with the hallway, where Daisy has filled each shoe with cornflakes to give them 'breakfast' (thankfully I caught her before she added milk).

Should tidy myself up too. Have experienced the usual overnight mascara slippage and look like a sad vampire. It's not a face a grieving person wants to see.

Evening

Alex has just come and gone. He had the eyes of a man who'd just seen a car crash – sad, shocked and afraid.

I gave him a long hug and cautioned him not to be alarmed about the hallway crunching – it was just cornflakes. Then we sat on the sofa and held hands in silence.

Eventually, I asked how Harold had died.

'A stroke,' said Alex. 'It was very sudden.'

'How is his new wife taking it?' I asked.

Alex said Nancy checked herself into the Priory today, where she will no doubt bump into Catrina – who also checked herself in.

Tried to think of something supportive to say and managed: 'At least it was sudden.'

Alex nodded, but I didn't feel he was listening.

After sitting in silence for a long time, Alex stood up and said he was going to the Dalton Estate.

'I need to be alone for a while, Juliette. I'm not good for anyone right now.'

Spent the evening Googling grief and its many expressions. The main flavour was that anything goes. Alex is allowed to do all sorts of inappropriate things in the next few months, including wanting to have lots of sex and/or blanking me completely.

I wish there was something I could do for him.

Sent a lot of heart emojis by text, but they seemed woefully inadequate.

Will keep trying to send love however I can.

Friday 5th October

Phoned Alex and had a very stilted conversation with one-word answers.

'How are you doing?'

'OK.'

'Who's handling the funeral arrangements?'

'Nobody.'

'And how's Harold's new wife doing?'

'Badly.'

'And Zach? How's he holding up?'

'Badly.'

Long silence.

'Are you still at the Dalton estate?' I asked. 'Should I come over and see you?'

'No. Best not.'

Encouraged by the extra word, I said: 'You really shouldn't be alone, Alex. It's good to have support when you're going through something like this.'

'No. Best not.'

'Why not?'

'Best not right now.'

I asked Alex if he'd seen a doctor, and he said no. Suggested it might be a good idea – he'd been overly hot and tired even before this happened. He said no again.

Will leave Alex alone today but will take Daisy to visit him tomorrow. Storm the castle, so to speak. We can pass the Co-op on the way and pick up that Thai ready-meal he liked.

Alex really shouldn't be alone.

Afternoon

Have called Catrina to offer my condolences. As usual, the call went straight through to answer machine. Left a voice message saying how sorry I am. I hope she knows that, despite our differences, I do care.

The nonsense cocktail-throwing argument and my need to hold Catrina accountable seem so petty now. All I feel for her is sympathy and I hope, even if I can't speak to her, she knows that.

Saturday 6th October

Thinking a lot about Alex. Sending heart emojis but I know it's not enough. How do you support someone who wants to be alone?

It's heartbreaking.

Have decided the only thing I can do is get on with my life and leave him to it. So went to work as normal.

Arrived at the pub to find Callum tapping away on Brandi's phone.

'What are you doing, Callum?' I asked.

'Messaging,' he said.

'Who?'

'I'll give you a clue,' he said. 'It's Angel Rain.'

He's never quite grasped guessing games.

Angel Rain is recovering well, but they're running lots of tests to make sure she'll be OK when she leaves hospital.

Hugged Daisy extra tight when I finished my pub shift, even though she was sleeping and I risked waking her up – a dangerous prospect for an exhausted parent.

Sent kind, loving thoughts to Alex, his family and every parent with a sick child.

Sunday 7th October

Mum, Dad and the internet say I'm not allowed to be angry with Alex because he's grieving.

Which is a shame, because I really want to be angry.

Daisy and I visited Alex today, but he refused to see us – sending his housekeeper, Mrs Hawks, to answer the door.

Mrs Hawks told us curtly that Mr Dalton wanted to be alone. 'He needs space and personal time,' she said.

'But I'm his fiancée,' I said. 'I am both his space and his personal time. It's not good for him to shut himself away like this.'

Alex appeared in the hallway then.

'Juliette,' he said, 'I do need to be alone. Daisy is welcome to play on the lawn if she wants. Hawksy can lay out a picnic. There's a ham in the fridge. I can't be with other people right now.'

'Other people?' I said. 'I'm your fiancée.'

'I just need to be alone,' said Alex.

It was both reasonable and totally unreasonable.

So I'm both sympathetic and angry.

Monday 8th October

Visited Laura in London today to talk about Alex shutting himself away.

Something good has come of Harold's sudden death – Zach has reassessed his priorities, is home more and Laura is no longer lonely.

'It's lovely having Zach with me,' said Laura. 'But I must admit, it's been hard work keeping baby Bear quiet for the grief counsellor's visits.'

I was surprised to hear that Zach is seeing a grief counsellor. Assumed he'd be the stiff-upper-lip sort who would weather emotional storms privately, but Laura said his father's death hit him hard.

'It's brought up a lot of questions,' said Laura. 'Questions that can never be answered.'

'What sort of questions?' I asked.

'About Harold's last will and testament.' Laura let that sentence hang in the air.

'What about the last will and testament?' I asked.

'Zach was left £100,000,' said Laura.

'Lucky him,' I said.

'Alex inherited five million,' said Laura.

'Why did Alex get so much more?' I asked.

'Because Zach isn't Harold's biological son. It's all come out now. The family scandal.'

No wonder Zach's going to grief-counselling. I thought our family were messy, with two single mothers and a nana who wears skin-tight Lycra. But this is something else.

'Zach has always felt like an outsider,' said Laura. 'He was given a pony for Christmas one year, whereas Alex got a stallion. The signs were there, but Zach never knew for certain.'

How awful.

Asked about Harold's funeral, and Laura said there has been backbiting and arguments over Harold's last wishes.

'Harold appointed Ronald MacDonald as the executor,' she said.

'What is an executor?' I asked.

'The will executor makes the final decisions after death,' Laura explained. 'They decide about the funeral and that kind of thing.'

'And who is Ronald MacDonald, assuming he's not the same Ronald MacDonald responsible for the obesity crisis?'

'Harold's business partner,' said Laura. 'Usually, a spouse or family member is named executor. But Harold has appointed Ronald MacDonald.' And then in answer to my unasked question, she added: 'He's nothing to do with Big Macs.'

'Why didn't Harold name his wife as executor?' I asked.

'Who knows?' said Laura. 'But it's probably for the best. Nancy isn't the most stable of characters. She's a creative, artistic lady. Very passionate. With strong opinions.'

I think that means she's nuts.

'What am I going to do about Alex?' I asked.

'Wait until he comes out of his cave,' said Laura. 'And love him while he's in there. There's nothing else you can do.'

Zach came home with an armload of organic groceries while we were chatting, and offered us stem-ginger biscuits and Rooibos tea.

'How are you feeling?' I asked.

'Raw,' he said. 'Finding out your father isn't really your father is bad enough. But right after the old guy carks it…it's been hard.'

Gave Zach my love and sympathy, but it sounds like he's doing all the right things. Talking about his feelings. Seeing a counsellor.

It's Alex I'm worried about.

Tuesday 9th October

Phoned Alex this morning.

I didn't expect him to answer, but he did.

'Laura told me there are a few arguments about the funeral,' I said.

Alex gave a curt laugh. 'I hadn't heard, but I would expect nothing less from my family. You saw how things were at my brother's wedding. My father and mother both making a point by their absence. A funeral is yet another opportunity for assertions of power and position. The one blessing is that the biggest power-player will be in the coffin.'

'Maybe the funeral will be a chance to bring everyone together,' I said. 'Death helps people see what's important.'

Alex made a strangulated 'Ha!' sound.

Asked Alex if he wanted to see me yet, and he said, 'No. Leave me be for a while.'

'I don't think it's healthy to shut yourself away like this,' I said.

'People handle things differently,' said Alex. 'Not everyone tells the world their problems.'

I think this was a subtle dig because I told Catrina's assistant about my diarrhoea. But it's healthy to be open about your issues. As the Amazon Echo mega-fart add-on says, better out than in.

Wednesday 10th October

Visited Nana Joan today.

Dad suggested I take her fresh vegetables from his allotment, but there was no point. She only really eats soft vegetables from cans, and even that is a rarity.

Nana Joan wanted to hear all about Alex's dad – cause of death, time of death, place of death etc.

'And how old was he when he died?' she probed.

'I think late seventies,' I said. 'He had that old-person walk, like a wind-up toy.'

'Oh, not old then,' said Nana Joan, shaking her head. 'It's a shame. But I suppose when it's your time to go, it's your time to go.'

Talked to Nana about Alex and how distant he's being.

'That's men for you,' said Nana. 'They go off into their caves, don't they? My new boyfriend's the same. Moody old sod.'

She lent me her copy of *Men are from Mars, Women are from Venus* telling me it would help me understand men better.

'This book is a godsend, Juliette,' she said. 'I'm telling you, it's cut my rages in half.'

I took the book, but I can't imagine it will help me re understanding men. From my limited experience, they're either unreliable womanisers or withdrawn workaholics.

Told Nana Joan that life might be better, just Daisy and me.

'What rubbish,' she said. 'Your Alex is going through a hard time. The last thing he needs is you giving up on him.'

But how can I be there for him when he doesn't want me around?

Thursday 11th October

Alex called with news about the funeral.

No one can agree.

Alex and Zach want to have the funeral in Ireland, where Harold's family are from, but Nancy Jane and Catrina have other ideas.

'Nancy Jane wants the service in New York,' said Alex. 'And my mother wants the service in Los Angeles.'

'So what will happen if you can't agree?' I said.

'I imagine it will go to court,' said Alex.

Asked Alex if he wanted me to visit, but he said no. He's still wallowing and 'not fit for public consumption.'

'But I'm not the public,' I said. 'I'm your fiancée. For better or worse, right?'

'Just let me do things my way, Juliette,' said Alex. 'I can't be with people right now.'

Alex sounded weird and distant.

This is hard.

Really, really hard.

Friday 12th October

Phoned Althea to talk about death. It's one of her favourite subjects because she doesn't fear it like most people – instead, seeing it as an opportunity to continue her karmic journey.

'Alex's father is still here,' said Althea wisely. 'He's part of the earth and the trees and the eternal energy moving and transforming.'

It wasn't especially comforting, because no one liked Alex's father. Who wants to imagine him in tree-form, sneering and swiping his branches at people?

Althea has invited me over for a 'death chat', so Daisy and I will head there shortly. First, I need to find two matching shoes for Daisy that aren't full of breakfast cereal.

Afternoon

Just back from Althea's house.

Wolfgang greeted us at the door in his 'dancing dress', then did performance art while Althea played the didgeridoo.

Three-year-old Wolfgang has quite a large selection of dresses now – a lot more than Daisy. I applaud Althea's non-gender specific upbringing. It should be an odd juxtaposition – an angry little boy in pretty pink frills – but Wolfgang carries it off with swagger and aplomb.

The dancing went on for quite a long time. Too long really, but that's performance art for you.

When Wolfgang finished, he gave Daisy her belated birthday gift: a My Little Pony Mega Collection, just like the two she already has.

'Sorry it's a bit plastic-consumer tat,' said Althea. 'But it was Wolfgang's idea. He's a real "Brony" right now. A boy who likes *My Little Pony*.'

Wolfgang found his own *My Little Pony* Mega Collection up-for-grabs outside a neighbour's house and has been mad for them ever since.

Sometimes, I wish I lived in affluent London. Althea gets the best haul of free stuff. Whenever I see a 'Free' sign in Great Oakley, it's inevitably taped to rubbish that's too big for the bin. As if anyone wants a broken gas hob.

'Alex sounds so spaced out,' I told Althea. 'It's like he's been body-snatched.'

Althea nodded sagely, and said Alex was a prime candidate for 'losing his shit'.

'Middle age, overwork and bereavement are a lethal combination for mental health,' she said.

Told her Alex was acting strangely, even before his dad passed away.

'Could he be having a nervous breakdown, like Uncle Ralph?' I asked.

'Almost certainly,' said Althea. 'But don't worry about it because there's nothing you can do. Power and control are illusions. Embrace the chaos and insanity that is life and don't forget the spray paint.'

Saturday 13th October

Alex still not picking up his phone or returning my calls.

I was so confused and desperate today, I even asked Nick for advice when he came to pick up Daisy.

'Why is Alex being like this?' I asked Nick. 'Shutting himself away. Not returning calls. Surely people need more love when they're unhappy, not less?'

'Why don't you dump him?' Nick suggested. 'And you and I can try again.'

'Thanks but no thanks,' I said. 'You don't go off in moods, *but you do* go off with bridesmaids.'

When Nick left with Daisy, the house felt too quiet and empty, so I headed to the pub for a bit of family love. I thought it would be relaxing without Daisy, but it wasn't because Callum was charging around the place naked.

He has now mastered a 'hobbling-run' technique in his moon boot, which enables him to move quickly while maintaining maximum clomping volume – either clothed or unclothed.

Mum was shouting at Callum to put some pants on when I arrived, but it was very half-hearted because she was laughing at the same time.

'Why is his bum so tanned?' I asked. 'Has Brandi been letting him apply her fake bake?'

'No,' said Mum. 'He's been on Brandi's sun-bed.'

'What sun-bed?' I asked.

'The one in Brandi's bedroom,' said Mum. 'She's hired it for the weekend. Can't you hear the thing, belting out UV rays? It's on day and night.'

'How could Brandi let Callum on a sunbed?' I said. 'She's done beautician's training. She must know the dangers.'

'She didn't let him,' said Mum. 'He snuck on while she was on

Tinder.'

'Then she shouldn't have it in the house,' I said. 'I'm going to give her a piece of my mind.'

Found my silly little sister lying on Callum's bottom bunk, completely naked, looking like a blackened piece of toast.

'Why are you naked too?' I asked.

'I'm in too much pain to wear clothes,' said Brandi. 'I've made my skin super sensitive with all the sun bedding. But it'll be better soon. I just need to give it a few hours.'

'You're setting a terrible example for Callum,' I said. 'Not to mention jeopardising your health.'

'Callum snuck on for a sunny when I wasn't looking,' said Brandi. 'You know what he's like. He doesn't listen.'

'His hearing is perfect when you offer him ice cream,' I said. 'You need to get rid of this sun-bed, Brandi. Don't you think being unable to wear clothes is a red flag?'

'Pain is a natural side effect of most beauty treatments,' said Brandi. 'This is nothing compared to lip fillers.'

Gave up after that.

You can't argue with stupid.

Have told Callum lots of horror stories about sunbeds, skin cancer and premature ageing. He wasn't fussed about the health dangers, but the vanity warnings were effective.

'People get addicted to sun-beds and end up looking awful, Callum,' I said. 'And girls don't fancy boys with wrinkly, Day-Glo orange faces and bright white teeth.'

Callum got scared then, especially when I showed him pictures of Donald Trump.

'I'll leave the sun-bed alone, Aunty Julesy,' he promised. 'I don't want to be an addict. It's not worth it. It's not *worth* it.'

Sunday 14th October

John Boy stumbled into the house early this morning with vicious scratches all over his face. I guessed (wrongly) that he'd offended a girl with good-quality fake nails, but it turns out he'd got drunk, fallen asleep in the park and been attacked by a badger.

John Boy was quite shaken but blamed himself for offering the badger pork scratchings.

'He looked like such a cuddly fella,' said John Boy. 'To think he'd turn like that.'

When John Boy and I got to the pub for our lunchtime shift, Dad took the opportunity to lecture John Boy about the nocturnal habits of badgers and their territorial instincts.

John Boy was interested at first but switched off when Dad started using words like *Mustelidae* and omnivore.

Wanted to ask John Boy about men and grief caves, but he was too busy telling his badger story to the enraptured pub regulars.

'And then he LEAPT at me, claws out, teeth bared…'

John Boy is always the hero of his own story, no matter what reality has to say about it. But then again, maybe that's true for all of us. Certainly, I see myself as a wronged heroine right now.

Monday 15th October

Still no word from Alex.

Have messaged to ask if there's a date for the funeral yet, but no reply. Didn't bother hinting about my birthday on Friday. Alex won't forget the date. But he might remain in his black hole and miss my birthday entirely.

Late afternoon
Just visited Laura in London to give baby Bear his birthday present.

Laura and Zach are taking Bear to Euro Disney on his actual birthday, so I wanted to shower him with pre-birthday love.

However, I had an ulterior motive: grilling Laura about Alex. Is Alex still going into work? Is he speaking to anyone at all? What does Zach know?

It was a useless grilling though, because Zach hasn't seen Alex since their father passed away.

'What about the funeral?' I asked. 'Has a date been set?'

'Zach and I don't know anything about that,' said Laura, her voice prim. 'We won't be attending. The grief counsellor says it's not good for Zach's state of mind. He's advised we take a holiday somewhere sunny and pass on the whole toxic affair. And that's exactly what we're going to do.'

'What kind of grief counsellor advises you not to go to a funeral?' I asked.

'A very expensive one,' said Laura.

I'm not sure Zach and Laura are doing the right thing, re missing Harold's funeral. It's not as though Zach will be able to change his mind further down the line. A funeral is a one-shot deal.

Also, on a selfish note, if Laura and Zach don't come, I'll be left alone with Alex's family and no sisterly life-raft. Assuming that Alex invites me to the funeral, of course. Given his current state of mind, it's entirely possible he won't. And maybe it's for the best – his mother and I still have unresolved issues, and I never liked his father.

If I'm entirely honest, I'm not Alex's biggest fan right now either.

Tuesday 16th October

Birthday in a few days. I don't feel excited about it, though, because the love of my life is still in his grief hole.

John Boy gave me my birthday present today (a 4.5 litre bottle of gin from Drinks Direct) because he's jetting off to Ibiza tomorrow on a super-cheap last-minute 'lads' holiday. The £150 trip includes flights, transfers and seven days in a hotel with unlimited food and alcoholic drink.

I'm a bit concerned about the hotel quality at that price, but John Boy doesn't care.

'As long as the beer is free, we'll make our money back on the first night,' he said.

'What about the hotel?' I said. 'It might be horrible.'

'I've slept in an army barracks,' said John Boy. 'When you've done that, everything else is a step up.'

He says he'll happily sleep next to a busy road, under a flight path, beside a loud disco or even in a room without windows – as long as there's a double bed for bringing back 'birds'. And no bed bugs, because that could put off 'the birds'.

There is a downside to John Boy's cheap holiday: the flight leaves at 3 am and doesn't include luggage unless he pays an extra £80. However, he has thought his way around this. He's going to wear all his clothes at once, including underwear and swimming trunks.

Wednesday 17th October

Daisy is asleep.

Alex still hasn't called or shown any indication that he knows it's my birthday tomorrow.

Feeling a bit sad, so have opened John Boy's birthday present and am drinking gin/wallowing in self-pity.

Knowing my luck, Alex will turn up for a surprise visit and find me glugging gin like a slattern. But my heart tells me he won't.

Feel quite low.

Thursday 18th October

My birthday and baby Bear's

Happy birthday to me. And baby Bear.

No contact from Alex yet, which feels pretty awful. However, I've done enough wallowing. Time to slap on a smile and appreciate what I've got.

Daisy and I have each other.

My family are down the road.

There's a big bottle of gin in the cupboard.

I have many reasons to be cheerful, 1, 2, 3 – number one being Daisy, who yelled 'HAPPY BIRTHDAY!' at me this morning, then gave me a pebble wrapped in a Domino's pizza flyer.

Aww.

Number two reason to be cheerful: my family.

Dad knocked on the cottage door this morning with a homemade wholemeal sponge and gooseberry jam cake, plus a book about medieval churches wrapped in recycled wrapping paper.

'Your mum and Brandi are on their way,' he said. 'But you know what they're like in the mornings. Hard to rouse. Where's Alex? Is he hard to rouse in the mornings too?'

Told Dad that Alex was currently in a grief hole and shutting himself off from the world.

'That's a shame,' said Dad. 'This gooseberry jam is one of the best batches I've ever made. Never mind, I'll save him a jar.'

'I don't think Alex deserves gooseberry jam,' I said. 'What kind of man misses his own fiancée's birthday?'

'It sounds like Alex is depressed,' said Dad. 'He probably wants to deal with everything alone, so as not to burden you. Would you rather be with someone like Nick? All amateur dramatics?'

'At least Nick paid me some attention,' I said.

'Alex pays you attention,' said Dad. 'But depression is a funny business. Sometimes, when men are having a hard time, they feel others are better off without them.'

'Alex isn't depressed,' I said. 'He's grieving.'

'Grieving is depression,' said Dad. 'And from what you told me, Alex had a lot on his plate beforehand, with business and travel and so forth. Your mum told me you were worried about Alex a few weeks back. That he was overheated and slurring his words. Maybe he already had some exhaustion-related illness. And then his father died. That's a lot to deal with.'

Saw things in a slightly different way after talking to dad. It's true – Alex *wasn't* quite right before Harold died. And his relationship with his father wasn't a normal one – he must have a lot to work through.

I need to be more considerate and understanding.

Afternoon

Have been considerate and understanding all morning, hoping that the universe would see how kind I am and make Alex call.

It didn't work.

Lost my considerateness and understanding by lunchtime, and phoned Alex to berate him for missing my birthday.

Alex answered the phone the third time I rang.

'I'm so very, very sorry, Juliette,' he said. 'I'm just not myself right now. It's hard to explain. I'm trying to hold it all together, but I'm struggling. I have no idea what day it is, let alone the date. I'm really, really struggling.'

Alex sounded so sad, almost on the verge of tears. It was impossible to be angry with him.

'Dad thinks you might be depressed,' I said.

'Yes,' said Alex. 'That's probably the word for it. Spending time with my mother hasn't helped. But she's back at the Priory now and I imagine she'll stay there until the funeral. They'll give her much more attention than I can.'

'Have you seen a doctor?'

'Not yet. But I'm beginning to think it's a good idea.'

'It is,' I said. 'You've got a lot to deal with. Has anything been agreed about the funeral yet?'

'Yes,' said Alex. 'Weapons have been put down and we've let Ron choose the date, time, venue etc. The funeral will be held next Tuesday at eleven o'clock. West London crematorium. The wake is at the Chelsea sorting office. May I have the pleasure of your company on this truly terrible day?'

'Do you want me to come with you?' I asked.

'I'd love you to,' said Alex. 'My whole family will be there. I need sanity more than anything.'

Thanked him for calling me sane. Said yes – of course I'd come.

Friday 19th October

Phoned Alex to get more details about the funeral.

'The funeral cars will arrive at the Dalton Estate around 8.30 am,' he said. 'And my mother will be with us. Just to warn you.'

'I still haven't spoken to Catrina,' I said. 'I've left a few condolence messages. Alex, I don't need anything from your mother to move forward any more. I can let it go. The last thing you need is someone else in your life holding a grudge.'

'Nice to know my father's death has led to something positive,' said Alex. 'God knows, it's caused enough squabbles and heartbreak.'

'Your mother won't mind me being at the funeral, will she?' I asked.

'Two of my father's ex-wives will be there,' said Alex. 'Anya has plenty of women to spar with. I doubt she'll even notice you're there.'

'Maybe it'll be a good chance to work on our relationship,' I said.

'If she sees how much I care about both of you.'

'Seems unlikely,' said Alex. 'My mother is like a violent tropical storm once angered. You're better off giving her a wide birth. Huddling below deck, waiting until the seasons change and the sun comes out again. Anyway, she's at the Priory right now, wallowing in self-pity and talking endlessly about herself to paid staff. She's in her element. Your use to her is limited.'

Will send Catrina flowers and a card. Have no idea what I'll write in the card, though. There is no off-the-shelf sentiment for 'sorry the husband you divorced twenty-years ago died'.

Saturday 20th October

Went shopping today for a funeral dress, while Mum and Dad looked after Daisy.

Thought I'd made a good, conservative dress choice, but am uncertain now because Daisy offered an unflattering assessment.

'Fat,' she announced, as I twirled in the bedroom mirror. Then she pushed my tummy for emphasis and said it again.

'Fat, Mummy. It fat.'

I was forced to re-examine myself through harsh, honest toddler eyes and have to admit the dress was a bit figure-hugging. I've put on weight recently. All the holidays this year have taken their toll, plus having a toddler is tiring.

I don't have time to sleep, so I eat a whole jar of Nutella instead.

Oh well. Funerals aren't about looking cute or showing off your figure. Plus Alex has already put the ring on my finger. He can't back out now and anyway it's me who's having second thoughts.

Sunday 21st October

Doubly good day for Callum – he was allowed to visit Angel Rain this morning AND has been unshackled from his moon boot.

When I arrived for my lunch-time shift, he was whizzing around at full speed.

'I brought Angel Rain a can of Coke and a David Walliams book,' he said, as he karate-kicked the sofa cushions. 'And she was really pleased. She gave me a kiss on the cheek. Then we did each other matching soulmate manicures. Look.'

Callum waggled his fingernails, showing off colourful hearts and flowers.

By the sounds of things, Callum has been an excellent hospital companion today. As well as offering gifts and manicures, he encouraged Angel Rain's musical dreams by giving her vocal training, via his karaoke app.

'She's an awesome singer,' said Callum. 'Really loud.'

Apparently, Angel Rain and Callum hit some extremely high notes before the children's ward nurses whisked the curtains aside and told them to be quiet or they'd get no jelly pot with their lunch.

Monday 22nd October

Mum was forced to go on an NHS alcohol-awareness course today by Doctor Slaughter.

She was annoyed about it but blamed herself.

'I shouldn't have been so honest,' she said. 'Everyone knows you say under twenty-one units when doctors ask about your weekly alcohol consumption.'

'Actually, it's fourteen units for women,' I said.

'I'm bigger than most women,' Mum reasoned. 'My boobs alone are worth at least five units each.'

Asked Mum if she'd learned anything from the course, but she said no.

'I was hungover,' she admitted. 'We were celebrating Mad Dave's fourth wedding last night, so it was a late one.'

'Did they at least warn you about what alcohol does to your body?' I asked.

'Oh yeah,' said Mum. 'And then some. It made me want to drink more. Watching graphic medical videos about liver disease – it's depressing, isn't it? I had a double vodka when I got home, just to get over the trauma.'

Afternoon
Feeling nervous about the funeral tomorrow. I don't know why – maybe because I haven't seen Alex for so long.

Not sure what to expect.

Tuesday 23rd October

It's Harold Dalton's funeral today.

The service itself hasn't started yet. I'm hiding in the powder room, where I've come to pretend to adjust my make-up.

It's been quite a day so far, and it isn't even lunchtime.

Arrived at the Dalton Estate this morning to find Alex and Catrina getting shit-faced, pre-9 am. They were both knocking back strong drinks from fancy glasses, while the housekeeper, Mrs Hawks, lurked in the background in a Queen Victoria-style silk mourning gown.

Mrs Hawks has a ghostly presence like she's died already, so it was a bit creepy the way she apparated to top up Alex's whisky tumbler and Catrina's fish-bowl cocktail glass, then blended back into the wallpaper.

I wouldn't usually drink so early in the morning, but the

atmosphere was dour. I heard myself shout 'White wine please!' and drank the whole thing within five minutes.

When the funeral limo arrived, Catrina and Alex brought their drinks to the car and drank stoically the whole journey – topping themselves up from the onboard drink cabinet.

I tried to get a little singalong going, but nobody was in the mood – which was a shame, because I'd downloaded Callum's favourite karaoke app especially.

Afternoon
Home from Harold Dalton's funeral.

Not sure how I'm feeling. It was a very surreal day – not helped by Nancy Jane Box Dalton's psychedelic decorating of the crematorium. Althea may very well disagree, but I feel orange and electric pink don't go well together. Also – peacock feathers and glitter have no place on a coffin.

'Harold would have hated this,' Catrina declared, mouth screwed in distaste as we walked to our garishly decorated bench. 'There is no style here. No class.'

In her black-velvet ball gown, black feather boa and cascading veil, Catrina cut a theatrical figure, striding between pews, ripping electric-pink flowers with her manicured fingernails.

Alex was stony-faced throughout his mother's complaints and remained stony-faced as we took our seats.

When Harold's coffin was carried down the aisle, covered in peacock feathers, neon rainbows and glitter, there were a few intakes of breath. But nobody said anything out loud. Alex had a tight grip on Catrina's arm just in case.

Nancy Jane Box Dalton – an ageing redhead in a black-leather biker jacket – wailed, sobbed and swayed in the pew beside us as the coffin came down the aisle. Her back-combed mountain of red hair shook as she rocked back and forth.

Catrina, noticing Nancy Jane's theatrics, upped her own grieving game – sobbing loudly and dabbing her eyes with a lace handkerchief.

Then came the speeches.

Nancy Jane spoke of Harold being a 'strong character who didn't suffer fools gladly'.

'Even in *death*, he won't get away from me,' she wailed.

After Nancy Jane's speech, Ronald MacDonald read out a Wikipedia-style statement about Harold's life, noting his place of birth, totting up his various business achievements and listing his marriages and children.

Then we sang two of Harold's favourite songs: 'My Way' and 'Je Ne Regrette Rien'.

Catrina sang with gusto, managing something like a fist pump during the chorus of 'My Way'. However, Alex was silent throughout – red-eyed, serious and unmoving.

When Harold's coffin slid behind the bright-orange and pink curtains, Alex's face didn't move a muscle. I took his hand, and he squeezed mine back.

'Let's get the wake over with,' he said. 'And put this whole sorry day behind us.'

Too tired to write about the wake now.

Will write more tomorrow.

Wednesday 24th October
Nice to be home.

After the wake yesterday, Alex took his mother to the Dalton Estate and I picked up Daisy and brought her to the cottage.

Daisy wanted to know all about my 'day out in London' so did my best to explain. Used simple three-year-old words like 'sad', 'bright colours' and 'lots of feathers'. Adult words would have been: 'garish', 'narcissistic', 'soulless' and 'odd'.

The wake was held at the old sorting office in Chelsea – a sort of shabby-chic, industrial venue popular with fashion-industry types.

On arrival, models in yellow boiler-suits smiled through red lipstick as they offered us luminous cocktails.

Nancy Jane Box Dalton strode among the guests in her own daffodil-yellow boiler-suit, pink cocktail in one hand, menthol cigarette in the other, talking loudly about 'getting closure.'

'I am deaf, that woman is talking so loud,' Catrina complained, eyes narrowing as Nancy Jane worked the room. 'And blinded by her outfit. Nobody but a prostitute wears yellow to a funeral.'

'A prostitute with her own highly successful fashion label,' said Alex. 'Careful Anya. She's coming your way.'

Nancy Jane tottered towards us then, and Catrina's lips snapped tight together.

'I think I got closure today,' said Nancy Jane, grasping our hands in turn. 'I loved him, but he's gone. Closure.'

'You never knew Harold as I did,' said Catrina. 'You met a tired, broken man. I knew the young Harold. Our romance was the stuff of movies.'

Nancy Jane gave a full smile and said, 'Grief is a journey. We all have our path. I wish you closure.'

Somehow, we made it through two awkward hours of odd-tasting food, overly sweet cocktails, Catrina's curt remarks and half a room of relatives who hated the other half.

It was a miserable afternoon, but I learned a valuable lesson.

Trying to bond with Catrina is pointless. My condolences fell on deaf ears, she ignored me all day and still thinks my name is Julianne. Furthermore, hearing her criticise Alex's grieving relatives told me everything I needed to know.

I do not want to bond with this person.

I don't know what this means for Alex and me.

It certainly doesn't make one big, happy, blended family.

Thursday 25th October

Alex is back at work already.

Phoned him at 8 am and discovered he was at the Chelsea Dalton, 'firming up some supply chains'.

'It was your father's funeral on Tuesday,' I said. 'Don't you think you should take the week off?'

'The hotel business doesn't sleep and nor should I,' said Alex. 'Of course, as mentioned, our guests should sleep well.'

Asked Alex how he was feeling.

'I have no idea,' he said. 'That's why I'm back at work. So I don't have to find out.'

'What about Christmas this year?' I asked. 'Any thoughts? Do you want to jet off somewhere to take your mind off things?'

'I don't know,' said Alex. 'Christmas is a sticky subject now Nancy and my father aren't hosting. I'll think on it and get back to you.'

Early evening

Just texted Alex to say that Christmas is entirely in his hands. One-hundred-per-cent his decision – even if he wants to take Daisy and me to the Caribbean for jerk chicken on the beach. Wrote that a few times, actually. Caribbean – just fine. OK with Caribbean. Christmas with rum and pineapple punch on a Caribbean island is OK, etc.

He hasn't replied yet.

Late Evening

Alex phoned. He's had an 'interesting thought' about Christmas.

'My father wanted to bring the family together this year,' he said. 'I didn't know why at the time, but now I understand. He knew he was dying.'

'Yes,' I said. 'Probably.'

'I'll never make amends with my father now,' said Alex. 'I can't put our feud to rest, nor tell him I loved and respected him. That chance has gone. But I can honour his wishes.'

'In what way?' I asked.

'By hosting a family Christmas at the Dalton Estate,' said Alex. 'I'll invite the whole Dalton clan. And your family too, Juliette. I know my father would have liked your parents.'

I seriously doubt that, but no one can prove otherwise now.

After Catrina's hideous behaviour at the funeral, I can't think of anything worse than spending Christmas Day with her. However, Alex is grieving, and I'm his supportive partner.

'OK,' I said. 'I already said I'd do whatever you wanted. You have written proof in that text I sent yesterday. So I don't have a legal leg to stand on.'

Alex laughed, but I was only half-joking.

'Excellent,' he said. 'Full-steam ahead then.'

Friday 26th October

Morning

Just dropped by the pub and told the family about Alex's Christmas idea.

They were surprisingly enthusiastic, especially Mum – who saw the advantages of Christmas in a house with a wine cellar.

'They've got a nice bit of land too,' Mum enthused. 'Room for professional fireworks in their garden.'

'Alex nearly burned to death on bonfire night,' I said. 'Fireworks are right out. Listen – are you sure you want to share Christmas with Alex's family? Won't it be cosier to stay at the pub while I do the fancy stuff with Alex?'

'You sound like you're ashamed of us,' Mum accused.

'I'm not ashamed of you,' I said. 'If anything, I'm ashamed of

Alex's family. Catrina is a very selfish person. She was awful at the funeral. But you have to admit, it's a culture clash. Our family tastes are very different.'

'Will Lord Dalton have Cromer crab on Christmas Day?' Callum wanted to know.

'How do you even know what that is?' I asked.

'I've been looking up nice restaurants for Angel Rain,' said Callum. 'She'll be out of hospital next week, so I promised to take her for a night on the town. And all the posh restaurants have Cromer crab.'

'Does Angel Rain like seafood?' I asked.

'No,' said Callum. 'Is that what Cromer crab is? Seafood?'

We've managed to steer Callum towards the best Chinese restaurant in town, which I think Angel Rain will enjoy. It has a fish tank and they're generous with the free fortune cookies and prawn crackers.

I feel nervous about my family descending on the Dalton Estate this Christmas, but these are Alex's wishes, and he's just buried his father.

Will try to make it a fantastic Christmas Day for Alex. I may fail, but I will try.

Can't help thinking that Alex has come out of his grief hole and walked right into La La Land.

Afternoon
Althea and Wolfgang just came by for a 'speed playdate', before heading to an alternative Halloween party in Brighton.

Told Althea about Alex's dad's funeral, Catrina's appalling behaviour and the Dalton Estate Christmas idea.

'I thought you wanted to bond with Catrina,' said Althea. 'Christmas Day sounds like a good love-bombing opportunity.'

'No way,' I said. 'I've had enough. I'm taking your advice and finding love and acceptance within. I don't know what the future holds for Alex and me, but it won't be at the Dalton Estate. There will be no love bombs. Catrina still can't get my name right. She's rude, selfish and self-obsessed. The love bombs will be chucked at more deserving people.'

'I suppose total nutcases can be an exception to the love-bomb rule,' said Althea. 'Maybe you're right about Catrina. You should let her go, let her go.'

Then she started singing 'Let It Go' again. And just like before, the children joined in.

'Wait a minute,' I said. 'Before you told me to let go of my anger and positively visualise getting along with Catrina. *Now* you're saying I should let *Catrina* go?'

'Yes,' said Althea. 'Some people are just a lost cause.'

I appreciate Althea's new contradictory advice, but she's timed it badly.

Why couldn't she have told me to cut Catrina loose months ago? It would have slashed my phone bill in half and Alex wouldn't now be suggesting that Catrina and I spend Christmas Day together.

Ugh.

Oh well. It's just one day.

I'll do it for Alex's sake. He has just lost his father.

Saturday 27th October

Morning

Nick picked Daisy up first thing. Meant to tell him about the Dalton Estate Christmas idea, but didn't. In my heart, I'm still hoping it won't go ahead. Alex hasn't asked his family yet.

They could all say no.

Afternoon

Alex came over for lunch and seemed more himself than he has in a while.

'This Christmas idea has cheered me up,' he said. 'I was so gloomy about my father. Thinking over and over all the things I never got to say. But this feels like a positive step. And Juliette, I have a request. Traditionally, the wives in our family host Christmas Day. I'd be honoured if you'd do the hosting as my fiancée.'

'You want me to host Christmas Day at the Dalton Estate?' I asked.

'Yes,' said Alex. 'Arrange the whole thing. Decide on the food, decorations, everything. I've never been a fan of Christmas. It's just not my thing. But you'll do a wonderful job. You'll bring the heart to it.'

Alex reassured me that we didn't need anything too elaborate this year. Only a small string quartet, not a full orchestra. And maybe a light entertainer. He thought David Blane might be free.

'I can't host Christmas Day for your family,' I said. 'I wouldn't know where to begin. Your relatives are used to much higher standards than me. I buy my fairy lights from Aldi.'

'You're too hard on yourself, Juliette,' said Alex. 'But if you need someone to hold your hand, here's another excellent thought. You wanted to bond with my mother, didn't you? Anya loves Christmas. Why don't the two of you host this thing together? You'll have a wonderful time, plotting and planning over a series of ladies' lunches. You might even become friends.'

Alex, perhaps noting my horrified expression, put serious hands on my shoulders then and added: 'Listen. I'm sorry about how I was before the funeral. I've been to see a doctor and had a few sessions with Zach's shrink. I didn't think tablets were right for me, but I took the advice. The grief counsellor said I should do something positive in my father's memory. Bringing everyone together... you, my mother…and honouring my father… It feels very, very positive. You asked how you could support me. Host Christmas Day. And let my mother help you.'

When he put it that way, I realised just how much Alex has gone through. And is still going through.

Ended up telling him that I would make this the best Christmas ever.

'And after the best Christmas ever,' said Alex, 'you can finally give me a wedding date.'

Admire his optimism, but one step at a time.

He has invited me to the Dalton Estate for brunch tomorrow, so we can 'firm up plans'. He's going to invite his mother too.

It's ironic that I've been calling Catrina for months, but the moment I give up the world throws us together.

As Althea says, the universe always delivers. Just not always the way you expect.

Hope Catrina will say no way to Christmas hosting and Alex, Daisy and I end up going to the Caribbean instead.

Have all fingers and toes crossed.

Sunday 28th October

Brunch with Alex and Catrina.

Catrina was in high spirits when I arrived and air-kissed me effusively.

'Oh Julianne. I am so happy we shall be hosting Christmas together.'

'My name is Juliette,' I said, eyeing her suspiciously. 'Not Julianne. Why are you being so nice? You ignored me at the funeral.'

Catrina hung her head. 'Yes, grief made a monster of me. I am so very sorry.'

'You weren't nice to me before the funeral either,' I said. 'Or my sister.'

'I am sorry for all of it,' said Catrina. 'You know, Harold's death has given me so much to think about. My ex-husband spent his life making enemies. And he brought pain to dear Zachary, even after his death. To die alone, with only that hideous, over-coloured woman for company… That is not an ending for me. I want my boys around me. And their families too.'

'What's brought about this change of heart?' I asked, turning to Alex.

'The Dalton Ball has been cancelled,' Alex explained. 'My mother has nothing to do, no budget to spend and desperately needs something to occupy herself. Juliette, by *agreeing* to share the Christmas Day hosting you've given Anya back her life purpose. Hostess with the mostess. *And* a Christmas Day with both her sons. She hasn't had that since we were boys.'

'Christmas Day was your idea Alex,' I said. 'I shouldn't take the credit. Please god, don't let me take the credit.'

'You were the inspiration, Juliette,' said Alex. 'You must take *full* credit. And accept my mother's gratitude.'

'Why has the Dalton Ball been cancelled?' I asked. 'Can't it be un-cancelled?'

'My father was a patron,' said Alex. 'Well, in truth he funded the whole thing. And it was felt by some, now he's passed, that it wouldn't be in the right spirit to hold it this year.'

'Isn't there a way to save the Dalton Ball?' I asked. 'I can make placards…'

'No darling,' said Catrina, pulling a little leather book from her handbag. 'I would not host that ball now, even if they paid me. The way they spoke to me at the meeting…imbeciles, all of them. We must look forward, Julianne. Always look forwards. What a pleasure it will be to host Christmas Day together. All that festive shopping! Now darling. We will want a signature fragrance for

Christmas Day. I had my favourite perfumery put some samples together.' She whisked heavily fragranced perfume wands from the leather book. 'I have my favourite. Cinnamon, rose and musk.'

'Anya loves Christmas just like you do,' said Alex. 'The two of you will have a whale of a time choosing the food, selecting the Christmas lights and so on. It'll be a wonderful opportunity to bond.' He gave me a wink. 'Just like you wanted.'

Alex looked so boyish and excited. I felt bad for all the many dark thoughts swirling around – now cinnamon, rose and musk-scented.

Monday 29th October

Told Daisy about Christmas at Alex's house today.

She seemed fairly indifferent and was more interested in finding Curry the rabbit – whom I'd shoved in the washing basket in the hope of washing his stinky body.

Eventually, Daisy located Curry by smell and pulled him out of the laundry.

'I love you ever, ever,' she said, twirling Curry around in an elaborate hug. Felt bad for stealing him, but he really does smell terrible.

'Alex and I want to bring our two families together,' I told Daisy. 'And if everything goes well at Christmas, we'll get married, move in together and live happily ever after. But all those things are unlikely.'

'Where will Daddy live?' Daisy asked.

'At his house,' I said. 'The one his mummy bought him. He can drive to see us in the car his mummy bought him.'

In adult language, I was saying:

'Daddy is an irresponsible mummy's boy and I couldn't care less where he lives.'

But luckily, three-year-olds don't understand subtext. I can passive-aggressively insult Nick for at least three more years. Maybe even five, if Callum is anything to go by.

Tuesday 30th October

In all the chaos of the funeral and the curve-ball of Christmas planning, I haven't thought about Alex's birthday – and it's only a week away.

How does one source a £30 present suitable for a multi-millionaire?

Have Googled this question, but no answers.

John Boy said I should get Alex a case of Stella Artois, because that's every man's dream.

Explained that Alex is a sophisticated fellow and therefore doesn't drink Stella Artois.

'I'm sophisticated,' John Boy insisted. 'I've got two Fred Perry shirts and three pairs of Chinos. But I still like Stella. All men do.'

Of course, it's not only the present I need to sort out. I also need to do something special for Alex. Cook a nice meal (Co-op Thai curry?) or take him somewhere romantic and meaningful. And preferably firework-free. Which rules out all of London and most of Great Oakley.

Cinema? Theatre? What do you get for a man who has flown all over the world, can buy anything he wants, has just lost his father and is afraid of fireworks?

Will keep thinking.

Wednesday 31st October

Took Daisy for her first eye test today.

The staff at Specsavers were celebrating Halloween in fancy

dress, so Daisy's eye test was performed by Dracula, aka a twenty-something trainee called Hazan.

Daisy couldn't understand why Hazan, a man, was wearing a silk cape.

'Why that lady have short hair?' she kept asking.

Told Daisy that clothes don't determine men and women and that, according to Aunty Althea, there are seven different genders.

Hazan smiled his plastic vampire teeth and said: 'She can call me a lady if she wants, just as long as she sits still.'

Daisy didn't sit still.

Alex called while we were in the opticians and asked why he could hear the Monster Mash.

'We're at the opticians,' I said.

'That doesn't answer my question,' said Alex. 'Have you and my mother met up to discuss Christmas yet?'

'Not yet,' I said. 'We only agreed to all this a few days ago. There's still time for your mother to pull out. She might pull out.'

'She won't,' said Alex. 'She's very excited. Now listen, it's nearly November. I'd hop to it if I were you. David Blane might already have made plans with his family.'

'I'll call your mother,' I said. 'But you know what she's like. She never picks up. And if we can't talk on the phone, I don't know how we'll organise Christmas together. Maybe we'll have to change the plan.'

'I'm sure Anya will answer the phone,' said Alex. 'I'll tell her too. No need to worry.'

Thursday 1st November

Phoned Catrina, praying she wouldn't answer.

She did.

This is typical. She's ignored at least 100 of my calls, but now I want her to ignore me, she picks up first time.

'I'm glad you called,' she said. 'We are already very late. The best Christmas wine is not just sitting around on British shelves. It needs to be flown in from France and Hungary. I will tell you the wine I like from my little black book of suppliers.'

'We're not going to be short on booze this Christmas,' I said. 'There's a massive wine cellar at the Dalton estate, and my parents run a pub.'

'Oh no, we can't use the cellar wine,' said Catrina. 'That is for every day.'

'Every day?' I said. 'The bottles in Alex's cellar cost more than my monthly wage. They're stored in a temperature-controlled environment, arranged by year and investment value.'

There was a stony silence, then Catrina said: 'So you will not order more wine, is that what you are saying? You won't lift a finger to make this day special for Alex? He buried a father this year. Can you be so heartless?'

'Catrina,' I said. 'No one's forcing you to help me. If you don't like my decisions, let me organise Christmas by myself.'

Catrina laughed gaily. 'Oh Julianne. You are getting cross. This is Christmas. It should be fun. I'll have Monique take care of the wine. Let's not fall out over this. Now then. There is something else I have to tell you. I have invited another guest for Christmas Day. Carlos has abandoned me, so I need an ally.'

'We're not going into battle,' I said. 'What do you need an ally for?'

'Of course we are going into battle,' said Catrina. 'Harold's sisters have been invited. And from what you tell me, *your* sister is angry because I missed her wedding.'

'Laura is never angry,' I said. 'It was me who was angry, but I'm letting it go for Alex's sake.'

'Oh, good darling!' said Catrina. 'Yes. So petty always to be looking at the past. But still. Those three Dalton Doris witches will be there. I need someone to fight my corner. As I say, an ally.'

'Who is your guest?' I asked. 'It had better not be a boxer.'

'Oh darling, I am far too heartbroken to bring a man,' said Catrina. 'No, I have invited a dear friend. A lady who understands my troubles.'

'Has this lady ever thrown drinks at people?' I asked.

'What a silly thing to say,' said Catrina. 'Of course not.'

'Then it's fine,' I said.

'My poor friend has nowhere to go this Christmas,' said Catrina. 'No one will have her, so I am doing her a kindness. She has had her share of heartbreak.'

Catrina probably shouldn't have said that. 'No one wants my sad friend' is hardly a glowing review.

Still. Maybe Catrina does have a good heart, somewhere in that well-preserved body of hers.

Buried deep down under a lot of silicon.

Afternoon

Had a bad thought.

Catrina is friends with Helen. Helen has had her 'share of heartbreak' this year. But it seems unlikely Helen would be alone for Christmas. She'll force Nick to keep her company. That's the trouble with letting your mum buy houses and cars for you. Bribery has its price.

Will phone Catrina and get the friend's name, just in case. But I'm probably just paranoid. I can't imagine Catrina describing Helen as a 'dear friend'. In fact, I can't imagine anyone describing Helen as a dear friend.

Evening

Oh holy Jesus.

The 'dear friend' is Helen.

Catrina has invited my ex-mother-in-law to spend Christmas Day with us. Worse, she insists Helen is a 'wonderful woman' and a welcome addition to any social gathering.

'You will enjoy her, Julianne,' said Catrina. 'Helen is ever so funny. And so charming.'

'Catrina,' I said. 'Helen Jolly-Piggott is the least enjoyable woman I've ever met. And more importantly, she's my ex-mother-in-law.'

'What a small world,' Catrina laughed. 'Well, that is villages for you.'

'We can't have Helen Jolly-Piggott over on Christmas Day,' I said. 'We just can't.'

'Well I won't cancel her now, darling,' said Catrina. 'The dear lady has had enough distress this year. Her husband left. Where is your heart? It's Christmas time.'

Tried to phone Alex, but he wasn't answering, so I called Althea in a panic.

'Well you did say you wanted to be one big, happy, blended family,' she said.

'I meant I wanted to get along with Catrina,' I said. 'Not Nick and Helen. And anyway, I gave up on the Catrina plan after Harold Dalton's funeral.'

'You asked for blending,' said Althea. 'You got it. Nick and Helen are family whether you like it or not. Be careful what you ask the universe. It delivers.'

Shit.

Shit, shit, shit.

Late evening
Finally got through to Alex.

He went silent when I told him about Helen.

Eventually, he said: 'She can't come. It would be totally

inappropriate. I'll speak to my mother.'

Thanked him. Then asked what he wanted for his birthday.

'To be ignored completely,' he said. 'I hate celebrating my birthday.'

'But what if a loved one, say a fiancée, wanted to show she cared on your birthday?' I asked.

'I'd tell her not to bother. I'll be working anyway. Meetings all day.'

Hmph.

11 pm

Alex phoned back. He thinks Helen should spend Christmas Day with us.

'We should look at this situation kindly, Juliette,' he said. 'Helen's husband left her. And she's always been good to my mother. Anya is trying to return the favour. Look, I know it's not ideal, but please recognise my mother is trying to do a good thing. It's a big house. Just keep your distance.'

'It's OK for you,' I said. 'Helen worships your family. I'll have to put up with her criticism all day long.'

'I'm sure Helen knows social boundaries,' said Alex. 'As a guest in our home, she'll be on best behaviour.'

'You don't understand,' I said. 'She hides her rudeness. She says things like, 'Why did you choose that dress, Juliette?' Meaning, *that dress is hideous*. It's very subtle.'

'I think you're big enough to ignore a few comments about dresses,' said Alex.

'No,' I said. 'I'm not. That's the trouble.'

'Think of this as your charitable Christmas deed,' said Alex. 'Helen's lost her husband. Have some sympathy.'

'Helen is a nasty piece of work,' I said. 'Henry leaving is karma. And it's easy for you to be sympathetic. She's never made you do a paternity test.'

'I'm sure you'll find it in your heart to forgive a woman who's clearly in a lot of pain,' said Alex.

'Forgiveness isn't the problem,' I said. 'The problem is spending time with her.'

It seems Alex's grief counselling has made him more empathetic and kind. This is bad timing.

I want the judgemental, stern Alex back.

Friday 2nd November

Have just held a crisis meeting at the pub re Helen coming for Christmas.

My parents weren't half as supportive as I'd hoped.

'You've just got to get on with it, love,' said Mum. 'The poor woman just lost her husband.'

'Why does everyone keep saying that?' I demanded. 'Helen didn't lose her husband. She was horrible to him for years, and he found a nice, soft-shouldered am-dram actress who I'm sure is kind and supportive and doesn't tell him to take showers.'

'But Helen will be all alone now,' said Mum. 'At her age, with all those bones poking out of her, it'll be hard to find someone new.'

'You were literally rubbing your hands together when you first heard the news,' I said.

'True,' said Mum. 'But I've seen Helen around the village since then. She looks dreadful. Even skinnier than usual. And Christmas is a time of forgiveness.'

'Actually Shirley, Christmas isn't a time of forgiveness,' said Dad. 'It's a celebration of Jesus Christ's birth.'

'Well Juliette can give birth to some forgiveness then,' said Mum. 'She said herself she wanted a big, happy, blended family.'

'That does NOT INCLUDE HELEN!'

Alex is coming to see me tonight after work.

I'm sure he's seen sense by now and has asked his mother to un-invite Helen. It would be ridiculous for her to come. She was horrible to me for years. Alex's job, as my fiancé, is to protect me from evil people, not ask me to host them on Christmas Day.

Evening

Alex has badly let me down. So badly, in fact, that I have sent him home in disgrace.

He is point blank refusing to get Helen uninvited, telling me it would just be kicking her while she is down.

'That's the best time to kick her,' I said.

'Juliette, I'd rather hoped you'd take a mature approach,' he said. 'My mother wants her friend over for Christmas. It means a lot to her after everything with Carlos. And Helen would be alone if it weren't for us.'

'That doesn't null-and-void Helen's evil harpy personality,' I said. 'She's a horrible human being.'

'You know, Helen and my mother had coffee yesterday,' said Alex, voice careful. 'I saw Helen. Maybe if you saw her in person, you'd soften a little. You're the host. Be a gracious one.'

Have just realised Alex has unwittingly given me a good idea.

I'm hosting Christmas.

All I need to do is confront Helen, face-to-face, and tell her she can't come.

Yes.

That's the solution.

Excellent.

Showdown time.

Saturday 3rd November

Phoned Nick to get details of Helen's movements and whereabouts.

I know she often helps out with Horry Horry Vom Vom (Nick's name for him, not mine) at weekends, so was hoping to identify a cafe/play-park/Tiny Tumbles showdown opportunity.

Nick was clearly panicking when he took my call, thinking he'd forgotten his Daisy weekend.

'I'm on my way,' he shouted. 'I haven't forgotten. I was just about to call. Don't hassle me, yeah? Horry's been a nightmare.'

When I told Nick it wasn't his weekend with Daisy, he managed an impressive swerve.

'Oh yeah, I know that,' he said. 'Just thought you might need help, so, you know… I can be on my way. If you need me.'

'I just wondered if your mother is looking after Horry,' I said, hoping Nick didn't detect the sneakiness in my voice. 'Daisy and I were thinking of meeting up for a play-date.'

'Mum isn't taking Horry today,' said Nick. 'She only just got her dry-cleaning back. She's taking him tomorrow morning. He does Sunday school at the Baptist Church.'

'And after Sunday school?' I probed, deciding a church showdown might offend God and many elderly people. 'Any plans?'

'I'm guessing the play-park,' said Nick. 'Mum's been banned from the deli because Horry pukes everywhere. Listen, if you want to meet up with Horry and me today –'

'No thanks Nick!' I said, then hung up.

So Helen might be at the play-park tomorrow with little Horatio. The trap is set. Time to catch a dragon.

Sunday 4th November

Showdown!

Intercepted Helen at the play park this morning. She was pushing Horatio on a squeaky swing and cut a lonely, stick-thin figure under the cold, grey sky. If she were a book, she would have been a dark, disturbing thriller with a shocking twist.

She wore substantial black sunglasses, even though it was overcast, and looked skeletally thin, with gaunt cheeks and a worried brow. Her usually sharp, neatly styled black bob was wavy and turning out at all angles and her long, hawkish nose was dry and flaking.

Helen has always been competitively thin to the point of bony, but this was a new level. She looked ill, frightened and tired. When she saw me, she gave a sad wave.

'I suppose you've heard the news,' she said. 'It must be all around the village by now.' Then her voice turned hard and angry as she added: 'That bastard. Running off with a twenty-something.'

I heard myself tell Helen I was sorry and that I wished her well. And I meant it – she looked terrible.

'There's only one chink of light in this long, dark tunnel,' said Helen. 'Catrina Dalton has invited me over for Christmas.'

'Yes, I know,' I said. 'I wanted to talk to you about that.'

Helen blinked at me. 'Why? Oh yes, of course. Your sister and Zach…'

'Actually, I'll be at the Daltons myself this Christmas,' I said. 'Alex and I got engaged this summer.'

'Engaged!' Helen leapt back in alarm. 'You and Alex *Dalton*? I thought that was just a flash in the pan. A bit of drunken nonsense.'

'It wasn't,' I said. 'We're engaged, and Alex has asked me to host Christmas Day. I'm the *hostess*. And Helen…you know we've never really seen eye-to-eye…'

There was a long pause, punctuated by a squeaky, squawking noise – which I realised was Helen crying.

It was awful.

'You won't get me un-invited will you, Juliette?' Helen sobbed. 'I've never felt so alone. Please don't take Christmas at the Dalton Estate away from me. It's the only thing I have to look forward to. Yes, we *haven't* been the best of friends, but I've tried to do right by you.'

'No you haven't,' I said. 'You've always been on Nick's side. Even when he cheated on me with my best friend and abandoned his daughter.'

'I'm sorry Juliette,' said Helen. 'I am so very sorry. Men are bastards. All of them.'

She collapsed against the swing post in distraught sobs. I felt awkward, and I could tell Horatio was trying to avert his eyes too, as he swung back and forth.

Gave Helen a clumsy pat on her bony back.

She flinched. 'No, no I don't need your pity.'

'You do need my pity, Helen,' I said. 'Because my pity means you keep your Christmas Day invite.'

Helen stopped crying immediately. 'Oh, that's wonderful. You really mean it? I'll take the pity then. Ha ha! Thank you, Juliette. I mean that. Thank you from the bottom of my heart.'

So.

My ex-mother-in-law is coming for Christmas.

This is not shaping up to be the best Christmas ever.

Catrina was right about the wine – we do need more of it.

Evening

Alex has just been and gone. Assumed he would stay over tonight, and we'd celebrate his birthday tomorrow, but he said share prices are falling so it will be all-hands-on-deck in London tomorrow.

'I'm taking the doctor's advice and not overdoing travel,' he said. 'So I'll stay in London tomorrow. I hope you don't mind.'

Told him of course not. Have decided that Daisy and I will head to London tomorrow and surprise him. I've taken a leaf out of Catherine Zeta Jones's book re Alex's birthday present, and will give him a simple framed picture of Daisy and me.

As Catherine Zeta says, it's love that's important in life, not Rolex watches. This is lucky because I can't afford a Rolex watch.

Daisy has made Alex a birthday card, aka a sparkly mess on some cardboard. She wanted to put her collection of squashed ladybirds inside as a present, but luckily I talked her out of it.

Really hope her psychopathic urges pass soon.

Monday 5th November
Alex's birthday

Daisy and I visited Alex in London today to shower him with birthday love and affection.

Alex was happy to see us and claimed to be 'delighted' with his fairly shit present.

'It's good news all round today,' he said. 'I have a beautiful picture for the office wall, a sparkly card for my desk and share prices are going up, up, up.'

We had a nice lunch at the Mayfair Dalton and chatted about Christmas, while Daisy tried and failed to escape her high chair.

Told Alex I'd made my peace with Helen coming, and he congratulated me on my maturity.

Which felt patronising.

Asked Alex if he wanted to do anything this evening for his birthday, but he said nothing sprang to mind.

'I promise not to let off any fireworks,' I said.

'I would hope not,' said Alex. 'Haven't you heard the weather warnings? Forty miles per hour winds tonight. Firework displays have been cancelled left, right and centre.

Suggested I cook him a nice dinner at the cottage.

'Thai curry again?' he asked, with a wry smile. 'Yes, why not?'

Evening

Fireworks are going off everywhere.

Alex is trapped in London due to the high winds, which started up sooner than expected. The weather is affecting overhead train lines and tipping lorries on the M25.

According to the news, nobody should be letting off fireworks in these conditions – which makes going outside dangerous right now.

Alex warned me to stay indoors. 'No late-night trips to the Spar for wine,' he cautioned.

'Of course not,' I said. 'I still have two litres of John Boy's birthday gin in the cupboard.'

Wish Alex and I could be together for his birthday, but we are sparkler-crossed lovers tonight, thwarted by raging winds and idiots letting off fireworks.

John Boy was nearly one of these idiots, but I've confiscated his Pyromaniac rocket collection, God Father shot cake, Ball of Fire and Satellite Killer mega-blast, putting them safely in the cellar.

Tuesday 6th November

Alex and I are still being kept apart by the weather.

Very high winds today, and predictions of heavy snow.

BBC news is telling people not to travel. This is serious, because they usually say, 'don't travel unless absolutely necessary.' But they are just saying, 'don't travel'.

Catrina and I have decided that Christmas planning is right

out until the weather calms down. She is having hysterics in her London apartment, talking about being trapped without cream cheese and smoked salmon.

I think I managed to calm her down a little by telling her that pickled herring and cheddar, which she had in stock, could be a substitute.

Wednesday 7th November

Snow!

But not the heavy type predicted. Just a millimetre or so – enough to make our pretty little village look chocolate-box beautiful.

My parents are panic-buying milk, fearing that a Siberian blizzard is just around the corner.

Dad bought three extra pints of semi-skimmed and Mum came home with sixteen pints of whole milk, two pints of double cream and a large box of Ferrero Rocher.

Alex phoned first-thing to say everything is functioning OK in London. However, trains are still down, the M25 is at a near standstill, and there is a shortage of fizzy water.

More snow is due, so it looks like Alex and I will go from being sparkler-crossed lovers to snow-crossed lovers.

Daisy and I miss Alex, but we're not having such a bad time of it. Howling winds and snow mean Christmas movies and junk food.

Pringles, Haagen Dazs and *Home Alone*, here we come!

Thursday 8th November

More snow.

There are over three inches now, which means Callum's school has closed, along with the local hairdressers and florists.

Mum wants to close the pub and take the day off, but Dad refuses

– calling the teachers, hairdressers and florists lazy and work-shy.

Dad grew up in Scotland, where shops stay open during freezing rain, floods, blizzards and 50mph winds. My dead Scottish granddad never missed a day of work – even though sometimes he was blown off his pushbike on the way to the factory.

Daisy and Callum are delighted because the snow is deep enough to have snowball fights and build snowmen.

I am less delighted, because panic-buying has emptied the Co-op shelves. This means ordinary non-panicked shoppers like me can't do a normal shop. I guarantee there are at least fifty OAPs in the village with fridgefuls of milk, but I can't buy one pint of semi-skimmed.

Alex and I had a lovely snow-crossed lovers' conversation tonight, saying how much we missed each other and what we would do when we saw each other again.

It got quite heated, in a good way, until the phone signal cut out.

A mast has gone down somewhere, so Alex and I are no longer in phone contact. Feel like a war wife, waiting for letters home and praying the Nazis don't bomb the sexy post wagon.

Friday 9th November

VERY bad snow today. A real blizzard.

Seven inches fell overnight, just as the news predicted, and there's more on the way.

Impressively, our post lady still delivered the mail. It probably wasn't worth braving the treacherous conditions to deliver my Tesco club-card vouchers, a flyer from a local estate agent and a bank statement I could have read online, but I appreciated her dedication. She looked like a White Walker from *Game of Thrones*, more snow than woman.

Got through to the Mayfair Dalton on the landline, and Zach

was summoned to speak to me because Alex wasn't available.

Zach assured me that Alex wasn't buried under snow, but simply in a different hotel. He's been trying to call me apparently, but can't get through.

Aww.

Snow-crossed lovers!

Saturday 10th November

It's Nick's visitation weekend, but it's too dangerous to brave the blizzard today, so Daisy stayed with me at the cottage.

Trees are falling left, right and centre, and only idiots, like Mum and John Boy are driving.

Am tucked up with Daisy now, watching Christmas movies with the heating on full-blast as thick snow swirls outside.

The newspapers and radio are running stories like 'Days of dread' and the 'beast from the east'. But actually, all that's happened is the shop has run out of milk, and we get to go sledging all day.

Callum is chuffed that his school has closed because one in a nearby village stayed open. According to the local paper this is, 'thanks to some brave teachers risking the treacherous roads, and one parent with an industrial snowplough'.

The idiots.

Spoke to Alex twice today, and on both occasions, he told me to stay put, wrap up warm and wait out the weather. Which is basically carte blanche to watch boxsets and overeat all day.

I have to admit, aside from missing Alex, the bad weather hasn't been all that bad.

Sunday 11th November
Remembrance Day

Still terrible snow and wind today, but the London remembrance parade went ahead.

Daisy, John Boy and I watched the parade on TV, and I phoned the pub to send Dad love because he always feels sad about Granddad on Remembrance Day.

Got through to Alex in the afternoon, and he told me he'd watched the parade from the Mayfair Dalton executive suite.

'It was very moving,' he said. 'So many people paying their respects, even in this awful weather. I must admit I shed a tear.'

None of Alex's family were in any wars. His grandfather was too old and his father too young. But I think he's missing his father today.

'How's the Christmas planning going?' Alex asked.

'It isn't,' I said. 'Your mother told me she couldn't think past day-to-day survival.'

'That's Anya,' Alex chuckled. 'Always first in line when the drama is dished out. Have you booked any entertainment yet?'

'I thought we might do something informal,' I said. 'Like charades.'

There was a telling silence, then Alex said, 'I'm not a fan. Have you *called* David Blane?'

Suggested we find a middle ground. Pictionary, perhaps?

Alex had to go then. But he didn't say no to Pictionary, so maybe it's an option.

Monday 12th November

Just tried to cancel my lunchtime pub shift today, but Dad insisted I come in.

'Snow days are for the feckless and work-shy Juliette,' he said. 'As a lad, I cycled to my potato-harvesting job in ten inches of snow. This is a mere seven. You need to toughen up. Or life will beat you down.'

'But there won't be any customers,' I said. 'Who's going to come out in this weather?'

'A good number of regulars were in yesterday,' said Dad. 'We're a life raft for the likes of Yorkie. If it weren't for this pub, he'd be sitting in a cold, dark room, shivering the day away with a bottle of cheap sherry. The drunks shall have their whisky in a fine glass.'

Grudgingly told Dad I was on my way, but warned if Callum threw snowballs I would snap his transformers in half.

Dad admitted Callum had a *small* snow arsenal at the ready. Just fifty snowballs and a pile of icicle knives.

'But he's bored with war games now,' said Dad. 'He wants to go skiing instead.'

'How?' I asked. 'He doesn't have any skis.'

Dad said Callum had got very inventive and strapped tea-trays to his trainers. God knows how he is going to operate those tea trays. If he can't do the splits yet, he'll be able to by the end of the day.

Tuesday 13th November

The wind picked up again today, so Daisy and I were housebound once again. We stayed in eating frozen pizza, ice cream, potato waffles, Pot Noodles and John Boy's stash of custard creams and chocolate bourbons while watching *Barbie's Dreamhouse* on Netflix.

The train-lines are still down, and roads are closed, so Alex and I remain young (ish) lovers, separated by trial and circumstance.

But my love and I will be reunited soon. Everything is supposed to clear up by the end of the week.

Daisy, John Boy and I will enjoy the boxsets and biscuits in the meantime.

Wednesday 14th November

Still snowing!

The steep road near the pub has been turned into a makeshift toboggan track by local kids.

Of course, Callum had to take things to the next level by turning his sledge into a dangerous snowboard. He has been pummelling down the steep road, shouting at shocked old ladies to 'get out of the way, Callum tornado coming through!'

Dad says the slope should be closed for health and safety reasons because there are parked cars nearby.

Mum disagrees and has already gone down the slope face-first with three kids on her back.

Thursday 15th November

Nice long chat with Alex. The snow is *definitely* due to clear by tomorrow, so he's going to hop on the train and spend the whole weekend with us.

Better put the house in order, get some decent food in etc. Hope the Co-op have restocked their shelves by now and have that nice Thai curry Alex likes.

Friday 16th November

Ugh.

It's stopped snowing, but the roads and pavements are thick with it and schools are closed because road-travel is dangerous.

So, no Alex. We are still snow-crossed lovers, although that joke is getting old now.

I miss Alex and want to see him. Plus I'm getting sick of biscuits and frozen food, and there are only so many *Buffy the Vampire* episodes you can watch without noticing the latex.

The only people on the roads are smug four-by-four drivers, crushing the snowdrifts under huge tyres while other poor saps wheel-spin in the sludge.

Saturday 17th November

Snow turning to mush today, but many roads are still closed, and most trains aren't running.

Went sledging on the last of the snow, but it was mostly slush. All we really did was watch Mum's bulky frame slide slowly down the slope and hear her bellow at children and dog walkers to get out of the way.

Alex is still trapped in London but says he'll brave the one train to Great Oakley later. Apparently, even First Class will be full because it's the only train to run in four days.

Alex doesn't care which carriage he travels in if the train is full. He has no specific prejudice against standard-class ticket holders. It's humanity in general he dislikes in travel scenarios.

Sunday 18th November

Morning

My love and I are still separated!

The train to Great Oakley was mobbed yesterday, and Alex kindly gave up his space to a stranded nun from Southend.

He's a good man.

Sunday trains are hit-and-miss at the best of times, so it's no surprise that there are motorway jams and no trains running today.

Alex did look into chartering a helicopter, but the wind has picked up again so it would be too dangerous.

Really miss him.

Evening

Mum just phoned to ask if I'd chosen the Christmas dinner 'for this great big bloody family get together'.

'We've just had a freak blizzard,' I said. 'I've been separated from the love of my life. I've had other things on my mind. Including stopping you sledging face-first into parked cars.'

'Well, you'd better get thinking about it,' said Mum. 'If you want me to do this twelve-bird roast, I've got to put the order in soonish.'

'I'll need to talk to Catrina,' I said, 'and find out if we can get the right wine for a twelve-bird roast.'

'Don't be bloody ridiculous,' said Mum. 'Roast bird goes with any wine, especially when you've got twelve different sorts to choose from. It'll be a feast, Juliette. A feast!'

Wish I knew more about wine-matching.

Need some kind of fairy godmother etiquette coach, like Julie Andrews in *The Princess Diaries*. The nearest I have is Catrina, which I suppose is better than nothing.

Monday 19th November

The trains are running, the roads are clear and Alex is finally on his way!

Can't wait for a passionate reunion. Must pop out and buy that Thai curry before he arrives.

Ooo – exciting!

Tuesday 20th November

Morning

Alex just left for London, despite my protestations.

'We've been apart all week,' I said. 'Separated by a devastating blizzard.'

'Exactly,' said Alex. 'During which my hotels have suffered power cuts, boiler difficulties and many gallons of spoiled milk.'

'But it's stopped snowing now,' I said.

'Snow turns to water Juliette,' said Alex. 'There's a lot of firefighting to be done.'

He *did* promise he'd take it easy and only work until 7 pm. Maximum 8 pm. Shouted that he must finish work at 5 pm. 'You exhausted yourself before,' I said. 'For goodness sakes take it easy.'

'5 pm is ridiculous,' said Alex. 'Who finishes work at 5 pm?'

'Everyone in a nine-to-five job,' I said. 'Hence the Dolly Parton song, "Nine to Five".'

'I suppose if I miss lunch…'

'No Alex,' I insisted. 'You need a normal working day. The doctor told you not to travel too much. Work is the same. You'll be no good to the business if you're collapsing with exhaustion.'

'I'll try Juliette,' said Alex, kissing my cheek. 'But this is an exceptional week. Why don't you get started on this fabulous Christmas? Keep yourself occupied while I put the fires out. We're halfway through November already.'

Afternoon
Phoned Catrina.

Once again, gallingly, she answered.

'My mother has suggested doing a twelve-bird roast for Christmas Day,' I said. 'I'm phoning for wine advice.'

'Is twelve-bird a kind of turkey?' Catrina asked. 'The British are obsessed with turkey. Such a tasteless bird.'

'It's twelve different roast birds,' I said. 'I think turkey *could* be one of them.'

'Julianne, why don't you come Christmas-decoration shopping with me tomorrow?' said Catrina. 'We can chat about the Christmas Day menu while we shop. Oh! I do so love Christmas shopping.'

It feels strange, Catrina being friendly. From Althea's point of view, the universe has delivered. From my point of view, I'm not too sure I want to sign for the parcel.

Dad will take Daisy tomorrow while I head up to Liberty in London for some first-class Christmas shopping.

Am looking forward to it, actually. Shopping for Christmas decorations in a fancy department store with a massive budget will be nice. And for all her faults, Catrina really is the perfect companion. I'm too humble to blow vast amounts of cash on overpriced, impractical items, but she will balance me out. She's made a career of spending other people's money.

Wednesday 21st November

Met Catrina at Liberty in London today for Christmas-decoration shopping. As predicted, she was an excellent shopping companion and had no qualms about spend, spend, spending. She even told me off for checking prices, calling this 'vulgar'.

The staff fawned over Catrina. They seated us in velvet chairs and served petit-fours and Champagne while various Christmas decorations were brought forth for our approval.

It was just like *Pretty Woman*, only without the pizza.

Usually, I'd feel exhausted after shopping, but Catrina knows the right way to do it. Tell the staff you're going to be spending a lot, then let them wait on you. Again – just like in *Pretty Woman*.

As the staff wrapped our pile of decorations, Catrina and I got chatting about Christmas Day – specifically the entertainment.

'You needn't worry about that, darling,' Catrina reassured me. 'It's all in hand. My dear friend Helen has arranged something to thank us for having her.'

'Helen has arranged entertainment?' I asked. 'What has she arranged? Please don't say amateur dramatics.'

'Yes, darling,' said Catrina. 'Helen's son Nicholas is a fine actor, and he has agreed to perform *The Seven Ages of Man* in the old barn. Won't that be fun? He will treat us to a solo performance, and we will treat him to Christmas lunch.'

'Catrina,' I said, my voice low. 'Nick is my ex-partner. There's no way he is doing the entertainment.'

'Your ex-partner?' said Catrina. 'Another coincidence! Vell I already said how villages are. Everybody knowing everybody.'

'I'm not watching Nick do a solo performance on Christmas Day,' I said. 'I lived with him for years. I've seen enough of his performances. Inviting Helen is bad enough, but Nick monologuing for hours on end is my limit.'

'It's all arranged now, darling,' said Catrina. 'It would be very unladylike to change plans.'

Told Catrina that I was prepared to be unladylike on this occasion.

'If Nick comes, Christmas is cancelled,' I said.

'Vell, he is coming,' said Catrina, eyes fierce.

'No way,' I said. 'I compromised for Helen. Now it's your turn.'

'I promised my dear friend, who is suffering so much and I VILL not let her down.'

So it looks like Christmas is cancelled.

Thursday 22nd November

Called Nick to shout at him for accepting Catrina's Christmas invitation.

He claimed he'd never wanted to accept, adding that Christmas Day at the Daltons sounded 'fucking awful'. But he'd reluctantly agreed for Helen's sake.

'Mum's *really* upset right now,' said Nick. 'Christmas at the Dalton Estate is her only shining light. She wants me to be there with her. She sees it as an epic event. It'll probably be written on her gravestone: I, Helen Jolly-Piggott, celebrated Christmas with the *extremely* affluent Dalton family.'

'I'll be *hosting* Christmas Day at the Daltons,' I said, my voice going all hoity-toity. 'And as the hostess, I'm telling you, you are *not* doing the entertainment.'

'What, you're doing the food and everything?' Nick asked.

'What's that supposed to mean?' I demanded.

'I'm just surprised,' said Nick. 'The Daltons are fancy. And you're a scampi-and-chips kind of girl.'

'Why do people keep assuming that pub families only eat breaded products?' I shouted. 'I mean, yes. I do like scampi and chips. Who doesn't? But I often give Daisy fresh pesto.'

'From a plastic tub,' said Nick.

'We're going off-topic,' I said. 'YOU need to get out of this Christmas one-man-show invite somehow. You always get out of things. It's one of your special talents. So get out of this one.'

'I can't,' said Nick. 'Mum's had enough heartbreak this year. I promised I'd come and support her. I can't let her down, Jules.'

Why are all the uncaring people in my life, aka Catrina and Nick, choosing *this* year to be caring?

'You won't be there Nick,' I shouted. 'Because if you are, Christmas is cancelled.'

Friday 23rd November

Met Alex in London to break the bad news.

'I know this was supposed to be the best Christmas ever,' I said. 'But that's impossible with both Nick and Helen there. So unless your mother changes her mind –'

'She won't change her mind,' said Alex. 'She's very stubborn. Will you change your mind?'

'No way,' I said. 'I've already bent on the Helen issue. I'm not bending on Nick too.'

Alex's next reaction was a surprising one: silent melancholy.

'You were right all along, Juliette,' he said. 'We were fools to think we could have a happy Christmas. We've fallen at the first small hurdle.'

'What are you talking about?' I said. 'This isn't a small hurdle. This is Christmas hell with Nick and his mother.'

'I was pinning a lot on this Christmas,' said Alex. 'I hoped you and my mother would bond. That our families would come together. Blend, as you put it. And you would see our future together. And of course, I wanted to honour my father's memory.'

'But *Nick* will be doing the entertainment – a three-hour Shakespearian monologue.'

'He's Daisy's father,' said Alex. 'For all your talk of blended families, I don't see you doing a lot of blending.'

It was a nauseatingly mature answer from someone who's probably in a far worse psychological state of mind than I am right now.

Perhaps I'm stubborn and unreasonable. But watching my ex-partner bellow Shakespeare while Helen claps from the side-lines is hell for all concerned. Better to cancel now before we ruin Christmas Day for everyone.

'It's just too much blending,' I told Alex. 'A blend too far. Like when you try for chunky salsa and end up with tomato purée.'

Alex said curtly that he needed a bit of space to think about things.

'Fine,' I said. 'Go in a strop about it. Back to your cave, I'm used to it now.'

'I'm not going in a strop,' said Alex. 'You had your time to think about things. Now I'd like mine.'

Evening

Told Mum and Dad that the Dalton Christmas is cancelled.

'So does that mean we're having Christmas at the pub?' Mum asked.

'I suppose so,' I said.

'I think you're running away from something difficult,' said Dad. 'Instead of facing a challenge head-on.'

'I'm saving us all from something hideous,' I said. 'Nick prancing around, over-acting in front of a captive audience. I *already* said yes to Helen. It's Catrina's turn to compromise, but she won't. Blame her, not me.'

'You wanted blending,' said Mum.

'SALSA NOT TOMATO PUREE.'

'I'm surprised at you, Juliette,' said Dad. 'Life isn't always easy. We face our problems.'

'I'm setting a healthy boundary and saving us from a day of hell,' I said. 'You should be thanking me.'

'You wanted happy families,' said Dad. 'Why can't that include Daisy's father?'

'No way, Dad,' I said. 'No way am I watching Nick do a pretentious one-man performance. I already said yes to Helen. Catrina should be backing down on this one. But she won't.'

'Right,' said Mum. 'We'll have Christmas here again, then. No biggie. I'll get the Baileys ordered and a few pounds of Murray mints for Mum.'

It all felt very simple. But I couldn't help noticing Dad's sad eyes and wondering if I'd done the right thing.

Saturday 24th November

Christmas is coming, and the goose for Mum's twelve-bird roast is getting fat, but I don't feel Christmassy.

I feel deflated.

After gearing myself up for a big Christmas do, a family meal at the pub feels like a let-down. Also, Alex isn't speaking to me. He's gone back into his grumpy cave and hasn't called.

Nick picked Daisy up first-thing, so I'm alone in the cottage, stuck with my overactive brain.

Maybe I should have gone through with this Dalton Christmas Day thing.

No.

No.

Nick is just a step too far.

It's the right decision.

Afternoon
Nick just rang.

Daisy isn't feeling well and wants to come home.

'Is she definitely ill, Nick?' I asked. 'Or are you struggling with two kids and want to return her?'

'No, she honestly is ill,' said Nick. 'She's got a runny nose, and her head feels hot. She's going on and on about wanting you. Can't you just come and get her?'

Agreed that I would – but only because I'm feeling sad and missing my little girl.

Alex still hasn't called. Am leaving him to his strop. Sort of see his point, but what can I do?

Evening
Nick was right – Daisy does have a bit of a cold. She's snuffling in bed right now with a hot-water bottle. Have given her some Calpol so, hopefully, that will knock her out. Treated myself to a little swig of the pink stuff too – it's sugar-free these days, zero calories.

Hope Daisy will feel better tomorrow.

Sunday 25th November

Daisy is worse today, and John Boy and I have woken up with colds too.

We are a house of misery and illness.

John Boy says there's so much hacking and coughing it's like being back in the army barracks.

Have told Nick that Daisy is staying here with me today. Nick understood. More than understood, actually. He said thank you at least three times.

It's horrible being ill as a parent, but even worse when your child is sick too, and needs looking after.

John Boy is OK. He's taken every painkiller in the house, drunk the remaining Calpol and is currently relaxing on the sofa with a *Sopranos* boxset, a pint of lemon-barley water and a Terry's chocolate orange.

However, I'm worried about poor Daisy. She's got a terrible streaming nose and keeps doing little fairy sneezes. She seems fine in herself and is making just as much mess as ever, but you do worry about them when they're so young.

Too ill to tackle our messy kitchen, so ordered takeaway pizza for lunch and am planning on Chinese for tea. I imagine my fortune cookie will say: 'You are a terrible slovenly parent and don't deserve children'.

I wish the Chinese takeaway made breakfasts.

Still haven't heard from Alex, and in my weakened state I'm too ill to chase around after him. Let him be grumpy. If he can't see where I'm coming from re Christmas Day, then we don't belong together.

It's as simple as that.

Monday 26th November

Mum kindly brought over a food parcel this morning to see us through our colds. She generally buys whatever is on special offer at the cash-and-carry, and today it was an entire roast duck covered in orange slices, a black pudding the size of a police truncheon and a catering tray of multi-coloured French macaroons.

My fridge now looks like King Louis' larder in Regency France.

Mum washed up before she left, but it was more of a hindrance than a help because she leaves things dirtier than they were originally.

I'm not too sure how she does it, but she covers cleanish glasses in a sheen of oil, often with a few herb strands clinging to their sides.

Texted Alex to say I have a cold. He didn't reply, which means he's definitely in a strop rather than needing his own space.

I think this is very childish.

Afternoon

John Boy has just come back from the Co-op with a trolley-load of essential medical supplies, namely Christmas chocolate. It was literally a trolley-load because he brought the trolley home too.

Feeling so deflated about Christmas, I just couldn't get excited about the dazzling array of festive treats. Instead, I criticised John Boy for stealing the trolley.

'I was just trying to do a nice thing and bring Christmas joy into the house,' he said, hanging his head. 'Everyone's been so miserable one way or another. We're all ill, and you've cancelled Christmas because you can't get on with Daisy's dad.'

'I can get on with him,' I said. 'I just don't want to spend the whole of Christmas Day with him and his mother.'

'Christmas is about forgiveness,' said John Boy.

'NO IT ISN'T!'

I suppose John Boy's heart is in the right place, and Daisy and I have been enjoying the chocolate. But his comments about Nick were just plain wrong. Forgiveness is one thing. Watching Nick perform indulgent one-man Shakespeare is quite another.

Tuesday 27th November

Very very sad day.

Angel Rain died in her sleep last night.

We've all been crying, even John Boy who never met her.

Visited the pub to see Callum and found him like a zombie, just saying, 'She's gone,' over and over again.

To think of Angel Rain's poor parents – it's devastating.

Mum is getting a care package together for the family. She's put three litres of caramel vodka and 200 bourbon biscuits in a promotional Pimm's hamper and is heading to the cash-and-carry to buy more items.

Callum picked red and white roses from the neighbour's garden and added them to the hamper. We were all too kind to tell him off.

Life can be so cruel.

Phoned Alex.

Told him I loved him and that I always would.

He said likewise.

Wednesday 28th November

Althea just finished (another) Buddhist course with Wolfgang and posted this on Facebook:

I am happy to announce I have reached emotional and spiritual perfection (I was already physically perfect). If anyone needs a guru, feel free to use my journey to help yours xxx

Am tempted to call Althea up and ask for advice re how nature can be cruel enough to take a young girl from her parents.

I suppose I should know how awful nature can be, having given birth.

Asked Brandi how Callum is. She says he's just sitting, staring at his tadpole tank.

There's only one tadpole left now – the half-ounce weakling, Judge Dredd.

Callum is telling him he loves him and to stay strong.

Poor Callum.

Thursday 29th November

Callum is very low today.

I found him in the pub garden, sitting under the bare-branched apple tree and staring into space.

If Callum is sitting still, you know something is wrong.

Asked how he was feeling.

'I don't think I'll ever get over a kid dying so young,' he said. 'How can the government let it happen? Why don't they make laws to stop children dying?'

Didn't have any answers for him, so we just sat together and had a cry.

Asked Callum if he wanted to go to the funeral and pay his last respects. He said no – it would be too sad.

'Her parents don't like me anyway,' he said. 'I taught Angel Rain all those funny fart noises. So best I stay away.'

Asked him if he was sure, because he wouldn't be able to change his mind.

He said he was positive. 'I don't want to see Angel Rain in a box,' he said. 'To me, she's everywhere. In the sky. In the flowers. Swimming with my tadpole. Everywhere.'

Callum's teachers say he's failing at school, but often he understands things other people take a lifetime to see. It's the school failing him really, and not the other way around.

Friday 30th November

Callum has become very attached to his last tadpole, taking extra special care of him and wrapping a Christmas scarf around the tank to keep him warm.

'He's a survivor,' he said. 'He'll make it through the winter. You see if he doesn't.'

He has put Judge Dredd on a high-protein diet to help bone development, and is giving him growth pep talks.

'Come on mate. You can do it. Grow those legs. Grow them!'

Dad is more pessimistic. 'There's no way he'll change this year Callum,' he said. 'Your only hope is that he survives until spring. Why don't you do him a kindness and set him free? Alex has a big pond at his house, hasn't he Juliette? Maybe Judge Dredd would like to live there.'

'Alex and I aren't speaking much right now,' I said. 'He's in a strop because I cancelled Christmas.'

'Why did you go and do a stupid thing like that?' Callum asked. 'Christmas at Lord Dalton's castle would have been brilliant.'

'Catrina asked Nick to do the entertainment,' I said. 'A three-hour solo performance.'

'So?' Callum asked.

'So I don't want to spend Christmas applauding someone who tried to take my daughter away.'

'Nick will always be in Daisy's life,' said Dad. 'You're running away love. You should face problems head-on.'

'I've dealt with Nick,' I said. 'I just don't want to spend Christmas with him.'

'You've got to find the love, Aunty Julesy,' said Callum. 'Even if someone isn't all good. That's what Angel Rain said. She loved everyone. And she never ran away from nothing.'

Then he started to cry.

Felt awful then.

Maybe I am running away from my problems. But goodness knows I have enough of them. Surely I'm allowed to run away from one or two?

Saturday 1st December

Angel Rain's funeral today.

Brandi and I paid our respects, while Mum, Dad and John Boy stayed at home with a distraught Callum.

During the service, Angel Rain's mother talked about her little girl living life to the full, and cherishing every minute. It was beautiful and awful all at once, and we were in floods of tears.

Seeing the child-sized coffin was hard to bear. There were no words, so Brandi and I just cried and held each other.

Left the funeral feeling thoroughly ashamed of myself. My problems are grains of sand compared to the mountain Angel Rain's parents are climbing. And they'll never reach the top. No one ever gets over losing a child.

I've been ungrateful, whining and cowardly. And I'm going to sort it out. I'm going to bring our families together for Christmas and honour Harold Dalton's memory. Nick may be a pain, but he's Daisy's father, and I can put up with him for a day.

Time to appreciate what I've got, rather than complain about what isn't quite right.

Sunday 2nd December

Phoned Alex.

Told him that Christmas Day is back on.

'We're going to have a big Dalton-Duffy get-together,' I said. 'And I'm going to host it. Just like I promised.'

'You haven't done anything terrible to Nick and Helen, have you?' Alex asked. 'Disposed of them in some way?'

'Nick and Helen are coming,' I said. 'Helen is your mother's friend, and Nick is Daisy's father. Let's do some blending. Proper blending.'

'What brought about this sudden change of heart?' Alex asked.

'Seeing a child's coffin has put things into perspective,' I said. 'I haven't appreciated everything we have. I've been scared and selfish. And I'm sorry.'

'I'm delighted,' said Alex. 'Not that you're scared. Obviously. But that Christmas is back on. And for what it's worth, Juliette, I don't think you're selfish.'

'You wanted to honour your father's memory, and I said no.'

'You were just trying to avoid unpleasantness,' said Alex. 'But if we want a happy family, we have to practise.'

'Thank you,' I said.

'For what?' said Alex.

'For not saying I told you so.'

Monday 3rd December

Called my family together today for a big announcement:

The Dalton-Duffy Christmas is back on.

Full steam ahead.

My family were disappointingly indifferent. There were no whoops or cheers or rounds of applause. I think they're expecting me to change my mind again, but I won't.

I'm determined.

'So I'll have to relocate my twelve-bird roast to the Dalton kitchen?' Mum asked.

'I don't know yet,' I said. 'Catrina and I still need to talk about the Christmas menu. The food all has to co-ordinate. You know, the starter and the main and everything.'

'Starter,' Dad snorted. 'It's nonsense, all this excess. In our day, we were given a bit of chicken skin and a bone on Christmas Day and counted ourselves lucky to have a whole roast potato each. Do you know what counted as a special meal when I was a boy? Cheese on a plate. And we felt like royalty, having that plate.'

While Dad rattled on about consumerism gone mad, Mum rearranged the overstuffed fridge to fit yet more food. She'd been on a supermarket spree and bought every Christmas novelty food going. Three Heston Blumenthal desserts, pints of cognac cream, cranberry-flavour cheese, cinnamon-and-spice custard, caviar canapés and a couple of roast hams heaved on the fridge shelves.

Mum fitted cheese, milk and butter around Christmas treats like a luxury jigsaw, while Dad droned on about festive excess.

Crazy that Mum and Dad, with their radically different values, have been married so long. But they make it work somehow.

I suppose it's proof that different people can harmonise, like when Bono and Pavarotti sang Ave Maria together.

Maybe there is hope for Alex and me.

Afternoon

Just stopped by Nick's house and told him about Christmas Day.

'So we're all going to be together?' he said. 'I get to eat Christmas dinner with my little girl?'

Said yes – we'll all be together on Christmas Day, and I'd try not to chuck roast potatoes at him.

Nick gave a little whoop of joy.

'That's brilliant Julesy,' he said. 'God, when I thought it was just going to be Mum and me…talk about depressing.'

Nick pretended he wasn't fussed about the one-man show being back on, but I knew he was lying. A Shakespearian monologue in front of a captive audience is every actor's dream – especially an actor who hasn't had work in a while.

Tuesday 4th December

Phoned Catrina and told her Christmas was back on.

'Good darling!' she trilled. 'Then I will open up my little black book and find us a good Christmas caterer.'

'Mum has offered to do the main,' I said. 'She has twelve roast birds stuffed inside each other's cavities ready to go.'

'Don't be silly, darling,' said Catrina. 'A lady doesn't cook her own Christmas dinner. That is what staff are for. Do you want your mother to be exhausted before her first glass of Champagne? No, no, the staff will cater. And I will prepare some delicious Hungarian pastries and liquors beforehand. There will be nothing to do on the day.'

'But Mum has her heart set on doing this big, extravagant roast,' I said. 'She's talked of using bread trenchers as plates and drinking from pewter mugs to mimic a real Tudor banquet.'

'That does not sound right for Christmas Day,' said Catrina. 'What about a traditional Hungarian butchering soup followed by a suckling pig? *Everyone* loves butchering soup!'

'Mum is very keen to cook,' I said. 'Her feelings could be hurt if a caterer takes over.'

'It is a foolish woman who cooks for fifteen people when there are caterers on hand,' said Catrina.

Can't deny that Mum is fairly foolish. She started a low carb diet today with toast for breakfast. But she is also surprisingly sensitive at times and can easily take offence.

Will see if I can tactfully negotiate a way forward.

Wednesday 5th December

Met Mum at the pub to delicately discuss the Christmas main course.

'Catrina wants the whole thing catered,' I said. 'But I know you have your heart set on this twelve-bird roast.'

'Oh, I couldn't give a monkey's, love,' said Mum. 'I'm happy to put my feet up and get drunk while someone else does the cooking.'

'But what about the birds?' I said. 'I thought you'd bought and prepared them already.'

'We'll just have them at New Year instead. Bob and I are throwing a hootenanny at the pub. The Dalton Ball is cancelled, isn't it? So half the village need somewhere to celebrate. And who doesn't enjoy roast bird as a bar snack?'

'Will the birds keep that long?' I asked.

'Of course, love,' said Mum. 'I haven't got around to preparing them yet. They're still in the freezer.'

Mum opened the kitchen freezer and showed me three shelves of exploding brown and white feathers.

I shudder to think of all the plucking and butchery needed to get those birds oven-ready.

'So what are these caterers going to do for the main?' Mum asked. 'The traditional dry turkey?'

'I don't know,' I said. 'But if the caterers are doing turkey, they'd better hurry up and buy it. The farm turkeys will sell out soon.'

'I know a few turkey butchers who'll have some birds left,' Mum mused. 'Ted the Turkey. Wayne the Turkey. But this is a bad time of year to ask. Turkey butchers are always grumpy in December.'

'Why?' I asked. 'Surely Christmas is their most profitable time.'

'They spend all day with their hand up a turkey's arse,' said Mum. 'It sucks the Christmas cheer right out of them.'

Am glad Mum isn't offended by the professional caterer plan, and also relieved – especially since she was potentially planning to cover Alex's spotless kitchen with brown feathers and bird guts.

I've never had a professionally catered Christmas before, but I'm willing to give it a try. As Mum says, it could be pleasant to put my feet up, get drunk and let someone else take care of everything.

Thursday 6th December

Catrina and I are coming to something of a compromise, re Christmas food.

She's agreed not to serve stuffed cabbage or fish-head soup as long as we can drink a strong Hungarian spirit called Palinka and eat some sort of rolled nut pastry with poppy seeds.

I have agreed to forgo pigs in blankets and three different types of potato (mash, roast and chips) as long as we can have Bailey's Irish cream and Yorkshire puddings.

We both agree on Christmas pudding (large booze-filled one with a side of double cream).

However, we're still at odds over the main and musical entertainment.

On the entertainment front, I think Burt Bacharach is way too elaborate for background music, and anyway he'll want to be with his own family.

'Nonsense darling,' Catrina insisted. 'The man will do anything for me. And what's one Christmas when you've seen so many?'

Friday 7th December

Catrina has invited me to Borough Market on Saturday.

'We'll choose the cheese and wine together,' she said. 'Oh Juliette, I do so love Christmas.'

'I thought your assistant was buying the wine,' I said.

'Monique has done her best,' said Catrina. 'But she only ever buys one of each kind. When it comes to wine, two is one and one is none. We must meet after 11 am because you *can't* drink wine in this country before that time, did you know? Honestly – they treat everyone like children here. In France, you can have wine with your breakfast.'

'I thought we were *buying* wine for Christmas,' I said. 'Not drinking it.'

'We have to *sample* the wine, darling. Otherwise, how will we know if we like it?'

Maybe my future mother-in-law isn't so bad after all.

Catrina rounded up the call by telling me not to drive to London.

'Take the train, darling,' she said. 'If you drink and drive these days, they can be very strict. Friends of mine have had prison sentences.'

I would never drink and drive but appreciated Catrina's concern.

Think we might be bonding.

Evening

Nice family takeaway at the pub tonight – Domino's pizza and Ben and Jerry's ice cream.

Mum has filled the house with even more Christmas tat this year, including a teddy bear that reads 'The Night Before Christmas', a jiggling, giggling snowman, two inflatable candy canes and a snow machine.

We chatted about Christmas at Château Dalton, and I think

we're all feeling excited. Although Callum was disappointed when I told him the Dalton Estate doesn't have a full-sized chocolate fountain or an unlimited-sweet machine.

'It's not Willy Wonka's chocolate factory,' I said. 'It's just a big, fancy house.'

'He's got a pond though, hasn't he?' Callum asked. 'For Judge Dredd. To let him loose and that.' Then he looked sad.

'Kids grow up,' said John Boy, putting a kind hand on Callum's shoulder. 'You can't hold onto them forever.'

'What if he's lonely in that big pond?' said Callum. 'And misses his dad?'

'Tadpoles don't experience emotions like you and me,' said Dad. 'He doesn't even know who you are, Callum.'

'Do shut up, Bob,' said Mum. 'Callum, of course, Judge Dredd knows who you are. But it's time to let him go now. You know that feeling when you run out the school gates? That's how Judge Dredd will feel in that pond.'

Hopefully, we've convinced Callum to do the right thing.

The alternative – Judge Dredd floating on top of the tank as Judge Dead – doesn't bear thinking about.

Saturday 8th December

Nick took Daisy this morning, so I've had a day to myself. Of course, when you're a mother you never really have a day to yourself, so have been working/tidying/cleaning.

During my lunchtime shift, there was fascinating – and possibly miraculous – news.

Judge Dredd might be turning into a froglet. It defies all natural laws, but he's greener looking and has feathery bits that could be arms and legs.

Dad has been mulling over global warming, the warm bar area, the good diet Callum's been feeding him etc. but he can't get his head around it.

Callum is in such a good mood, singing Moana songs to himself and smiling away. It's the happiest we've seen him since Angel Rain passed away.

Sunday 9th December

Got a leeetle bit merry yesterday and consequently am a leeetle bit hungover this morning.

I feel guilty about the hangover, but Nick has Daisy today, so I've spared her my bad-mother grey face.

Catrina and I had a fun afternoon choosing cheese and wine for Christmas. And best of all we've agreed on the main: boring, traditional, inoffensive, dry turkey.

Catrina has texted the caterers to let them know, so everything is taken care of.

Christmas is coming!

Catrina was in a good mood at the cheese cave, laughing and whooping when she saw me.

'Oh Juliette! I have such very good news. Carlos and I are engaged!'

Was taken aback for two reasons:

I had no idea Catrina and Carlos had got back together. The last time Catrina spoke about her ex-boyfriend, she called him a 'disgusting pig with pointed dog teeth.'

Catrina got my name right.

'Thank you for calling me Juliette,' I said.

'Well, you will be my daughter-in-law,' she said. 'Why wouldn't I know your name?'

'When did you and Carlos get back together?' I asked.

'Yesterday,' Catrina gushed. 'You know me, darling. I am a

romantic. Swept along by love. My heart says yes, yes, yes.'

Catrina was in such a good mood that we ended up having a fabulous time, shrieking and laughing like schoolgirls, trying all sorts of different wines and cheeses.

At one point, Catrina picked up some empty black cheese plates, put them above her solid blonde chignon to make mouse ears and squeaked, 'I am Minnie Mouse! More cheese please!'

We even joked about her throwing the Martini, pretending to chuck glasses of wine at each other.

When all our wines and cheeses were wrapped and packed, Catrina clasped my hands in diamond-encrusted fingers.

'Juliette, I understand what it is Alex sees in you, darling. You are very vital. Full of life. What do you think? Alex says you want us to be friends. Can we be friends? And we'll have a truly wonderful Christmas together.'

Agreed on all counts.

Maybe Christmas miracles really do happen.

Monday 10th December

Pleasant Christmassy pub shift today, serving all the regulars Baileys and other novelty Christmas spirits.

Mum was outside on a ladder when I arrived, hanging tasteless Christmas decorations around the pub.

'Why are you hanging even more lights?' I asked. 'The pub already looks like a disco.'

Mum explained that she is having a passive-aggressive Christmas lights showdown with the stylish neighbours next door.

'The miserable sods said the pub looked gaudy,' said Mum. 'They were whispering behind the fence, saying we're making the street look bad. I shouted they should come say it to my face, but they wouldn't.'

The neighbouring house is a tasteful historic cottage with sandy walls, a slumpy tiled roof and real Tudor beams. They've decorated their doorstep bay trees with simple white lights and hung a single chain of glass icicles from their guttering. It's all pretty and understated – the opposite of the pub, where flashing Santa climbs up and down a tinsel chimney, before pulling his trousers down to reveal a porcelain pink bum.

To upset the neighbours further, Mum has bought herself a sexy Santa outfit, which she wears around the village and behind the bar. It has a fluffy marabou trim and low-cut front – so low that the regulars have made a game, trying to land dry-roasted peanuts in Mum's cleavage.

She has barred a customer already and administered two black eyes. Rumour has it that there's a fifty-pound prize for whoever can land two peanuts and a pork scratching at once.

Silly really.

Fifty pounds isn't worth a broken leg.

Tuesday 11th December

Have made a final task list for Christmas at the Dalton Estate:

Find the dining room. Am guessing it's somewhere on the ground floor, but there are so many rooms at the Dalton Estate it's been challenging to pin down so far. Once found, note how many chairs can fit around the table. Doubt there'll be any problems here but should make sure.

Finalise guest list and seating plan. Make sure conflictual guests (i.e. Helen and me, Helen and Mum, Helen and Brandi etc.) are sat at opposite ends of the table and not in direct eye-line. We don't want any food thrown on Christmas Day.

Consider entertainment. Nick is doing his one-man performance, but we need something more interactive for the afternoon. If I don't arrange activities, Dad will pull out old-fashioned games like dominoes (boring), Happy Families (inappropriately titled) or Monopoly (could remind people of bad feeling over Harold's will).

Find out if Zach and Laura are staying overnight, and if so organise a guest suite with cot for baby Bear.

Ditto Catrina and Carlos, but without the cot.

Talk to Mrs Hawks about her holiday arrangements. Does she have time off at Christmas? I assume so, but you never know. If not, she'll need adding to the seating plan. And does she have a plus one?

High chairs for Daisy and baby Bear. Some kind of strap restraint for Callum, if poss.

Make sure there are adequate bananas and boiled sweets for Nana Joan, and sugar for John Boy to add to his vegetables.

Have a serious word with Mum and John Boy about burping, farting etc. during the Christmas dinner.

Wednesday 12th December

A wonderful, miraculous thing has happened.

Judge Dredd has turned into a froglet.

Dad is both bewildered and delighted, declaring Callum's tadpole a wonder of nature. He has called up the National Trust, WWF, the Natural History Museum and various other wildlife bodies to have spirited conversations about the Great Oakley miracle tadpole.

Dad has also phoned our local newspaper, *Oakley Gazette*, to see if they want to write a story. I'm sure they will – *Oakley Gazette* are incredibly short of news. Some of their headlines have included:

+ 'Man Falls off Ladder'
+ 'Tool Kit Stolen by Teen'
+ 'Co-op gets Facelift'

I am so happy for Callum. It really is a Christmas miracle.

Daisy and I have been invited to the pub later to dig a pond for Judge Dredd. Callum wants Judge Dredd close to home in case there are any grandkids to take care of further down the line.

Evening

Lovely day at the pub digging Judge Dredd's pond.

Daisy bought her mini gardening kit (thin gloves, a trowel that would bend in butter, fork with rounded, blunt points, plastic shears), but was largely obstructive, throwing dead leaf 'wedding showers' at Callum.

Mum was obstructive too, bossing us all around while she sat with a cup of tea and the biscuit tin, complaining of a bad back.

The ground was cold but not frozen and digging the damp earth was easy. This was good, because Callum wanted a sizeable 'mansion' pond for his DF (darling froglet).

After we lined the pond, Callum carried Judge Dredd carefully into the garden to see his new home. The little froglet kicked around his pimped-up tank but refused to hop into the pond.

It's not surprising, really.

Callum brings Judge Dredd food, cleans his porcelain castles with a mild, pond-friendly solution and chats to him every night before bed. If I were Judge Dredd, I wouldn't want to move into brutal, unforgiving nature either.

Callum thinks Judge Dredd will be the toughest frog in the village and run a 'mean gangsta pond'.

'But he'll be a nice gangster,' he was quick to add. 'He'll have a girlfriend who is ill, but he looks after her and she gets better.'

We were all quiet then, remembering Angel Rain.

I suppose clichés are there for a reason because we all said things like 'another star in heaven now' and 'only the good die young'.

'Do you think Angel Rain turned Judge Dredd into a frog?'

Callum asked.

We all told him yes – we were sure of it.

Thursday 13th December

Callum has made the *Oakley Gazette* front page with his miracle froglet. There's a picture of him grinning and pointing at the tank, under the headline: 'Christmas Miracle'.

Callum is pleased to be in the papers but disappointed at how Judge Dredd photographed. I can see why – Judge Dredd is just a shadowy blob in the murky water.

'You can't even see his legs,' Callum complained. 'And they haven't spelt his name right. It's an insult.'

If he thinks that's an insult, wait until he fulfils his ambition of becoming a Champions League footballer. The papers do far worse than spell their names wrong.

Callum hasn't seen Judge Dredd since we put him in the pond, but he's still singing to him and giving him fish food every day.

Mum always says love makes things grow. If that's true, Judge Dredd will be the biggest frog in the village.

Friday 14th December

All the Christmas arrangements are in hand. Staff and caterers are taking care of everything – hanging decorations, sourcing food etc.

It's Alex's last day at work, and he's taking time off to spend Christmas with us.

I should be relaxing but feel there's something still to do.

Not sure what, but...*something* important. Probably I'm just paranoid because I'm not used to having things taken care of for me on Christmas Day.

Off to Althea's house now. She and Wolfgang are heading to Sri

Lanka in a few days, so I want to wish her happy Christmas before she goes.

Althea told me not to buy her a Christmas gift because she is doing a 'crap we don't need' amnesty.

Wolfgang is getting nothing for Christmas, except his mother's love – which Althea claims is 'more than enough'.

Evening
Just got back from Althea's. She was in the back garden when I arrived, chain saw in hand, sawing down a silver birch tree.

'What are you doing?' I asked. 'A bit of winter coppicing?'

'Wolfgang wants a Christmas tree,' Althea explained. 'But the shops only sell those boring firs, so we're cutting down our own.'

Helped Althea drag the grey, bare tree into her house, its spindly, spider-web-covered branches ripping the hallway art to shreds. Then we stood the scary, dead tree in a bucket of black sand.

It exuded the opposite of Christmas joy.

'It's not supposed to be joyful in an obvious way,' said Althea. 'It's an art installation. You have to *look* for the joy. We should give it a name.'

Suggested 'dead winter' or 'widows tears'.

8 pm
Just remembered. CHRISTMAS TREE!! That's what I've forgotten.

ARG!

8.10 pm
Alex is ten minutes away. Have just phoned to share my Christmas-tree panic.

'Calm down,' he said. 'We'll buy a tree tomorrow. There's plenty of time.'

When he put it that way, I felt a bit silly.

Better go. The microwave just pinged for Alex's Thai curry.

Saturday 15th December

A fun day.

Alex and I went Christmas-tree shopping.

John Boy and Callum wanted to come, but I banned them due to their new hobby: Christmas-tree jumping.

Whenever the pair of them see Christmas trees on sale in town, they hurl themselves into the thick, fir branches, giggling like maniacs.

A few greengrocers have chased them down the street, but they haven't been caught yet.

Alex was a little disappointed by the size of trees in town. Apparently, Harold used to get twenty-foot Christmas trees from friends in Norway, but those friends are dead now.

Personally, I was delighted by the beautiful, bushy green trees on sale. They were a big step up from my cheap one at home, or the fake one at the pub which Dad douses with pine aftershave for that 'authentic' Christmas smell.

We eventually settled on the biggest tree we could find, which Alex thought was a bargain at 'just' one hundred pounds.

Alex and I held hands as we shopped, and it felt magical and fluttery. Like old times. I know he's still sad about his father, but we're moving forward.

As a family.

Sunday 16th December

Alex presented Daisy with a surprise present this morning: the dreaded Elf on a Shelf.

He bought it in town yesterday, after noticing Daisy stroking Elf's striped legs in a department store.

Alex was a little upset with my reaction to the gift, which was unbridled rage.

'Why would you bring something like that into the house,' I ranted. 'Christmas is already a busy time. The daily demands for biscuit making, snowflake cutting, advent calendars and all the rest of it. Now I'll have to get up early in the morning to set up cute, mischievous elf things.'

'I'll do that,' said Alex. 'Daisy is worth getting up early for. Leave it to me, Juliette. Daisy will have the best Elf on the Shelf there ever was.'

Alex has fallen into the classic parenting mistake of being too enthusiastic. He'll do a fantastic Elf on the Shelf tomorrow, then get bored – like everyone else does – and wish he'd left Elf on the toy shop shelf.

Monday 17th December

Alex created an inspiring Elf on the Shelf display this morning, involving a circle of Daisy's soft toys, a *Christmas Carol* picture book, electric candles, real holly, a miniature Christmas tree and flour mixed with glitter sparkles.

Daisy retrieved Elf from the storytelling circle and told him off for running away.

'Naughty elf. You get up too early. Mummy sleeping. GO BACK TO BED!'

It was an embarrassing re-enactment of me in the mornings, but I tried to smile my way through it.

'But look at what Elfy was doing!' Alex enthused. 'He was telling stories to all your soft toys. He's a dear little thing.'

Daisy looked at him blankly. 'He naughty elf.'

'No, no – he was being very kind,' said Alex, with a fatherly smile. 'Reading to your toys.'

'Mummy doesn't like noise in the morning. NAUGHTY ELF!'

Alex says he's going to try again tomorrow.

I bet he gets sick of it after that.

Tuesday 18th December

Alex made a zip wire for Elf this morning and had him abseiling across the lounge with a rucksack of sweets on his back. Some sweets were artfully scattered on the lounge floor, with dustings of icing sugar making magical, edible snow.

Daisy didn't notice the elf dangling from its hairy-green zip wire. However, she ate all the sweets before breakfast and has been a nightmare all day.

Wednesday 19th December

As predicted, Alex is tiring of Elf on the Shelf.

This morning was a lack-lustre display. Naughty Elf had taken a decoration off the tree.

Neither John Boy nor I noticed, and Alex didn't bother pointing out Elf's bad behaviour to Daisy. Without sweets, she just wasn't interested.

Might put Elfy quietly away. Daisy is seeing Santa at the Co-op later, who'll be giving away shopping vouchers and cheap, breakable plastic toys.

That's more than enough magic for a three-year-old.

Late afternoon

A bad developmental milestone.

Daisy is now terrified of Santa.

She loved him last year. What happened?

We stood in line for the kindly Co-op Santa, with his real white beard, authentic fat stomach and delightful chimney and magic key story, but when we reached him, Daisy ran away screaming.

'Don't want scary Santa man,' she yelled. 'Want Father Christmas.'

Tried to explain that Santa and Father Christmas are the same person, but she wasn't having any of it.

'Nasty Santa,' she said. 'Fat Santa.'

Admittedly, Santa was a bit fat. As mentioned, his tummy and beard were both authentic.

I hope Santa didn't take Daisy's comments personally.

Thursday 20th December

So close to family harmony, and yet so far.

Catrina is kicking off big time because I want to send Mrs Hawks home on Christmas Day.

Poor Mrs Hawks hasn't spent a Christmas with her family since 1972, and she has quite a large family – five children and twelve grandchildren.

Am putting my foot down, though.

There'll be plenty of other staff to do the catering. Young, twenty-somethings with no children, delighted to be earning double-time while hungover.

Catrina put her children in boarding school – she doesn't understand that most people like spending time with their kids.

'How can we have a Christmas without dear Hawksy?' Catrina demanded. 'She is the very heart of the home.'

But 'heart' isn't a word I'd use to describe Mrs Hawks. 'Unsmiling' would do the job better. Stern, aloof and oddly fragranced are a few more.

Friday 21st December

Alex, Daisy and I visited the Dalton Estate today and found events staff making unnecessary final touches to decorations. The house already looked fabulous, but they were fussing over everything, tweaking and moving things an inch to the left, an inch to the right.

The huge Christmas tree twinkled in the hallway. Real holly sprigs hung from the cornicing. The marble floors gleamed. Everything smelt Christmassy too, thanks to an organic spice humidifier that wafted Christmas cake smells into the air.

Really, there was nothing to do, but Catrina was running around in a flap.

'Those red apples are not glossy enough – somebody polish them. Have staff memorised the Christmas meal courses, *with photos?* It looks so ugly when they check menus and ask what is this, what is that. And fix that door handle, for goodness *zakes*. Nobody wants to hear squeak, squeak when they are relaxing with their family.'

Catrina was especially stressed because Alex's American aunts will be arriving tomorrow.

'They are so fussy, eyes over everything,' she said. 'And you know, of course, they have never liked me. Such plain women from a plain time.'

I have to admit, Alex's aunts weren't overly smiley when I met them at the funeral, but funerals aren't smiley places. They might be a real laugh on festive occasions.

We all had a chat about Christmas Eve, and decided that Daisy, Alex and I should stay at the Dalton Estate overnight so we can wake up together on Christmas morning.

Catrina also wants to host a 'little' Christmas Eve carol service.

'You know, Christmas Eve is special in Hungary,' she said. 'We will put candles on the tree and sing carols. Your family will love it,

Juliette. You will see.'

'My family aren't scheduled to come on Christmas Eve,' I said. 'Just Christmas Day.'

'Oh they simply must come on Christmas Eve,' said Catrina. 'They will miss all the singing. Christmas Eve is such a joy. *Such* a joy.'

I suppose – in for a penny, in for a pound. And Dad loves singing carols.

Alex is going to stay at the Dalton Estate with his mother this weekend because Catrina feels 'stressed' about paparazzi while Carlos is in Spain visiting relatives.

Daisy will be with Nick tomorrow, so I'll do the last of my Christmas wrapping, etc. then and pack for Christmas at the Dalton Estate.

Starting to feel magical and Christmassy.

Ooooo Christmas!

Saturday 22nd December

Nick turned up this morning with baby Horatio struggling and gurning in a sling.

'Daisy boo boo!' he called. 'Ready for a day with Dadda?'

'You're chirpy,' I said. 'Is Helen taking Horatio today?'

'No, Daddy is doing the double,' said Nick, adjusting the sling straps. 'Two for the price of one.'

'Then why are you so happy?' I asked suspiciously. 'Usually, you're terrified to take both of them.'

'I've invested in equipment,' said Nick, patting the sling, then pulling colourful straps from its zipped front pocket. 'The sling and these bad boys.'

'What are those straps?' I asked.

'Reins,' said Nick. 'Daisy will be leashed and tethered so she can't make a run for it. Daddy has the power.'

'Good luck,' I said. 'But in my experience, equipment is hit-and-miss. Remember the bumbo? The bounce and play? The vibrating chair? The jungle gym? They don't give you a *real* break. Just a few moments of distraction.'

'Stop being a Nelly neg head,' said Nick. 'It's Christmas. And speaking of which, let's talk about the Christmas Day highlight – my performance. Do you know anything about the size of the stage? How well sound carries in the auditorium? Do you reckon I can do a proper stage rehearsal before the big day? To put on a professional show, you need to *know* your venue.'

'It's only a small Christmas Day skit in front of family and friends,' I said. 'Your most interested audience will be three-years-old. And she'll only be interested for the first five minutes. Get things in perspective.'

Nick chuckled then. 'You don't understand, Jules. I aim for perfection. That's what marks me out from the am dreamers.'

'I thought paid work was what marked you out from the am dreamers,' I said.

'Look, I'm trying, OK?' said Nick. 'I'm losing hair by the bucketload. There's a lot of hair-loss prejudice out there, Julesy. It's a real thing.'

I have to say that Nick has lost a lot of hair. Coupled with his face, which has the ring of a smarmy womaniser, it gives him a sleazy air, which is generally bad for leading roles. Unless *Chitty Chitty Bang Bang* enjoys a resurgence.

Reminded Nick that maintenance payments are still due, whether hair-loss prejudice is a real thing or not.

Afternoon
Nick just called with two kids howling in the background.

'It's not been a good day,' he admitted. 'Daisy found an equipment loophole. She bit my hand in the Co-op and I dropped the reins. I caught her at the Cadbury's chocolate stocking promo shelf, stuffing Fudge and Freddo bars into her face.'

'She unwrapped the chocolate by herself?' I asked.

'Yes. *And* ripped open the Christmas stocking netting to get to it.'

Daisy's so clever!

Asked Nick to put Daisy on the line and told her to behave for Daddy because Mummy had to wrap presents. Then back-tracked, realising I might have blown the Santa illusion.

'I mean I'm helping *Santa* wrap presents,' I said.

'He come from North Pole, Mummy?' Daisy asked.

'Yes,' I said.

'I speak to him,' said Daisy. 'He very naughty. He leave his elves. I tell him – NO COOKIE FOR YOU!'

She's *so* articulate.

Told Daisy that Santa was too busy right now but am already regretting the lie. Predict more questions about where Santa's sledge landed, if he liked our Poundland Christmas tree, etc. To lie effectively, you have to have a good memory, and no mother has a good memory. Our heads are far too full, especially at Christmas time.

Sunday 23rd December

Alex's widowed aunts, Blanch, Betty and Barbara, arrived today from West Virginia.

Since Daisy was still with Nick, I had a nice opportunity to meet and greet them at the Dalton Estate without Daisy hanging off me, demanding attention.

They were friendly enough, but remembering their names was difficult. They all looked identical in their loose jeans and ski jackets, with NYC baseball caps over clipped, grey hair.

After the aunts had unpacked, they sat and slowly chewed a traditional English cream tea while asking lots of questions.

I think I gave helpful information – explaining that you don't put cream in your cup of tea when having a cream tea. The cream is for the scone.

'So it's just a cute name for a dessert combo?' asked one of the aunts.

Said yes, pretty much.

Then Alex's aunts wanted to know about my family, taking turns to ask about who was married to whom, if there'd been any bad separations, who the patriarch was and whether there had been any inheritance disputes.

'We only have matriarchs in our family,' I said. 'Dad thinks women are superior to men. He's a committed feminist.'

'And your daughter?' one of the aunts asked. 'Where's her daddy this Christmas?'

'He lives in the village,' I said. 'You'll meet him on Christmas Day.'

'Well that sure does sound mature,' said one of the aunts.

'Yes,' I said. 'It does, doesn't it?'

We talked about Christmas Eve carol-singing tomorrow, and the aunts said they couldn't wait to meet my mother, who sounded like 'a character', and my father who must be 'a sweetheart'.

Mum certainly is a character, for better or worse. And Dad's special talent is conversing with old ladies, so I'm sure they will find him a sweetheart.

Think carol-singing will be OK tomorrow. Carlos is flying back from Barcelona, so Catrina will have someone to lavish her with attention. And my family have been cautioned to be on their best behaviour – no swearing, wiping hands on anything other than napkins, discussing toilet habits etc.

The Dalton Estate doesn't have an Amazon Echo, so Callum can't ask Alexa to make fart noises.

It's Christmas Day when shit will get real.

That's when Nick and his mother arrive.

Monday 24th December

WOOOOOO!

Blended family bliss here we come.

I'm writing this in Alex's big downy bed at the Dalton Estate. My family are still downstairs, 'blending' with Catrina, Carlos and Alex's aunts.

Things are going *very* well.

Dad is entertaining Alex's aunts with his local history knowledge, enjoying 'oos' and 'aahs' as he talks about the famous 17th-century peasant shoe found under the Co-op car park.

Mum, Brandi, Nana Joan, John Boy, Carlos and Catrina are bonding over cocktails by drinking a lot of them.

I am currently upstairs relaxing, while Alex takes Daisy for a 'tire her out' bedtime walk around the grounds. Mum did offer, but it was half-hearted because Jonny the bar guy had just rustled up another round of Christmas Sparklers.

Unbelievably, it's been a GOOD day – give or take the odd Catrina tantrum. We haven't experienced the Helen and Nick bomb yet, but if today is anything to go by, it could be OK. Nice, even.

Feel full of cosy Christmas magic. Possibly because the staff added a brandy shot to my hot chocolate.

We've sung carols, lit Christmas candles, eaten Christmas cake and some Hungarian nutty pastry, drunk Christmassy cocktails and had a thoroughly lovely time.

Better go.

I can hear Daisy coming up the stairs with Alex.

'One step, two-step, three-step, one-hundred step, nine-step'.

Alex is so sweet. 'That's a wonderful job, Daisy, but let's try again. One, two, three, *four*.'

Hope Daisy goes down easily tonight. Suspect she won't. Christmas Eve is very exciting for kids. My sisters and I used to stay up until gone midnight, telling each other we could hear Santa's sleigh.

I remember one year, Mum lost her temper and offered us a shot of brandy each to shut us up. Fortunately, we didn't drink the brandy because it smelt disgusting.

Quite a shocking lapse in parenting, looking back. Mum should be ashamed of herself.

Midnight

Daisy is still awake.

I can see where Mum was coming from now, re brandy.

Tempted to follow her example and offer Daisy brandy-laced hot chocolate but have refrained.

I am a good mother.

I am a good mother.

Tuesday 25th December

1 am

She's asleep!

Christmas Day here we come.

Morning

Well, we tried.

You can't say we didn't try.

Some things are not meant to be.

The big, blended, family Christmas Day did not go well.

I am writing this from the cottage, having fled the Dalton Estate with my daughter clutched to my breast.

I can't bring myself to talk about the worst bits of Christmas Day just yet. But let me write about the morning.

Waking up to Dalton Estate staff making breakfast was nice.

It would have been even nicer if Daisy hadn't woken at 5.30 am, but you can't have everything.

Of course, Alex didn't mind starting the day at 5.30 am, saying this was 'a standard wake-up time for many'.

'For who?' I demanded.

'*Whom*,' said Alex.

'OK,' I said. 'For whom is it a standard wake up time?'

'Anyone who commutes,' said Alex. 'Also, personal trainers, farmers, soldiers etc. The kitchen staff start the breakfast patisserie at 5 am. And when Zach and I boarded, the older boys would hit us with sticks if we didn't wake before six.'

Thinking back, maybe it was the 5.30 am start that set us up for a bad day. But I can't blame Daisy. It's the adults who are culpable, me included.

Breakfast was, of course, delicious. You can't go wrong with three French pastry chefs in the kitchen.

It was lunch that was problematic.

Will write more tomorrow.

Wednesday 26th December

Mum says the cocktails were to blame. They were very strong, but we needed a little bit of social lubrication – especially when Nick and Helen arrived mid-morning. However, sadly we can't blame the cocktails. We can only blame ourselves.

The first kick-off was minor, looking back. Unremarkable,

considering what followed. It started when Catrina objected to her present from Carlos.

'What kind of man are you, to think a woman would wear something like this? I wear diamonds. Not costume jewellery. After everything this year, you insult me.'

Carlos knew the drill. He gave Catrina big wounded puppy eyes and told her a pearl necklace was a token of her purity and that he adored her and would do anything for her.

Catrina broke the necklace and flounced off upstairs, leaving Carlos to scrabble around picking up pearls. Alex tried to help, but Carlos got tearful and tried to fight him. Then Carlos sat in a chair and fell asleep, snoring loudly.

There were a few more petty rumblings, but again – nothing too serious.

When Nick and Helen arrived, Alex gave Nick one of those Alpha-male bone-crushing handshakes, teeth gritted. Then Nick asked if Alex's big house was 'compensating for something'. But we managed to push past that without incident.

Then my family arrived, and Helen rudely winced when Mum or Nana spoke.

In some respects, this was understandable because Nana Joan kept talking about 'the shits'.

'Ooo, is that a mince pie? Go on then. Only you'll have to point me towards a toilet because I'll never find one in this place and mince pies give me the shits. No, no, love, I don't do canapés. They give me the shits.'

But as I say, these were all minor things. Nothing to what followed during lunch. Taking Daisy out now to stretch her legs. Will write more later.

Afternoon
OK. Daisy is napping. Time to write more Christmas awfulness

out of my system.

Pre-Christmas lunch, Catrina had flounced off to her room in a strop, but everything was still at a low simmer. Nothing was boiling over just yet.

Alex wasn't worried about his mother's absence.

'There's no Champagne or cocktails in the guest suite,' he explained. 'I've instructed staff not to respond to her ringing bell. We'll starve her out.'

Alex was right. Just before lunch, Catrina glided downstairs, Santa hat jingling with every step. She demanded a cocktail for her headache, then sat at the dining table right by the Champagne bucket.

Things seemed like they might be OK during lunch. The food was terrific, and Catrina even wore her Christmas-cracker hat.

Then the cheese course arrived, and things got real. Really real.

Mum says it's just one of those things. Families fall out at Christmas. But I think the universe is giving us a sign.

Proceed with caution. Danger lies ahead. Do not blend this family. Stay at chunky salsa stage. Purée at your peril.

Thursday 27th December

Back to reality and working at the pub today.

Alex turned up with a bunch of red roses and a roll of masking tape. The masking tape was supposed to be a joke about sticking our families together. However, it all looked a bit *Fifty Shades of Grey* – a man in a suit turning up with flowers and bondage equipment.

Of course, John Boy immediately congratulated Alex on 'decking that twat'.

'Let me get you a shot of Aftershock, mate,' said John Boy. 'We've got to celebrate. I've wanted to punch that drama dickhead for ages.'

'I didn't mean to hit him,' Alex insisted. 'It was a complete accident.'

'Citrus or cinnamon flavour Aftershock?' John Boy asked.

'What are we going to do, Juliette?' Alex asked. 'Nobody believes me.'

'I believe you,' I said. 'But that doesn't mean you shouldn't apologise.'

Alex went all tight-lipped then and said he saw no reason to apologise to *that man*.

'You gave him a black eye,' I said.

'True,' said Alex. 'But he's an adult. I'm sure it's not the first black eye he's experienced. The person I need to apologise to is Daisy.'

'You did,' I said. 'But she's three-years-old. She had no idea what 'thoroughly ashamed of my mistake' means.'

'We should be celebrating,' said John Boy. 'Not apologising. Nick had it coming.'

'There's nothing to celebrate here,' I said. 'Nick is Daisy's father. She could be traumatised.'

'She'll be OK,' said John Boy. 'When I was growing up, my dad was always punching people. And I turned out fine.'

'I DIDN'T PUNCH HIM!' said Alex.

There was a long silence. Then Alex said: 'I'll apologise to Spencer. Just…give me some time. I need to work up to it.'

Then he downed his Aftershock and left.

Friday 28th December

Met Althea today for herbal tea and sympathy, re Christmas Day. Althea had five different types of herbal tea, but no sympathy.

'What did you expect?' she demanded. 'Family bliss in one day?'

'Yes,' I said. 'That's exactly what I expected. Catrina and I were getting along so well. She's even started calling me Juliette. But now everything's worse than ever.'

'Keep trying,' said Althea. 'Don't give up at the first hurdle. Wolfgang PUT DOWN that carving knife.'

'It just feels like a sign,' I said. 'I promised Alex I'd give him a wedding date if Christmas Day went well. Now I feel like getting married is a terrible idea. I'll be dragging Daisy into a whole world of dysfunction and instability.'

'Just because of one Christmas Day punch-up?' said Althea. 'Do me a quaver. Life can get a lot worse than that. What about your miscarriage? And that little girl who passed away this year? Come on. If you can't weather this storm Julesy, you're not up to the job.'

'What job?' I asked.

'The job of life. What do you want to say at the end of it all? That you gave it your best shot with the James Bond sexy scar man? Or that you didn't try hard enough and regret what might have been?'

'It's not just about me,' I said. 'It's about Daisy too. If this is what blended family gatherings will be like in the future, I think I'll pass. She'll grow up traumatised.'

'Oh, she won't be traumatised,' Althea scoffed. 'You're from a shouty household, and you're fine. Family conflict gives you backbone. Anyway, kids are self-centred. They barely notice adult shit. I'm always asking Wolfgang how he feels after I've shouted someone down, but all he cares about is his next spoon of damson jam. It's New Year in a few days. Let the past shit go and start again.'

'Exactly,' I said. 'A clean slate. Just Daisy and me. No mess.'

'But that's not what you want, Julesy,' said Althea. 'You want things to work out with Alex. So get out there and make it work. God loves a trier.'

Saturday 29th December

Phoned Alex again and asked if he'd apologised to Nick yet.

'No,' he said. 'I'm planning on doing it the next time I see him.'

'And when will that be?' I asked. 'You're not a regular musical theatre-goer, as far as I'm aware.'

After a long silence, Alex said: 'What's Spencer's number? Let's get this over with.'

'It might not be too bad,' I reasoned. 'Nick has changed a lot in the last few years. He's grown up.'

'Has he?' Alex asked. 'Or has he been forced to calm down because he's been left holding the baby?'

Said I wasn't sure. But the apology still needs to take place.

Have given Alex Nick's number and told him to call me when there's news.

Alex hasn't called yet. Probably, this means Nick isn't picking up. He does that. Ignores unknown numbers just in case it's someone he's borrowed fifty quid from.

Afternoon

Alex has confirmed that Nick isn't picking up the phone.

'I'll try twice more,' said Alex. 'Then I'm drawing a line. I'm not humiliating myself.'

Pub shift today.

Asked Dad if he thought we could ever move on from Christmas Day.

'Depends what you mean by moving on,' said Dad.

'Alex apologising to Nick. Nick accepting the apology. And everyone else forgiving and forgetting the many slaps that rang out over the Christmas Day dinner table.'

'Mmm,' said Dad. 'Well, if Callum's little froglet has taught me anything, it's that miracles are possible.'

'But many gallons of water need to go under the bridge,' I said. 'We're talking a positive flood. I've given Alex Nick's number, but Nick's not picking up.'

'Sounds like you need a bit of trouble-shooting,' said Dad, putting on his serious glasses and pulling out his problem-solving notepad. 'Let me ponder on this. See the opportunity in every difficulty, that's what Winston Churchill said. Of course, Churchill's second-world-war strategy got many soldiers killed, according to your grandfather. But he was a stirring public speaker, nonetheless.'

I'm not optimistic about moving forward, though.

Callum's tadpole has used up our share of Christmas miracles – probably for the next decade.

Evening

Have just realised I haven't written about the full Christmas Day nightmare.

I suppose it could have been worse. There weren't any hospitalisations, just five slaps and one black eye.

Embarrassed to admit the first slap came from me, but when someone grabs your arse, you react on instinct.

The bottom grope was, I believe, an innocent mistake. Carlos meant to grope the waitress's bottom, but I was serving the veg too, and he grabbed mine by accident.

After I slapped Carlos, Catrina gave an outraged scream and reached across the table to slap me.

Then it all kicked off.

Laura passed baby Bear to Zach, and calmly slapped Catrina.

Helen, eyes blazing, told Laura she should never slap a lady of Catrina's standing. And slapped her.

Then Mum put down the cracker she'd been loading with cheese and slapped Helen.

Alex tried to get between whoever seemed to be slapping each other, but it was hard for him to keep up and required a sprint around the dinner table.

Then Daisy tried to throw herself from her high-chair, I'm guessing in an effort to get more dessert now the boring cheese course was out.

I shouted, 'DAISY!'

Alex whirled around just as Nick leaned forward, and Alex's elbow hit Nick in the eye.

Nick clutched his face and talked about a violent assault. Then Helen hustled Nick out of the house, glaring at me and whispering to Nick about legal action.

Catrina finished her glass of wine, marched out to Carlos's sports car and demanded he take her back to London.

Alex's elderly aunts sat like startled cattle in their identical sparkly party dresses, chewing their cheese and crackers.

It was all awful. Absolutely awful.

I don't think a dozen rolls of masking tape can fix it.

Afternoon

Oh my god!

Dad has invited Alex and Nick to the pub on New Year's Eve to 'settle their differences'.

I know Dad meant well, but this is quite unbelievable.

'Was Christmas Day not enough?' I demanded. 'You want to ruin New Year's Eve too?'

'You've got to do something pro-active, Juliette,' Dad insisted. 'Or your problems will never be solved. This is a logical solution, as promised. You said Alex wanted to apologise to Nick. Well, this will give him a chance, won't it?'

'Alex is phoning Nick,' I said.

'You said Nick wasn't picking up.'

'Yes,' I conceded. 'But a public meeting is a terrible idea. A Nick apology should be made in private. Nick milks apologies for all they're worth. He's even worse with an audience.'

'I'm sure Alex and Nick can manage an adult discussion,' said Dad. 'For Daisy's sake, if nothing else. And most chats are better when others are watching. It keeps people in check.'

'Were you not there on Christmas Day?' I asked. 'Five women slapped each other publicly. An audience didn't put us off.'

'It'll all turn out fine love,' said Dad. 'You'll see.'

'I thought that about Christmas Day,' I said. 'And I couldn't have been more wrong.'

Late afternoon
The New Year's Eve Hootenanny/showdown at the Oakley Arms is the talk of the village. Hootenanny tickets have now sold out, and most of the Duffy family have booked themselves to work behind the bar – even Aunty Trina, who lives miles away.

Mum is quite blatant about her desire for drama.

'We'll have ring-side seats,' she cackled. 'This'll be better than the Tyson-Lewis fight. I'll make sure there's plenty of popcorn.'

Sunday 30th December
Nana Joan is working at the bar tomorrow.

'I thought Shirley would need a hand,' she said coyly, not meeting my eye. 'What of it?'

'This is my life we're talking about,' I said. 'Not a reality TV show.'

'Well if Nick comes in looking for a fight, he should be warned,' said Nana Joan. 'I've got twenty-pound coins in a sock, and I'll start swinging.'

Am now picturing something like a Wild West brawl in the pub, with Alex and Nick throwing chairs and whisky bottles.

What on earth was Dad thinking?

Monday 31st December

So here we are.

New Year's Eve.

When all parents secretly want an early night.

Alex and I...yet again, I don't know what we are. I love him, but, but, but...

Let's see what tonight brings. Most likely violence and panic attacks, but if this year has taught me anything, it's that – for better or worse – life often surprises you.

Afternoon

Real anxiety about this evening now.

Phoned Alex to try and talk him out of coming. 'I just don't see things going well,' I said. 'Nick can be a real idiot when people apologise. Why not just send him a text message? Job done.'

'No, Juliette,' said Alex. 'That's the coward's way. I need to make a proper apology for Daisy's sake. Your father is right. The best way is man-to-man.'

The way Alex said 'man-to-man' sounded very much like a man wanted to punch another man.

Can NOT see this going well.

Tuesday 1st January

Althea is right about life: expect the unexpected.

It was the worst Christmas Day ever, but New Year's Eve brought surprises.

No miracles, perhaps.

But surprises.

I'll say one thing – Mum and Dad hosted a very profitable New Year's Eve. By 6 pm the bar was rammed. There were no queues either, because so many of my family members were serving behind the bar.

Alex arrived at the pub around 8 pm, having just dropped his aunts at the airport. He was greeted to cheers and slaps on the back.

'I *didn't* punch Spencer,' Alex kept insisting, as people offered him congratulatory drinks. 'It was an accident.'

'It might be better if you call Nick by his first name,' I said. 'In the spirit of making amends and moving forward.'

'Well, is he here?'

'No,' I said. 'Not yet. What did your aunts make of Christmas Day? Were they traumatised?'

'They haven't even mentioned Christmas Day,' said Alex. 'They were more interested in their airline meal and what movies will be showing on the flight. They're hoping for the new *Spiderman*.'

Alex and I had a few glasses of wine, tried different meats from the twelve-bird platters and waited.

At 10 pm we were still waiting.

Nick finally swaggered into the bar at 11.30 pm, by which time all the quail, squab and duck were gone. And Nick had an unexpected guest with him:

Helen.

Mum was furious to see Nick's mother and bellowed across the bar: 'Who invited you, you posh tart? What do you think this is, a spectator sport?'

This was hypocritical, given that half my family were spectating from behind the bar. But it was a fair point – Helen had no invite, and it was a ticketed event.

'I'm here to support Nicholas,' said Helen. 'He might need a witness. An assault took place on Christmas Day. Who's to say there won't be another?'

'There will be an assault if you don't bugger off,' said Mum. 'Go on, sling your hook.'

'It's OK, Shirley,' said Alex. 'We're here to move forward, aren't we? If Nick needs his mother, so be it.'

Nick approached the bar then and asked if the pub had got with the times and put Peroni on tap.

'Peroni is an Italian lager, Nick,' said Dad. 'Hardly fitting for an old-fashioned English alehouse. We don't move with the times here, as you young people say. Ours is a venue steeped in history. For centuries, the Oakley Arms has provided rest and refreshment for travellers riding the old cart-track to London, and local villagers seeking good food and companionship. The traditionally brewed ales we serve are similar to those provided by 18th-century publicans all those years ago. You know, the garden outside used to be stables for –'

As Dad began his history rant, Alex shook Nick's hand in a jerky way.

'I'm deeply sorry about Christmas Day, Nick,' he said. 'It was an accident, but you were injured so I apologise. Can we be men about it and agree to move on?'

'Oh, come off it,' said Nick. 'How can you accidentally give someone a black eye? Listen – I've been traumatised, psychologically and physically by all of this. I'll never enjoy a cheese course again. I had a *panic* attack this morning when I saw the cranberry brie in Mum's fridge.'

Helen nodded vehemently. 'And Nick is an actor,' she said. 'His face is his career.'

'That's right,' said Nick. 'It's going to be hard finding work while this thing heals.' He pointed at the tiny bruise on his cheekbone.

'Nick. You've been hit loads of times,' I said. 'You've had your nose broken twice. Alex only gave you a small black eye. It's your mangy head that's stopping you getting acting work. Just shut up and accept the apology.'

'I don't want this guy around our daughter,' said Nick, jabbing a finger at Alex. 'He's shown his true, violent colours. And if you defy me on this Jules, we're going back to court.'

The bar was silent at this point, except for the light 'scratch scratch' of Aunty Trina scrubbing a beer tap with wire wool. Then the bar door squeaked and there, in the pub doorway, stood Catrina Dalton.

We all stared.

Catrina's glamorous, fur-covered frame was silhouetted by cigarette smoke from the smoking area, and her green eyes sparkled pink under the light of Santa's flashing bottom.

'*Alex?*' said Catrina. 'What are you doing here?'

'I'm apologising to Nick,' said Alex. 'For Christmas Day. What are *you* doing here?'

Catrina laughed. 'That is so funny! I am here to see Juliette. To apologise for Christmas Day.'

'I'm sure you'll find Juliette very forgiving,' said Alex. 'But sadly, Nick isn't of a mind to move forward.'

'Nicholas, you *must* move forward,' said Catrina, striding to clasp his shoulders. 'Juliette wants us all to be a happy family, and that is what we all must be. No, Nicholas, you must FORGET Christmas Day. Helen, please tell your son. You tell him to forget it, or we cannot be friends. I do not like ungracious, unforgiving people. The handbags will be over.'

'Nicholas.' Helen hissed. 'We *are* gracious people. We are forgiving. Accept the man's apology. Alex – yes, of course, we do accept your apology. Don't we Nick?' Then, turning to Catrina, she said, 'Is that a new gilet, Catrina? Beautiful. I saw one just like it in Florence this year. Fur is so stylish.'

'We can talk about fashion some other time,' said Catrina. 'Juliette. I would like a very cold white wine. And we shall talk.'

Mum placed a bottle of wine on the bar counter with a large glass.

'There you go, Catrina,' she said. 'Help yourself. I must warn you, this bottle *could* have been in the fridge a while, so if it tastes like vinegar, proceed with caution.'

'What do you want to talk about?' I asked Catrina.

'Juliette,' said Catrina, filling the large glass to the top. 'I want to apologise. Poor Carlos was too frightened to tell the truth before. He was reaching for a gravy jug and found your bottom instead. Such a silly mistake! But he should have been honest sooner. Before the other girl – the waitress – made me watch the security footage. I understand, now. I am sorry for slapping you.'

'It's fine,' I said. 'What are a few slaps between family?'

'Yes indeed!' Catrina declared. 'That is the way I see it too. So now we can all be friends. Happy New Year! You know, there is a toast we say in Hungarian. It means to your health. When the English say it, it sounds like, here's to your arse. Ha ha! But I am not English. So I will pronounce this toast perfectly. *Egészségedre*! To your health. To your health!'

We all joined in Catrina's toast, even Nick – who was not about to turn down one of the free toffee vodka shots Mum placed on the bar.

'I must bid you adieu Catrina,' Helen called, after Nick had downed his shot. 'I have an appointment at the sailing club. Henry is there with his twenty-something marriage wrecker. Let them see me, the ex-wife, and feel ashamed as the New Year bell tolls. We must meet up for coffee soon and talk handbags.'

'Yes, yes darling,' said Catrina, as Helen hustled Nick out of the door. 'Now, Juliette. I am told you haven't given Alex a wedding date yet.'

'Anya,' said Alex. 'That's something for Juliette and me to discuss privately.'

'Fine, fine,' said Catrina. 'Yes, you two young people talk amongst yourselves.'

She turned around.

My family did something similar, pretending to busy themselves at the bar, while blatantly listening.

'Juliette,' said Alex. 'Should we talk outside?'

'There's no need,' I said. 'I have a wedding date for you.'

'Really?' said Alex. 'You don't want to forget about weddings for the foreseeable future?'

'No.'

'So what date do you have in mind?'

'A spring wedding is always lovely, Juliette,' said Catrina. 'The flowers are beautiful at that time of year. You could walk down an aisle of Dutch tulips. Quite spectacular.'

'You don't want spring in this country,' said Nana Joan, polishing the bar with a tea-towel. 'It rains too much. Summer's the thing.'

'Actually, I'm thinking winter,' I said.

'Good idea, Juliette,' said Dad. 'Very economical. You'll save a fortune getting married out of season.'

'So what's the date?' asked John Boy.

'Christmas Day,' I said.

'You're serious?' said Alex.

'Yes. Safe is risky and risky is safe. Wasn't that your father's motto? So this has to be the safest day. Since so much went wrong this year.'

'I'm not sure you quite understand the motto,' said Alex. 'It's not about repeating past mistakes. But let's not quibble over terms. Christmas Day it is.'

The New Year's Eve countdown started then, and Mum turned up the radio, so we could all hear the chimes.

'10, 9, 8…'

'Well, Mrs Dalton,' said Alex, sweeping me into his arms. 'In a few moments, we can say we're getting married this year. How do you feel about that?'

'7, 6, 5…'

'Good. Really good.'

'And do you think we can be one big, happy, blended family?'

'4, 3…'

'Miracles can and have happened this year,' I said. 'I have faith.'

'2, 1, HAPPY NEW YEAR!'

As the New Year chimes rang out, Alex gave me a long, romantic New Year's kiss.

It would have been a perfect moment, except:

a: My family were watching from behind the bar

b: Mum kept tapping Alex on the shoulder, asking if he wanted a toffee vodka shot.

But that's life for you. Even the most perfect moments aren't perfect. Then again, if you look hard enough perfection is everywhere.

Thank you for finishing my book.
If you have a minute, please review
on Amazon and GoodReads.

Suzy xx

BOOK IV:
The Bad Mother's Wedding

will be along soon.
And just in case you haven't yet read the
first three books in the series, there are
some summaries to tempt you in the
following pages . . .

The BAD MOTHER'S DIARY

Suzy K Quinn

Why Mummy Drinks meets Bridget Jones
The first in the bestselling comedy series

Juliette is a new mother, but life isn't going the way she'd hoped. She doesn't live in a cottage with roses around the door. She doesn't own a rolling pin. And Daisy's out-of-work actor father still hasn't proposed.

While Juliette sobs her way through sleepless nights and nappy changes, Nick drinks Guinness and plays computer games. Meanwhile, his helicopter mother is always on hand to find fault – with Juliette. At least when Nick pops the question, things will look up…won't they?

With a supporting cast including Juliette's over-honest mother, potty-mouthed grandmother, militant hippy best friend and handsome-but-scarred hotel magnate Alex Dalton, the first in Suzy K Quinn's hilarious, bestselling Bad Mother series is a sassy, uplifting, addictive treat.

Lightning Books 2019
ISBN: 9781785631566
£7.99

The BAD MOTHER'S DETOX

Suzy K Quinn

Why Mummy Drinks meets Bridget Jones
The second in the bestselling comedy series

Juliette Duffy has made a lot of mistakes. They include falling in love with the wrong man, having a baby with the aforementioned wrong man, and googling 'haemorrhoids' then looking at the image pages. This year, however, she is hoping for joyful, post-baby romance with Alex Dalton – a man who has loved her since childhood and owns half of London.

Can she really make it work with Alex? Living in a country village and working in her parents' local pub is a world away from Alex's high-powered life in London. And there's another big problem, which there aren't enough four-letter words to describe: Daisy's cheating, irresponsible father, Nick.

The second in Suzy K Quinn's hilarious, bestselling Bad Mother series is another addictive treat.

Lightning Books 2019
ISBN: 9781785631573
£7.99

The BAD MOTHER'S HOLIDAY

Suzy K Quinn

Every mother deserves a holiday
The third in the bestselling comedy series

Juliette Duffy is knocked up again. Preggers. Up the duff. To put it
another way…whoops.

While she and her hotel magnate boyfriend Alex get their
heads around unexpected parenthood, Juliette is having all the
usual pregnancy symptoms: throwing up, indigestion, sciatica,
constipation, migraines and brain-fuddling tiredness. Because
Mother Nature is a psychopathic old hag.

She needs a distraction and this summer she is determined to
get away. Her party-loving mother is demanding the usual Duffy
family all-inclusive Greek holiday. Her dad wants to go camping
in Norfolk. And Alex? Well, he has asked her on a five-star luxury
cruise. The trouble is, his mother is coming too…

The third in Suzy K Quinn's addictive Bad Mother series, where
Why Mummy Drinks meets Bridget Jones, is another laugh-out-
loud treat.

Lightning Books 2019
ISBN: 9781785631597
£7.99

Praise for the Bad Mother books

'A witty, warm, real, observational and poignant page-turner. I loved it!'

Nicola May

'Brilliantly funny and so real – the perfect pick-me-up page-turner'

Kate Harrison

'Frank, disarming and hilarious, it's the best women's fiction I have read since the last Marian Keyes and it made me spit more coffee out than *Bridget Jones' Diary* ever did. I can't wait to read books 2 and 3'

Rachel Read It

'This book made me laugh so much it became dangerous for a mother-of-four to continue'

Books In My Hallway

'Suzy K Quinn is a born storyteller'

Erin Kelly

'One to watch'

Julia Gregson

About the author

Suzy K Quinn writes in three different genres: psychological thriller, comedy and romance.

She was first published by Hachette in 2010 with her debut novel *Glass Geishas* (now *Night Girls*), then self-published a romance series, *The Ivy Lessons*, which became No 1 Kindle romance bestsellers in the US and UK. After her second daughter was born in 2013, she self-published the *Bad Mother's Diary* series, which also became Kindle bestsellers. Her novels have now been translated into seven languages and her books have sold over 750,000 copies worldwide.

She lives in Wivenhoe, Essex, with her husband Demi and two daughters, and travels to Mexico every year to write and study Mayan story-telling.